SANCTUARY

Tom Gaisford

Published April 2025
ISBN 978-1-917447-02-7
Text © Tom Gaisford
Typography © Bath Publishing

Published by Cinto Press (an imprint of Bath Publishing Limited)
Email: info@bathpublishing.co.uk
Tel: 01225 577810
www.bathpublishing.com

Printed and bound in Great Britain by Clays Ltd, Elcograf S.p.A.

Bath Publishing Limited is a company registered in England: 5209173
Registered Office: 27 Charmouth Road, Bath, BA1 3LJ

EU RP (for authorities only)
eucomply OÜ
Pärnu mnt 139b-14, 11317 Tallinn, Estonia
Email: hello@eucompliancepartner.com
Tel: +3375690241

Praise for *Sanctuary*

'Passionate and atmospheric, both as a love story and a ferocious drama set in the murky world of asylum policy and practice, written with deep insight, exciting twists and insolent good humour.'
Robert Bathurst, actor and writer

'Every scenario was beautifully done whether amongst lawyers or asylum seekers, convincing and moving in some cases, and excellent and believable characters...I could not stop reading it.'
Rebecca Fraser, author and broadcaster

'People have been moving around in search of a better life since time began, but few subjects generate gloomier air. Tom Gaisford's close knowledge of the law makes *Sanctuary* not just clever and gripping, but also heartfelt.'
Robert Winder, author of Bloody Foreigners and former literary editor of The Independent

'Tom Gaisford's gripping novel explores an urgent subject – the UK's inhumane treatment of asylum seekers...(it is) both affecting and memorable.'
Lucy Popescu, Chair of the Author's Club and the Best First Novel Award

'Very clever...the storyline about an immigration lawyer posing as an asylum-seeker to expose iniquities is a real brainwave.'
Anthony Gardner, author and founding editor of the Royal Society of Literature's magazine RSL

'Timely and hugely well-informed, Tom Gaisford's debut novel shines a light on the UK's asylum process and from inside brings us a novel that is ambitious, entertaining and amusing in equal parts.'
Peter Hanington, author and journalist

'A startlingly unique legal thriller with beautifully drawn characters.'
Anna Stothard, author

Praise for *Sanctuary*

'I really loved this book, which is nothing if not original. Gaisford combines rich and humorous dialogue, beautifully filmic description, searching questions about our treatment of asylum seekers, and a deftly-woven, romantically-charged plot, to create something truly unprecedented.'

Lorelei King, actress and award-winning narrator of audiobooks

'Inventively structured, packed with vivid characters and replete with rich depictions of London and Andalusia, Tom Gaisford's entertaining debut novel shines a light on the plight of asylum seekers and the dedicated human-rights lawyers who fight their cases.'

Ben Hinshaw, author

'I loved how the plot twists and writhes, and how it left me at times racing to catch up. I could easily picture this as a television series as it felt so visual and connected to events that currently surround us. Smart as heck and containing a taut energy, *Sanctuary* is an exciting and convincing read.'

Liz Robinson, Head Reviewer for LoveReading and former judge of the CWA Gold Dagger Award

To my beloved Sarra

When the gods and demons disappear a different world appears, rich in sunlight and storm but without fear.

Arthur J. Deikman

FIGHT

1

Stansted airport, Immigration Control. Spanish holiday over. I find the toilets, bin my false passport and make for the international arrivals queue.

#

Twenty long minutes later, an expressionless border control officer beckons me forward and holds out her hand.

'No have *pasaporte*,' I say.

Her eyes widen, but before she can get too animated, I claim asylum.

#

And so it begins. They take me to a breakout room and tell me to wait. It is empty but for a couple of chairs. An hour passes. Another. With my story well rehearsed and still no sign of anyone, my mind starts to wander; I find myself recalling the testimony of a former client of mine, left in a room for two days without food, water or access to a toilet. And now other vicarious memories of abuse start resurfacing in my mind: chokeholds, broken bones, images of cut and bloody faces. My thoughts spiralling, I lie down on the floor and try to focus on my breathing.

No joy.

And it's not just the fear that's getting to me. It's the rage.

At last, a door opens and into the room strides a tall man in a navy suit and striped cravat. With him comes a waft of aftershave so intense I can almost taste it. The man speaks slowly and firmly.

'My name is Gianluca De Rossi,' he begins, dusting down one of the chairs and lowering a leather holdall from his shoulder. 'I am a senior immigration officer. I am going to ask you some questions, understand? We call this a screening interview.'

I nod and get up.

'Good. I'll start by asking you to confirm your full name and where you are from.'

'I am Alejandro Guerrero.' I slightly overcook the double-r sound.

De Rossi's eyes flicker, then refocus on the interview pad in front of him.

'I am,' I announce, 'from *la Argentina*.'

He fiddles around with his laptop for a few moments, then proceeds to ask some questions about my purported home country – all pretty straightforward by Home Office standards: local currency, description of the national flag, popular Argentinian dishes, the origin of Tango, average wingspan of the Andean condor, approximate number of Patagonian-Welsh speakers in Chubut province, and so on.

He seems satisfied with my answers and invites me to summarise my claim: there will be time to elaborate at my asylum interview.

I tell him I am an English teacher from a rural village called Uspallata, in the foothills of the Andes. A couple of weeks ago, I was targeted by a minority sect, known locally as *La Vereda Frondosa*, for refusing to worship their leader. The government failed to protect me and I was left with no option but to flee the country – in disguise, of course, which explains the hairstyle. I escaped to Spain on a tourist visa and an agent secured my onward passage to the UK.

Scarcely five minutes have passed when De Rossi stops the interview. He raises a hand in the air, flicks a speck of dandruff from his shoulder and passes me a proforma to confirm and sign. There is a large 'W' firmly printed at the top of the first page. Other than that, all standard, and the summary of my account is pithy but accurate, as far as I can see.

He takes a mugshot with a digital camera and briefs me on what is to follow.

'Your asylum claim will be fast-tracked – I mean to say prioritised. Shortly, you will be transferred to Herringsworth Immigration Removal Centre, where you will be detained pending resolution of your case. Understood? Any questions? No? Fabulous.'

He leaves and a couple of men replace him. One handcuffs me – 'Just a precaution, mate' – while the other, a stockier fellow with a bandaged left ear, grimaces and fans his clipboard backwards and forwards, only revitalising the lingering scent.

'Who was that man?' I ask.

'De Bossy?' answers the bigger of the two, wiping some dribble from his mouth. 'He's the head honcho, right Novak?'

Novak. The name makes me shudder.

'Mr De Rossi manages Herringsworth,' Novak confirms. 'The removal centre across the runway there. All of us answer to him.'

'Removal?' I repeat.

'Ha!' the big one jeers. 'He's bricking it already!'

Novak shakes his head wearily. 'Pay no attention to Mr Hog here,' he says. 'It's called a removal centre, but not everyone we detain is removed, OK?'

I nod as if this were news to me, and with his free hand, he stuffs a finger between his collar and his sweaty neck, and wiggles it about.

'Why does it have to be so fucking hot in here?' He frowns. 'Come on, outside.'

#

They escort me into the back of an unmarked van and five minutes later, they are dragging me out towards a yellow brick building with high walls decorated in rolls of shimmering concertina wire. I flinch and suppress an instinct to bolt. For all the adrenaline, inside those walls lies a place so joyless the prison inspectorate described it as 'sub-Pentonville'. But I'm getting ahead of myself.

2

The previous morning

I'm standing on a hotel balcony in Zahara de los Atunes, looking out over the glistening sands of the Playa del Carmen and across the straits to Africa. I'm naked but who cares: the sun's barely up and besides, little could be as humiliating as the last few weeks. First the demotion, then Amy, now this. I take another slug of *Cruzcampo*.

In fairness, this 'leave of absence' was the GP's idea. 'Suggestion,' he said. 'Use this time to do *whatever* you like.' And here I am again, in the peaceful place I picture when someone says, 'picture a peaceful place'. Yet peace, it appears, is more an internal thing.

The stillness of the morning is broken by the hollow sound of footsteps on the boardwalk below. A Senegalese merchant is traipsing down to the beach, back buckling under a sack brimming with colourful throws. If previous summers are anything to go by, he'll work all day for next to nothing and, as it's Ramadan, without a drop of water passing his lips. My mind flits back to London, to Hatton Taylor Solicitors and to the asylum seeker clients we turned away. Even if they weren't refugees fleeing persecution, but migrants risking it all for a better life, the truth is undeniable: we failed to help them.

The thought of failure whisks me back to an hour or so ago and the call I received from Jedrek, our Senior Partner. He was his usual brisk self and for a moment it seemed he was going to restore me to the Refugee Team. When, instead, he suggested I try a stint in the billing department, I assumed he was joking… Then I couldn't breathe,

7

picturing myself in the office basement, hunting through other people's files for missing attendance notes.

Later in the call, he revealed the reason: the partners no longer believe I am cut out for asylum work.

'On reflection,' he explained, 'we feel you lack the requisite judgement and – sorry to say this, old boy – the emotional hardiness.'

It felt like a bad dream.

'Rest up, Alex, and we'll see you in ten days.'

When the line went dead, my first thought was of Amy. There'd be no keeping this from her. There was nothing for it but to climb back into bed, switch on the ceiling fan and try to make peace with my fate. Cool air on my face, I shut my eyes. And reopened them. Does it have to end like this, I thought, then got up and raided the minibar.

The second beer is never as good as the first. I leave it half-finished, sling on some shorts and a t-shirt and head outside in search of a plan.

Ten days.

Ten days to prove I have what it takes…

#

Walking down to Café Paco past yuppies, kids, widows, junkies, hippies, holidaymakers and stray animals, I clock a familiar face. It's my old friend, Javi.

'*Que pasa*, Javi?'

'*Chiquillo*, *picha*, how are you, broder? Can't keep away, can you? What's it been, two months?'

I see he is carrying clippers.

'You've taken up hairdressing now?'

'Ha! You saw Hans the German's mohican last time you were over, right?'

Hans is a third-generation immigrant but as Spanish as a leg of iberico ham.

'The peroxide job? Yes! Did you do that to him?'

'Got it from *la farmacia, tío!*' he says, laughing. 'Shit's so strong it would even bleach your dark mop!'

An image forms in my mind of Jedrek at his desk. He's looking at holiday snaps in which I look so relaxed and well it's hard to imagine I was ever not...

'Got any left?' I ask Javi.

'Wait...you're joking, right?'

#

The makeover doesn't take long. We return to Paco's and are tucking into some tapas, when who should find us but Hans himself.

'*Oye, imbécil!*' he shouts, crossing the street to join us. 'That's my look!'

He's right. Plus, it looks absurd. Jedrek will be more worried about me, not less – perhaps more so if I shave it all off...

'*Otra?*' Javi asks, pointing to the empty plate of baby squid he has just troughed.

#

Ten minutes later, I am up to speed. Hans is out of work again and has moved back in with his ageing father. In the meantime, he is, as ever, selling anything he can get his hands on: weed, blow, bikes, IDs and other stolen goods.

'And the waitering job?' I ask. 'What happened?'

'He couldn't keep his hands to himself,' Javi interjects. 'Stole a keg of beer and they kicked him out.'

'Oh Hans...'

'I know, I know...it was shit anyway.'

'The beer?'

'The job.' He laughs, producing a little plastic bag from under his baseball cap. 'Here, have a little present for your stay. It's marijuana pollen – smoother than the normal shit you get. You like it, I get you some more.'

I hesitate, then take the bag. Hans moves closer and whispers in my ear.

'Hey, *inglesito*, you still interested in that *pasaporte*, *sí o qué*?'

'No,' I reply. 'Don't think so.'

'You sure? *Seguro, segurísimo*? I can get you a good price, eh?'

'What are you *idiotas* talking about?' Javi interrupts.

'Nothing,' we reply in unison.

'Let me know, *vale*?' Hans insists, fixing me with his beady blue eyes. 'There's a guy in the village. I can have it for you today…'

The bloke is nothing if not persistent.

'I'll text you,' I answer, rather than confess that I had been winding him up.

#

I wander up the beach, away from the village and smoke the pollen. He was right, it is exquisite. In the calm evening light, the sea is a rippling sheet of pewter. I take off my clothes and wade in up to my waist. Across the water lies Africa. To the right of me, some ten kilometres down the coast, I can just make out the bobbing fishing boats of Barbate and above them, gleaming white on the mountain-top, the majestic Moorish village of Vejer de la Frontera. I lie on my back, buoyed up by the salt water and, watching the vast sky darken over me like a shroud, let the current carry me out. In all the beauty, it is almost possible to forget that scattered across the seabed below, entombed in sand and rock, rest the drowned remains of myriad men, women and children.

#

It's hard to say how ideas come to you, where and when the seeds are sown, how they grow and take shape in your mind. Sometimes it's a tiny observation, it seems, a jolt or a simple change of scene that sets your complex, fragile brain in motion. Other times, they appear to bubble up from deep inside you; memories, perhaps, of things that did or did not happen. What is certain, I am discovering, is that whatever its provenance, an idea can quite literally save your life. I turn against the outgoing tide and paddle back towards the lights of the shoreline.

#

A mile or so down the beach, Zahara glows gold against the shadowy mountains of the Sierra del Retín. I drag my heavy body out of the water and flop on the sand. And there I lie, alone, motionless, a washed-up corpse. Only, I am still alive.

#

It is midnight when I awake. I text Hans, then find my way through the dunes and back into town. The bars are just getting going. I pass an acquaintance in La Calle Peñon – Guillermina, from Argentina. She's with the same enormous bloke I clocked the last time I was over.

'*Hola* Alex,' she says breezily. '*Te presento a* Gustavo, my husband.'

'*Mucho gusto*, I've heard a lot about you,' I lie, styling it as well as I can.

'We're off to The Green Whale for *copas*, if you want to join us?' she says, without a hint of unease or embarrassment.

'That's kind.' I keep walking away as fast as I can without actually running. 'But I have plans.'

And so I do.

#

When, eventually, I reach the hotel, Hans is there waiting for me. I give him the money, he hands me the envelope and I take a quick look. Pretty poor likeness, but it will do. Now to see how this plays out.

3

It starts with waiting, watching, listening; guards, radios, voices, keys jangling, big reinforced doors sliding open and banging shut. Eventually, I am ushered into reception. It's a large white room with an empty row of plastic chairs, a desk and little else but surveillance cameras and some brightly coloured instruction posters dotted around the walls. *Have you provided emergency details of your next of kin?* one says. *Have you considered voluntary departure?* reads another.

'Guerrero?' The receptionist beckons me forward and hands me a plan of the place, mapping out the facilities – library, canteen, courtyard, prayer rooms, recreation area, TV room, cell blocks, showers and so on – and it is then, out of nowhere, that a female officer catches my eye.

She is midway down the corridor, reading the riot act to a fellow detainee. But the serenity of her poise belies the admonition in her voice. And when, moments later, the detainee bursts into tears, to my astonishment she puts an arm on his back and moves it in a circular motion, until the crying stops. When she clocks me, I manage to hold her gaze for just enough time to affect a relaxed smile. Yet before I can address her, she has trotted off down the corridor, shiny black ponytail swinging in sync with the clean clip-clop of her heels.

A sort of exhilarating desperation comes over me, and I stay standing there motionless. I know this feeling. Or did once. Eyes shut, I can almost hear the shimmering sound of the steel drum and for a moment, I have forgotten where I am.

Footsteps behind me.

I turn around to find Novak standing there, holding a standard-issue grey tracksuit and blue flip-flops in a transparent plastic bag.

'Here.' He presses the bag into my stomach and points to the toilets. 'Still sorting where you're sleeping so you'll have to change in there. When you're done, leave your clothes with reception and await further instructions.'

#

I manage to change clothes without treading in any piss puddles, then I kiss goodbye to my Hawaiian shirt and best Bermuda shorts. As for the espadrilles, they were never me anyway. Then I wait.

#

As dusk begins to fall, Hog appears. He escorts me to a small, white cell with a pair of beaten-up bunk beds and an exposed toilet in the corner.

'Your room, sir,' he says mockingly. 'Get used to it.'

'I take it.'

'Oh, I know you will,' comes a gravelly, West African voice from the bottom bunk.

I glance back at the officer, who smirks and shuffles off, locking the door behind him.

I crouch down and see a man so tall that his legs have poked through the gap at the foot of the bed and his feet are resting on the floor. Gingerly, I extend my hand, which the man grasps and begins to squeeze. I try to pull away but find myself being winched into the space between the man's chest and the metal slats of the top bunk.

'The name's Alejandro, but you can call me…'

'Biiiitch,' the giant responds.

I wince and brace myself. Mercifully, however, the man releases his grip and shoves me back out into the room.

'Got you there, white boy!' He holds out his hand again and introduces himself properly. 'Abayomrunkoje.'

I wipe a bead of sweat from my temple, lean forward again and shake his hand.

'How long you been in here, ahm, mate?'

The man sucks his teeth. 'Ab-ay-o-mrun-ko-je,' he says. 'It is really not that hard, Ah-leh-hand-roh. Oh, call me Abay.' His tone softens. 'The cops picked me up last night and called Immigration – I was like, no, this cannot be happening.'

'Have you claimed asylum?' I ask.

'Yes, I have told them.' He pauses. 'Basically, in Nigeria I was abducted by Islamist extremists.'

'Ouch.'

'Tell me about it. I escaped, but you know how it is? These maniacs have people everywhere…'

'Do you have a lawyer?'

'You ask many questions. Not yet, but the interview man promised me I'll see a solicitor tomorrow, on the legal aid. That reminds me,' he says fiddling with his watch, then he puts it to his mouth: '*Man interviewed me around 7pm – short one – asked about school, age I left, work – shit like that. Told him I want to claim asylum – seeing a lawyer tomorrow – on the legal aid.* What?' he laughs. 'Take it from me, you have contact with the authorities, you document it!'

I ask how the hell he got a smartwatch past Compliance and he shows it to me. It has a simple analogue face with green and white striped background.

'Not everything is as tacky as it looks.' He smiles. 'Ten full days of battery life per charge – beat that!' His eyes twitch. 'My father gave it to me. "A proper watch, for a proper athlete", he told me. It is true as well.' He looks up again. 'Tells you everything, this thing, from your heart rate to your favourite Fela Kuti song!'

I try to reply but my roommate just closes his eyes and lets out a long, easy yawn which glides down the bass clef like the slide of a trombone.

'Goodnight, *amigo*,' I whisper.

With no response from Abay, I have no option but to turn in too. Before climbing up to my bunk, I consider attempting to use the screenless loo but think better of it.

The top bunk proves more comfortable than it looks. I lie back, arms behind my head, heart still racing. I've done it, I'm in! I shut my eyes, and, 'Ffff...' Short inbreath, and again, 'Ffffff...'

Distracted from my fears for a moment, I muse about what I might do to obstruct operations before they bust me. And when nothing occurs, I remind myself that it matters little, that anything I achieve in here, any inside information I can glean, will be a bonus. My mission is accomplished already: I've fooled the bastards, soon all this will be over and I'll be harnessing the inevitable media attention to raise critical awareness and funds for asylum seekers. 'Emotional hardiness', was it? 'Judgement'? I yawn and fall into a deep, delicious sleep.

#

I am awoken in the night by the sound of a door shutting. Forgetting where I am, I reach for my bedside light and rap my knuckles on the wall. Yelping, I clamber out of bed, drop six feet and whack my head on the porcelain toilet bowl.

#

When I come to, I am lying in pitch darkness, flat on my back. Raising a hand to my swollen forehead, I trace a trail of dry, crusty blood through my hair and to the floor beneath me.

The cell door opens, the light comes on and in bounds a male immigration officer. 'Rise and shine, it's breakfast time!' His voice grates, then, 'Christ, look at the state of you…we'll get Healthcare to take a look.'

When the officer leaves, I sit up, bum-shuffle myself up against the wall and look around the room.

Odd. There is no sign of Abay and his bed has been stripped.

4

'Healthcare' comprises a makeshift surgery in the bowels of the building with no natural light, an old examination couch and a middle-aged woman in a grubby lab coat, staring at a TV.

The programme is Good Morning Britain, and today it features a ruddy-looking man in a flat cap, motoring about in the English Channel with a megaphone to his lips. As the camera pans out, you can see he is barking something at a group of some thirty or so people, of all ages, who are crammed into a dinghy which is barely afloat.

'You're not refugees!' flash up the subtitles. 'You're benefits tourists! And terrorists!'

I cough and the woman turns around, switches off the TV and introduces herself: 'Carole,' she says, handing me a medical form to fill in. 'Pop your clothes on the couch there for me.'

I hesitate. 'Everything?'

She peers at me over her glasses. 'Well, I need to examine you, don't I?'

I explain that it is only my head that hurts, but she simply puts her hands on her hips and asserts, 'The body is the sum of its parts, is it not?'

#

The medical consists of her revolving around me, scribbling notes on an A4 outline of a human body and making the odd comment. 'Height…six foot plus, build…athletic.' We are nearing the end, it seems, when she moves in closer and examines the six-inch scar on my lower abdomen.

'How did you get this?' she asks.

'It was *them*.' I fix her with an anxious stare. '*They* did it.'

'Right, OK,' she says. 'And who are "they"?'

This time I lower my mouth to her ear. '*La Vereda Frondosa*,' I whisper, and inhale sharply before returning to full height.

'Nope, you're going have to write that down for me, love,' she replies, handing me the pen and paper without batting an eyelid. I oblige and, squinting, she asks, 'Who are "Luh Vreda Frondowsa"?'

'Very bad people,' I tell her. 'They try to kill me!'

'I see.' She goes over to the corner of the room and picks up a phone. The voice on the other end is audible and familiar.

'Yes, who is it?'

'Mr De Rossi, sir, it's Carole from Healthcare.'

'Yep.'

'Have you got a moment?'

'Make it quick.'

She freezes up. 'I, ah, have a Rule 35 here,' she says. 'Patient is a victim of torture in his home country of Algeria.'

'Argentina,' I interrupt.

'Sorry – Argentina, sir.'

There is a pause.

'Don't tell me: tallish man, ridiculous hair?'

'Yes, sir,' she confirms, without a moment's hesitation.

'Thought as much. What's he claiming now?'

'Says he's a victim of torture, sir.'

'Of course, he does,' De Rossi replies. 'Strange he didn't mention it to me at screening, isn't it? Evidence? Scarring?'

'Sir, indeed there is a scar.'

'Is there now? Where, may I ask?'

'Lower right-side abdomen, sir.'

There is another short silence, followed by a scoff.

'Let me guess – six inches or so?'

She squints. 'Yes, sir – roughly.'

'Inguinal hernioplasty. Or an appendectomy.'

She does not respond.

'Carole, do not tell me you have never seen a hernia scar?'

'Well, yes…yes, I have, sir. It's just not my place to pre-empt…'

'You are medically trained, are you not?'

She replies but her voice is so diminished it is inaudible.

'Is that a "yes"?'

She is now visibly shaking.

'I…I thought we were supposed…' she squeaks, her eyes welling up.

'No, you didn't. You didn't think at all, did you?'

By this point, I have heard enough. I walk over and gently take the phone from her. She doesn't resist, just stares blankly at the receiver. I then introduce myself and De Rossi responds: 'Well, that's just wonderful. Now kindly pass me back to Healthcare immediately. Carole!'

Of course, I do no such thing.

'She cannot speak,' I reply.

'I beg your pardon!'

'Too upset.'

The man is incensed. 'You have no idea who you are dealing with, cretin. I could have you transferred!' He draws breath. 'Deported. I meant deported.'

Eh? He hangs up and I'm left wondering how someone so experienced could confuse moving someone to another detention centre with removing them from the country altogether? I hand the phone back to Carole, who steadies herself then looks at me quizzically. 'Your English is good, isn't it?'

'Thank you,' I reply. 'I studied it during many years.'

'It's *for* many years.'

I thank her again and go to pick up my clothes. 'If you excuse me, *señora*?'

'Yes, of course.' She looks away. Not for long. 'That one, what's that one?' She is pointing at my left thigh.

I tell her the truth: it is a map of La Janda, a district in the province of Cádiz, a place of spectacular beauty, 'marshlands, bordered by white villages, mountains, sea...'

'Not the tattoo,' she interrupts. 'That long scar there. I can't believe I missed it.'

Poor Carole has suffered enough today.

'Dancing,' I confess.

'Ouch, sounds painful.'

Not half, I reflect. I fractured my femur... Hangover the next day wasn't much fun either, now I remember it. Worst of all though was the regret: that was supposed to be the night I kissed Amy...

#

The door bursts open and in marches Novak with a baton. The bandage has been removed from his ear, revealing several stitches. He conveys a message from the boss – no Rule 35 report needed and he's to take me to my room.

'But this gentleman may be a victim of torture,' Carole protests. 'I have to file the report – detention centre rules.'

'No, he definitely is not.'

'Oh no?' She steadies herself on her feet.

'Boss saw him personally, at screening. He's satisfied he's low risk.'

'But that is not the test...'

'Is now. Direct orders of the Home Secretary herself to Mr De Rossi – all part of a department-wide crackdown on immigrant malingerers.'

'But, but...' Carole stutters.

'Oh, you want to tell De Rossi he's got it wrong, do you?'

'No, of course not. It's just, with the greatest respect, Mr De Rossi's not a medical professional.'

'And you are?'

She bites her lip.

'Well?' Novak prods.

At last, Carole stands up for herself: 'I am a fully accredited first-aider, I'll have you know.'

'Well, then,' Novak laughs. 'You'll be perfectly qualified to call a hernia scar a hernia scar.'

He turns his attention to me: 'Right, you – this way.'

'And my head?' I reply, looking at Carole, and pointing to the bump above my temple.

'So sorry, dear, I nearly forgot.' She digs out some paracetamol and a manky bandage for me.

'Thank you, Carole,' I reply with my best smile. 'You are…a life saver.'

#

I am escorted back to my cell, and we are passing the removal centre's rear entrance when the double doors open and I catch a glimpse of a large woman wearing a hijab. She's being wheeled into the back of a van; it's hard to see but she appears to be resisting.

'Where is she going?' I ask.

'Oh, that's the Onward Transfer Team,' Novak replies. 'They'll be taking her to a different removal centre.'

'Why?'

'Any number of reasons. Most likely to be closer to family, amenities and suchlike, while her case is progressed.' He stops and looks me in the eye.

'You ask a lot of questions,' he says, and for an anxious second, I fear he is on to me. But no, it seems, he wants to explain.

'Look, I don't know much about transfer – not my domain – even if I did, I wouldn't tell you. Confidentiality, mate.' He smirks. '66, 67…here we are. Room 68. One further down and you'd be having the time of your life!'

I smile dutifully and ask if my roommate is coming back. No response. And before I can ask again, he has ushered me into the room, unhooked an enormous bunch of keys from his belt and stepped outside again.

'Wait! What is this?'

'Boss's orders, mate. It's for security reasons.'

'Eh?'

'That, or you pissed him off.' He laughs. 'Calm down, won't be for long, all right?'

'Not all right!' I yell. But he has gone.

#

The shock of being doubly detained soon passes and I am half glad of the time alone. I climb onto my bunk and listen to the muted whirr of planes taking off and landing outside. It is perversely soporific. I take out my smart new notebook and begin jotting down the events of the last 24 hours in as much detail as I can – where I have been, who I have seen, my conversations, observations, reflections, and so on. This was always the plan, in so far as there was one.

#

It has been an hour now. Every so often, my attention is knocked off course by the throbbing pain in my temple, loud voices outside, or more distressingly, the faint sound of muffled weeping. I finish the note for now and read over what I've written, only to observe that it seems disappointingly insignificant. A creeping sickness appears in the pit of my stomach; for the first time since embarking on this stunt, doubts are surfacing about its efficaciousness. Is it certain to attract media attention, for instance? If so, what sort? Might it backfire, even?

With hindsight, an exit strategy might not have been a bad idea. I throw my pen across the room in frustration. So much for judgement.

#

Crazy how quickly one's perception can shift. In just a few minutes, I've gone from visualising my acceptance speech at next year's Human Rights Lawyers Awards to wondering how I got myself into this sorry mess in the first place. Not *this* mess – I mean the disaster that led to it. It would be funny if it weren't so tragic. I turn over onto my side and a frivolous thought occurs: when this is over, when I'm back in the real world, I could write it all down, make a virtue of necessity – mine, that is, to understand how the fuck it all went wrong! 'FAIL', I'd call it. And, yes, my imagination is running away with me. But what's a man to do in a lock-up but explore his thoughts?

#

Another hour and still no sign of anyone coming to release me. Some twenty minutes ago, there was an eruption of noise from the corridor outside my room: footsteps and chatter, doors opening and shutting. Then, just as I was thinking someone might be coming to let me out, I heard something that made my heart sink. I remember a former client described it to me as a 'mechanical clunk', and it's the sound of all the cell doors being locked at the same time. I must have been too deeply asleep to hear it last night, and it would have given me a jolt then for sure, but to hear it now, at noon, on a warm day in mid-summer, feels more than oppressive. It feels downright cruel.

Once more I sense my breathing becoming shallow. It seems there is a limit to how long one can distract oneself from this…this fucking uncertainty. How long can they keep me cooped up in here? Have they forgotten I've done two hours already? I wipe the sweat from my brow. It's tempting to shout for help, only...well, there is this image I cannot get out of my head, of an officer digging his fingers into my client's bleeding neck, whispering, '*You fucking piece of shit...I'm going to put you to fucking sleep.*' The officer's name was Novak.

5

Eventually, I hear the clunk again, doors opening and detainees leaving their cells. I jump out of bed, only to find that my door remains shut. There is, I notice, a little red button on the wall next to the handle – a panic button? I hesitate a moment, then press it and wait. Nothing. I try again. Useless! Is the bloody thing even connected?

#

At long last, Novak returns to release me. 'Here you are, shouty,' he says, heaving the door open. 'If you're lucky, there may still be some food for you.'

I scurry off towards the canteen and am halfway down the corridor when a burst of exclamations rings out from a door marked Staff: 'Whoa!' 'No wayyyy!' 'Oh My God!' 'Awwwww…'

I creep up and peer through the glass. Inside, I see the same female officer I clocked yesterday. She is surrounded by colleagues and camouflaged by one of the biggest pot plants I have ever seen.

'It's a Saharan date palm!' shrieks a woman with pink hair. 'You're one lucky lady, Priya – wish my Ron was a transport mogul…'

'He's scarcely a mogul,' Priya contests.

'Darling, he literally runs all our chartered removals.'

Just then, I catch Priya's eye. She stands up, walks over and opens the door. 'Can I help you?' she asks and looks up at the top of my head. 'It's you…'

I ruffle my mohican. 'You know me?'

'Not yet,' she replies. 'Alejandro Guero, right?'

'Guerrero, madam. At your service.'

She studies me playfully for a moment. 'You know, I had a glance at your file, and couldn't find your full name?'

I confess, it takes me a moment to see what she is up to. 'Are you asking for my maternal surname, madam?'

'I am,' she confirms with an air of disappointment.

'I did not say before because…'

'No,' she cuts in, 'you didn't, did you?'

There is something unconvincing about this display, dare I say comforting even. I am reminded of something a certain junior barrister once told me: 'There are natural cross-examiners, and then there are nice people…'

'You do realise this omission adversely affects your credibility?' she continues, and I try to suppress the urge to laugh – I mean, seriously, for this lot is there anything an asylum seeker can do that *doesn't* adversely affect his credibility?

'Is something funny?' she asks.

'Priya, darling,' her colleague intervenes, putting a hand on her shoulder. 'Perhaps you should save your questions for interv…'

'My mother's family name was Topito,' I volunteer – it's the first name that pops into my head, straight from my subconscious, and I instantly regret it. I make my excuses and leave while I still can.

#

I'm kicking myself. 'Little mole'? Is anyone even called that in real life? What would have been wrong with 'Lopez' or 'Gonzalez' or something? But then again, I reflect, chances are none of them picked up on it, and my thoughts move to Priya. Notwithstanding the credibility crap, was that compassion I detected in her eyes? And didn't she have a beautiful voice…I check myself. This is ridiculous, not to mention traitorous.

The canteen is like a big American diner with the charm stripped out. Rows of grey plastic booths bolted to the floor, surrounded by walls of pink, vanilla and brown pastel stripes that could almost be Neapolitan ice-cream. Running along one side of the room is a tray rail leading to a food hatch, and on the opposite side hangs a faded photograph of the London skyline.

Queueing up, I receive a prod in the back, and I turn round to find a diminutive old man glaring up at me. He is hard to place – Turkish perhaps? – but his English is near perfect.

'Life here is poor enough without big bodies blocking the food,' he says.

'Food, you say?'

'Easy sunshine,' a dinner lady cautions, and dishes out each of us some sloppy stew and mash on a styrofoam plate.

We find the least occupied table, where a tall, white man with cropped silver hair and a corporate-logo polo shirt is finishing his lunch.

'Mind if we join you?' I ask.

'Not at all,' the man replies in an American drawl, and ups and leaves.

#

Ten minutes later, we are deep in discussion about the old man's native Chechnya, his long career as an English Literature lecturer, persecution by the Russians and escape to the UK. It is when he is describing his treatment in immigration detention, though, that he becomes most animated.

'I always had admired the United Kingdom,' he confesses, 'until I actually came here!'

I point out that here in detention, he might not be seeing the nation in its best light…

'No, but that is the point!' he exclaims. 'How this country treated foreigners was one of the things I most admired. But what do they do to me? They try to take me away in a plane without so much as hearing my asylum claim!'

'They did what?' I ask.

A look of confused panic sweeps across the man's face.

'Who are you? W-where am I?' he stutters, looking around.

'Wait here.'

I check that he is sitting securely in his seat and rush over to get help. The nearest officer I recognise is the woman from earlier with the pink hair. She gallops over but on seeing the man, she slows down.

'Not to worry about old Tapa,' she says to me. 'Been happening a lot this, I'm afraid. He has these little strokes called "TIAs".'

'Poor man,' I whisper back, and attempt to elicit information from her about what medical care he is getting, if any. When she seems defensive, I put to her what Tapa said about her colleagues trying to put him on a plane, without processing his asylum claim.

'What? Not a chance!' she laughs. 'Listen, with the best will in the world, the man's barely, you know, with it.'

I glance at him again and am about to respond, but the old man beats me to it: 'I certainly am, young lady!'

'I meant...I meant in that particular moment, my dear,' she says.

'Ah, do not worry your little pink head about it,' he replies angrily. 'You know nothing about this condition.'

'I beg your pardon?' she says.

I try to intervene but there is no stopping him.

'And, you clearly know nothing of the effort to take me away in a plane either,' he continues. 'I am not surprised. These things come from higher up.'

The lady takes my arm and pulls me aside.

'I want to reassure you,' she says *sotto voce*, 'Tapa was never put on any plane. Far from it.' Funny thing to fabricate, I want to say, but I hold my tongue. 'He is *confused*,' she adds, like the word were some closely protected passcode or something – loath to say it aloud, but it's actually quite endearing.

'I still don't get it,' I say.

'All right, strictly between us, De Rossi said they tried to transfer him to a different facility better equipped to deal with his needs.'

'On a plane?' I ask.

'There was no plane,' she insists, smiling.

I think for a moment, then ask where they were hoping to take him, 'so I can explain to him', I say.

A blank look comes across her face.

'As I say, somewhere better equipped,' she replies. 'Look, what matters is that he understands he is in a safe place and that his claim will be processed. I've told him all this a million times but…well…you just can't help some people.'

I am reluctant to risk drawing more attention to myself, but my inner lawyer proves irrepressible.

'Is he fit to be detained at all?' I ask, and instantly I know that I have gone too far.

'I'm sorry,' she says, reverting to type. 'Who exactly do you think you are? His solicitor or something?' And with that, she flounces back over to her spot in the corner of the room by the food tray stacks.

'Dessert?' my new friend asks.

#

Over a piece of old rock cake, Tapa returns to his lucid self and a clear picture of his detention history emerges.

He tells of how, a week or so ago, he resisted removal by biting an officer's ear. A day or two later, officers called for him again, only this time to ask him what assets he had in Chechnya and whether he had considered applying for entry clearance to the UK as an investor. And when he confirmed that he did not have the requisite two million pounds, they tried to charge him a fee for his detention. This, they said, was because of his condition, in other words because he required more care than other detainees.

Even I am shocked by what he tells me. I am curious, too, as to why they did not just try to remove him again. But he reveals that after the biting incident, he obtained legal representation. And it now makes sense: if anything were to happen to him, his solicitors would know about it.

I am just getting my head round all this when Tapa drops another bombshell.

'There is something else,' he says, almost as if it were an afterthought. 'The others they pushed on the plane...they were mostly negroes.'

'You mean black?' I ask politely.

'Yes. And I remember some of them were wearing really bright, colourful clothes. I could swear I heard French spoken, and other tongues. They were boarding Indians too,' he insists.

I query whether, possibly, they were sending him somewhere else.

'The same thought occurred to me,' he confirms, eyebrows raised. 'But where could they have been sending me? Africa? Or perhaps they planned to send us via another place, or places, and drop the others off en route?'

Scarcely.

'Wait...do they have your passport?' I ask. Something has occurred to me.

'No,' he confirms. 'I was advised to destroy it.'

'OK, so maybe they *were* transferring you internally or how would they have been able to get you off the plane the other end?'

The old man stares at the floor a moment. Sensing he might be deteriorating again, I gently place a hand on his shoulder.

'You OK?'

'Of course, I am!' he shouts. 'I am thinking, that's all.'

I take my hand away.

'No,' he continues. 'It doesn't make sense. An expensive, internal flight, when they could have put us on a bus for so little money?'

'Then?'

'I don't know,' he confesses. 'But that plane was leaving this country. Of that I am sure.'

6

After lunch, back on my bunk, I note down the salient details of my conversation with Tapa with fresh urgency. As I do, I find my mind racing back to the distressed disabled woman I saw being bundled off in the back of a van. If they were transferring her to a better place, why did she seem so resistant? And why have I never heard of an Onward Transfer Team for that matter? I'm speculating, but then there is Abay too. Where did he go? Even if he managed to see a lawyer, even if he has a strong case, they can't have granted him immigration bail already, can they?

I down tools, roll onto my back and feel my stomach rising and falling with each breath. Nope, I sit up again. I need answers.

There is a knock. I freeze, then hide my notebook under my pillow. And when the immaculate Priya pokes her head around the door, I release an involuntary little yelp.

'It's OK, I don't bite,' she says.

I clamber down, but land on my bad leg and find myself genuflecting at her feet.

'You can get up, Mr Guerrero,' she says, then opens a file and begins scribbling on a bit of green, regulation foolscap. 'I haven't come to hear your confession. That's tomorrow.' She explains that she is here to tell me about my asylum interview. A short way into describing the process, however, she stops writing and lifts her head.

'If you don't mind my saying, you seem very calm for someone in your situation.'

'I'm sorry?'

'A bit cocky even.'

'Cock?' I reply, throwing her a confused look.

'Your word, not mine.' She hands me the form, and I spot a quite staggeringly large diamond on her ring finger.

'At the interview,' she continues, 'you will have the chance to expand on the answers you gave to Mr De Rossi in your screening interview and, from what I have seen of your claim so far, you will need to…'

On the top of the form is written: "04 or 43". Which one are you, I wonder. Casually, I ask if Priya herself is going to interview me.

'Gosh, someone is quick on the uptake,' she says. 'Or knows the system…?'

Christ she is sharp!

'11:00 – 15:00?' I scoff, reading on down the form. 'What about lunch?'

'Sandwich.'

'And my *alérgia al trigo*?'

'Your allergy to what?'

'*Cómo se dice*?' I mutter. 'Wheat?'

'The allergy you have developed since your medical this morning?' she replies. 'We do read the medical notes, you know, Guerrero.'

Floundering, I congratulate her on the perfect pronunciation of my name.

'*Hablas Español*?' I ask her.

'*Italiano*, if you must know – my mother's side.' I nod and she sighs witheringly.

'My father's Bengali, they met in London, OK? What? Thought I was a freshi, did you?'

'Freshi?' This is the first time I've heard the term.

'Fresh off the boat.'

Bloody hell, what a racist pit our country has become. I feel an acute need to apologise to her. But I can't. In fact, I am about to make it worse.

'Don't be *absurda*,' I tell her. 'For a start, you are air traveller.'

'Meaning?'

'Look at you: your perfect hair, the shiny buttons on your suit, your blusher so *sutíl* – everything – it screams high-flyer!'

'Oh god, please, I'm going to throw up. Spare me your grotty little mile-high fantasy. Anyway.' She closes her file. 'I am not wearing blusher.'

I smile. 'So, you are blushing.'

'And you are a cock.'

She turns and makes for the door. I wolf-whistle, and she turns back towards me.

'Correction. A sexist cock.'

#

Alone once more, I go over the conversation in my head and shudder with shame. Then again, what choice did I have? It seems if I am to learn anything about what the hell is going on in here, Priya may be my best hope. And who in her position now would pass up a chance to interview and dismiss a sexist cock like me?

7

I make for the recreation area in search of answers. It is a large, quadrangular space, decorated with torn 80's-style posters of paradisiacal holiday destinations, platitudinous slogans and staff Christmas party pictures. In one photograph, there's a group of three men holding up cans of Red Stripe. I do a double take and notice they are wearing afro wigs and 'blackface'. The state of them, I balk. The state of this place – it is like a time capsule, designed to educate future generations on where we went wrong. I pour a coffee from a large, steel urn.

'Yuck!' I spit it back out into my cup.

'What did you expect? A gingerbread latte?' comes a familiar-sounding voice from the football table. The antisocial American from earlier.

I tell him that too would be disgusting, and introduce myself.

'Whatever,' the man drawls.

I move closer and ask him if he's going to tell me his name. At first, he just blanks me, and spins the row of strikers, one of which connects with the little white ball, shooting it against the back of the goal.

'Spinning is cheating,' I tell him. 'And anyone can score when there is no opposition.'

He grimaces and holds out his hand. 'Frank,' he says. 'You can throw in.'

#

The best of three becomes the best of five and the best of five, the best of seven.

'I am surprised. An American good at *fútbol*?'

'Soccer.'

'*Fútbol.*'

'Soccer.'

I cough.

'*Fútbol.*'

'Perhaps you could agree to differ, gentlemen?'

I look up from the table and see De Rossi, who appears to wink at Frank. And, to my embarrassment, standing with him is none other than his protégée, Priya. Still, once you've started something…

'You cannot leave me alone,' I say.

'Drop it, Guerrero,' she snaps back.

De Rossi seems amused by this. 'I see you two are already acquainted.'

'Enough to know we don't want to be,' she whispers back, raising an eyebrow.

'Don't be like this,' I respond. 'How is it you say? The path of the true love, it never…'

'…runs through a removal centre,' she interrupts. 'See you tomorrow. And do not be late, or I shall assume you have withdrawn your claim.' She turns to De Rossi, whispers something in his ear, and the pair continue on their way.

#

'Christ, she's fierce!' says Frank, when they are gone. 'He's OK, though, isn't he?'

'Del Monte?'

'Dude, that's a bit racist.'

'True…sorry,' I reflect. 'You like him?'

'Well, he's been good to me. Can you keep a secret?'

'You are shit at *futbolín*?'

'Seriously!' he whispers, and looks nervously around to ensure no one is in earshot. 'De Rossi knows my case is horseshit, but he's hooked me up with a decent attorney – says everyone deserves representation, or some shit.'

'Legal aid?'

'Ha! No siree. I'm in oil, monkey. What? You didn't hear the Texan accent?'

I ask him why he is here and he tells me about how he 'met a gal' and overstayed his visa. I laugh – 'met a gal' – the man must be 60. He forces me to explain why I am laughing and, of course, he doesn't like what he hears.

'Hey, fuck you, man!' He grabs me by the collar. 'I'm not even 57 yet.'

I peel the man's chubby hands off my shirt and ask if he minds my asking how old this 'gal' is.

'I do, actually…' he huffs. 'All right, she's 31.'

I give it a moment or two, then ask him why he doesn't just go back to the US and apply for a visa.

The man scans around him, then continues.

'Seems there's another way for me,' he whispers. 'Investor route! My attorney's shit hot. Says I'll be out of here today or tomorrow and the paperwork will be sorted by next week latest.'

Sounds like utter bullshit to me. I ask how much he's paying this cowboy.

'It's a she, doofus brain.' He snarls. 'And that's none of your business.'

'Wait, you say De Rossi introduced you?'

'Keep your voice down, schmuck! He gave me her number, that's all.'

'That is introducing…e'schmuck.'

Frank goes to hit me, but I block and parry, get him in an arm lock and pin his head to the football table. A group of fellow detainees quickly assembles around us. But it is done.

'Sorry, gentlemen,' I announce. 'Fight finished...*terminado*.'

I pull my new friend back up to his feet, straighten his jacket and offer him some parting advice.

'Listen, *hermano*, it's a scam.'

'Oh yeah? What would you know?'

I give it one last shot and tell him in my best broken English that they are going to refuse him. To change from visitor to investor, he will first need to leave and apply from the US.

'Anything else?' he asks sarcastically.

'They will not let you out of here.'

'Oh no? Why not, hot shot?'

'Convenience, but they'll *say* there is a risk you will run away.'

Frank is having none of it. 'No offence, but I'll take my attorney's advice over yours.'

'Get a real lawyer,' I hit back, and turn to leave.

'Hey, come back!' the guy shouts after me. 'You never told me why you're in here.'

'Long story,' I reply and continue on my way. With people missing and my asylum interview tomorrow, I've precious little time to waste on this guy. Pink hair lady said it – some people can't be helped. Question is, can any?

8

Framing the communal spaces are four long corridors, the other side of which lie our cells, immigration offices, storage holds and at one end, a glass-fronted viewing gallery of the runway. There, detainees can watch the planes and, one assumes, contemplate their fate.

'Nice touch, isn't it?' says a trendy-looking young man, taking his hands out of his pockets. 'Amir. And you are…'

'Alejandro.'

'Cool. Been in here long, mate?'

'Two days. You?'

The man laughs. 'Me? Too long. Can you keep a secret?'

I am starting to wonder if there are in fact any secrets in here. 'Of course.'

'The Bengali lady, foxy one, what's her name?'

'Priya.'

'Ha! That's the one! Well, she interviewed me yesterday and said she's "inclined" to grant me asylum. That means she's going to, right?'

I shrug my shoulders. 'Sounds positive. Where were they trying to send you back to?'

'Algeria, mate. Came here illegally, by boat. I was a nipper, just 13 years old. Worked some 18 years before they picked me up.'

'They came to your work?' I guess.

'Fuckin' traffic offence, wasn't it? Fuckers! Still, my fault for coming here without a visa.'

'You were 13…'

'Yeah, plus we had like literally nothing… It was like, starving

40

versus drowning; drowning versus starving. I chose drowning. And, well, I made it, didn't I?' He smiles and points to my head. 'Nice, erm, "do" by the way!'

'Thanks.' I run a finger over the crest. But I'm curious to know why he has claimed asylum. For instance, has the political situation in Algeria deteriorated since he left?

'All right, I'll tell you,' he says, without much hesitation, 'but a word to anyone and I'll break your legs! That Priya, if you can, get her to do your interview. She's – how do I put it? – on side.'

I affect a look of surprise.

'Seriously,' he continues, 'I made my case up and she knows it's bollocks, I'm sure of it. But she's allowing it anyway.'

'Why?'

'I as good as asked her that myself. She said what I told her was "reasonably likely" to be true – or something like that. Truth be told, I think she felt sorry for me. I told her about my upbringing, the poverty back home, the crossing, my experiences here, the racism, my music, et cetera.'

'You are a musician?'

'Of sorts. I write code really, but I've worked with some of the big music labels – remotely, of course: it's easier to stay anonymous as a virtual colleague, and to keep up the, ehem, hacking...'

'The what?'

'Keep it under your hat, but yeah. It's a lot of fun. And easy enough – all you need is someone's email address and a click-enticement, and Bob's your uncle.'

'Are you serious? I am sure I have opened those things...'

'Bah – I wouldn't worry. Most scammers don't have a clue. They faff around trying to get you to part with your bank details when, if they tried a bit harder, they could just nip inside your desktop and find them for themselves!'

This revelation causes me to second-guess myself about Priya: call me cynical, but might there be another reason she seems to be waiving this guy through?

'Was your coding part of your asylum claim?' I ask.

'Nope,' he replies. 'I said I was gay. Why?'

'Ah, never mind.'

'I told the tall guy, though.' My ears prick up. 'As I remember, coding was virtually all we spoke about.'

'Which tall guy?'

'The boss – you know, the arsey guy with the dandruff.'

'De Rossi?'

'That's him.'

'When?'

'When they brought me in here for – bollocks! – what's it called again?'

'Screening. Did they offer you a lawyer?'

'Not exactly. I had no savings, so old Dandruff sent me to the Advice Surgery and I got one there – same one my mate Ali's got – she's good! I'll give you her digits. Hey,' he reiterates, 'don't tell anyone about this.'

'Of course not. Can I meet Ali?'

'Come, I'll introduce you.' He glances back at the runway. 'You know, in a funny sort of way, I'll miss this view.'

Sure he will. Like I miss chargeable hours.

#

On the way to find Ali, we see Frank, dressed in a shiny beige, double-breasted suit, walking towards the exit with a security officer in tow, pulling a large suitcase.

'*Hijo de puta…*' I mutter under my breath – just like that, "welcome to Britain".

I ask Amir if he met him.

'Did I fuck,' he replies. 'Only spoke to white folk.' He yawns. 'Shame about old Tapa, isn't it?'

'Eh?'

'The Chechen bloke, old, nice guy…'

'Yeah, I know him. What happened? He OK?'

'You didn't hear? They dropped him, didn't they?'

'What? Who?'

'Solicitors, mate. I was there when he got the fax. "No merits" or something – basically, his claim was a bag of shite.'

Was it? I reflect. The man told me he had been tortured by the Russians…

'Where is he now?' I ask.

Amir sucks his teeth. 'Too late, they've taken him.'

'What the hell?' The man had an asylum claim pending. 'Where have they taken him?'

'To another centre, I'm told.'

I feel sick.

'Who told you?'

'Scrappy.'

'Who?'

'Ah, sorry, it's what we call Novak. We have names for all of 'em, you know – Priya's "Foxy", De Rossi's…hey, you OK mate? You look like you've seen a ghost.'

'Bastards.'

#

We find Ali in the prayer room. When he sees us, he stands up, folds up his mat and steps outside.

'This is Alejandro,' Amir tells him.

'Hello, I am Ali.'

'I hear you have a good solicitor,' I say slowly, sensing the man's English is weak, but Amir translates anyway. It is impressive. 'You understand each other?'

'Sometimes things get a bit lost in translation,' he replies, 'but we get there in the end, don't we, Ali?'

'Inshallah.' He smiles, bowing.

Amir turns to me again: 'This champ grew up in Mogadishu – basically his whole life has been a civil war.'

I struggle for something positive to say. 'They do say the situation in Somalia has improved a little, no?'

Amir contorts his face. 'You reckon? Bro, you should hear some of his stories…'

As he says this, I remember some of the horrors my old clients described: the constant shelling, the militias, the extortion, the camps, the rape, the torture.

'Who is your solicitor, again?' I ask.

'Our lawyer is best,' Ali responds. 'Her name is…I forget…'

'It's Martina or something,' Amir confirms. 'Hatton Taylor.'

'Marina?' I ask.

'Yes! Only met her once. She does everything though – takes statements, prepares your case, prepares your appeal. I can ask her to write to you if you want?'

'Erm, thanks Amir…can I think about it?'

He confers with Ali again. 'Yeah, that's right,' he says laughing. 'Ali's reminding me that if it weren't for her, he might not even *have* a lawyer. Get this – they met in Camden on a night out and she helped him claim asylum, gave him her details and stuff.'

Ali pipes up again.

'Says she contacted the Home Office,' Amir relays, 'and told them she was his lawyer, before he went to Lunar House to claim – wait – what was that? Oh yes!' he laughs, as, pouting, Amir lifts his elbows and rocks his head from side to side. 'She said it was to prevent any "monkey business"!'

'She sounds great,' I laugh with them. 'But tell me something: why is he in here at all?'

Amir sighs. 'Because the bloke can't turn up to an appointment. He skipped his reporting event, like six times in a row, so they took him in. She's made bail applications for him, but they've been unlucky with the judges – he has another chance next week.'

#

Relieved the men are in safe hands, I decide to head back to prepare for my asylum interview. Before leaving, however, there's one last question for Amir – a discreet one.

'*Amigo*, don't translate this. Your tech skills…are you able to, you know…?'

'Can I get porn for you?' he asks.

'No. Let's try again…'

'You want me to design an app or something?'

I take a deep breath. 'All right, suppose I wanted to hack a laptop…'

He laughs, but I am serious. As any immigration and asylum lawyer worth his salt will tell you, sometimes you need to think outside the rules.

9

Seven days left

Well, she is true to her word. Once seated in the interview room, a middle-aged man with a comb-over pops in and presents me with a sandwich menu. 'Bespoke Bites', reads the header, and below it, three options: 'North African tuna mayo', 'Nigerian fried chicken' and 'Zimbabwean corned beef'.

'Can I ask about the names?' I begin.

'I'm sorry?'

'I think he is asking about the names of the sandwiches, Terry,' Priya explains, ordering her papers.

'Oh, yes. Well, here at Herringsworth, we endeavour to cater to the various different tastes of our detainees. Obviously, we can't do all the countries, like, but we do our best to match the nationalities of whoever's inside. Several years ago, we had lots of Sri Lankans in, didn't we?' he says, turning to Priya.

She smiles. 'I think that was before my time.'

'Of course, silly me. Anyway, we did a marvellous curry paste baguette.'

'Thank you, Terry, we really must crack on now.'

He pauses like a bit part actor relishing his moment on stage. 'My pleasure, my lady. Have you made a choice, then, sir? What is it to be?'

'Ah yes,' I reply. 'I'll take the North African. Thank you, Terry. Or, as we say in Argentina, *gracias chabón*.'

Priya rolls her eyes at me as she stands up to usher Terry out. 'Terry, careful with the doo…'

Too late. The door slams shut behind him, blowing half of her file onto the floor. She frowns and turns to me. 'All right, all right, so we're not the world's most sophisticated caterers, but we do our best with what funds we have. Let's get on with it, shall we?'

#

'First things first: it says here on your screening interview form that you refused legal representation, correct?'

Lying bastard never offered me a lawyer. I nod anyway.

'Good, right.' Priya reaches into her jacket pocket and produces a digital voice recorder. 'Pressing *record*.'

Just then, the sandwich arrives. I lift the top layer of bread and peer inside – tuna paste…it can wait – and Priya begins in earnest:

'Now it also says here that you came to the UK via Spain on a false document, correct?'

'Correct.'

'And, what's this in your medical note about a tattoo?'

'Yes, it's of La Janda.' I offer to show it to her.

'No, that won't be necessary,' she says. 'It's a gang, I assume?'

'No.' I laugh – no doubt she was hoping to reject my claim under one of the Refugee Convention's exclusion clauses. 'It's a beautiful *comarca* in the province of Cádiz, Spain.'

'Com-what?'

'I think you say "county",' I explain, and off I go: 'Along with the coastal villages of Zahara de los Atunes, and Bolonia next door, it is the most beautiful place on the earth.'

'Yes.' She looks at me with a mixture of bewilderment and disdain. 'I want to clarify something – you've been to this place on holiday?'

'I have.'

'Several times, I take it?'

'*Correcto.*'

'And it's in Spain, you say, so you obviously speak the language.'

'Andalusian is actually a dialect…'

'It's Spanish, right?'

'Well, yes.'

'And it is safe for you in Spain?' She looks up. 'You don't dispute that, do you?'

Tempting as it is to say something flippant about, say, the recent reintroduction of the Iberian wolf, I resist the urge.

'I do not,' I reply, and I think I know where she is going with this.

'But you didn't think to claim asylum there? Or perhaps you did?'

Yep. She is exploring whether she can send me back to Spain. She can't: no one took my fingerprints in Spain, the UK has lost access to the Eurodac fingerprint database anyway, and there is no legal obligation on asylum seekers to claim asylum and remain in the first safe country they reach – at least, not as yet.

'I didn't have to,' I say, and she puts her pen down.

'Not my question… Right, I am going to ask you a few questions about this group you say you fear, this *Vereda Frondosa*,' she says, and against my better judgement, I have a go at developing my ridiculous story.

'It means the Leafy Path,' I begin.

'Yes, so I gather…'

#

Midway through the interview, Priya stops me.

'OK, it seems only fair that I put this to you directly. I researched *La Vereda Frondosa* this morning, exhaustively, and – guess what? – I found no trace of them. Not a single reference. Now, either that is because they are the most secretive, furtive organisation in history, or it is because they do not exist.'

'Madam…'

'Before you answer,' she interrupts, 'I'm going to make a further observation: you speak remarkably good English for an Argentine.'

'I...'

'And, before you answer that...'

'*Mierda!* Are you going to let me answer anything?' I ask. 'What is this?'

She pauses, 'Funny you should ask that. I believe you know exactly what this is...'

'OK, I am confused.'

'Are you really, though?' She composes herself. 'Let's just say that for a man who's been in the UK a little under 48 hours, you know a lot about asylum procedure.'

I shrug.

'Permit me to summarise,' she says. 'You claim to be at risk from a group that doesn't exist, you speak perfect English – yes, you do – and you know more about the asylum procedure than many of my colleagues.'

Well, that is not saying much.

Last try.

'Alternatively...'

'Yes?'

'...you have poorly researched *La Vereda Frondosa* – one morning is nothing. I went to the international school in Mendoza – look it up. And I know about asylum here because, you know, I am claiming asylum here – I have *indagated* it!'

Priya laughs. 'You mean "researched" it. But, then, you know that is what you mean, don't you?'

'I am confused,' I say a second time, but it's hopeless.

'I was warned your account was most likely fabricated,' she says, 'but this...this is quite special. Tell me, Mr Whoever-you-are-in-the-real-world,' she presses, 'just what exactly is going on here?'

I freeze. The fun's over.

'Fine, have it your way. I am concluding this interview. Time 15:05.'

'Wait!' I try to buy more time: 'You haven't asked about my family or private life.'

'Oh, you mean your Article 8 claim? There you go again,' she says, laughing. 'What are you – a journalist? A lawyer?'

It's no use. 'All right, stop recording.'

'Certainly not.'

'I need a comfort break.'

'No, you don't.'

I reach over and press the stop button on the voice recorder, then I close my hand around it.

'What on earth do you think you're doing?' she snaps, trying to prise the device off me.

I keep hold of it and, against all my human instinct, place my free hand over her mouth.

'Shhhh,' I whisper. 'I'm not Argentinian.'

'No shit!' comes her muted response. She reaches for a panic button under the desk; I release the recorder and block her. She is looking at me in disbelief. This is horrible. But it's make or break.

10

Very slowly, I remove my hand from Priya's mouth. She makes as if to shout, so I replace it. Again, I remove my hand and, again, she tries to shout. This continues for several rounds. Several times, I appeal to her to hear me out. Eventually, she nods and I remove my hand.

Silence.

Then...

'You have thirty seconds.'

'Just listen.'

'Twenty-five.'

'Give me a chance!'

'19, 18, 17...'

'OK, there's something weird going on.'

'You're telling me!'

'My roommate. Where is he?'

'Who?'

'Abay, the towering Nigerian guy.'

'Oh him, yes. Not your business.'

'Where is he?' I press.

'If you must know, he was transferred, OK? Can we get back to the interview now, please?'

'Where to?'

'Where was he transferred to? I don't know. That's the Onward Transfer Team's domain.'

'Ha! I thought as much.'

'Yeah, the clue's in the name, Einstein.'

'You don't know where they took him, do you?'

Priya laughs, then leans forwards until she is right in my face.

'No, I don't. So what? Enough of this!' She reaches for the panic button again. Again, I stop her.

'Can you at least find out for me?' I plead.

'Certainly not!'

'Wait. Abay told me he was seeing a legal aid solicitor in the morning. Could you just check for me that he did?'

'Absolutely not.'

I search for another way through:

'The big lady!'

'What?'

'Disabled? Middle-eastern looking?'

She looks blank.

'Come on! How many people are detained here? Can't be more than a few hundred? She was taken yesterday.'

'Transferred, you mean?'

'Yes, where have they taken her?'

'OK, I'm calling time on this.'

'And…Tapa?' I find myself choking up. 'The elderly Chechen gentleman? The man is very unwell.'

She shakes her head. 'Then he has probably been moved to somewhere better equipped to his needs.'

'They already tried to bundle him off once – he thinks to Africa, or the Indian Subcontinent…'

'What?' Priya is incredulous. 'That is absurd!'

'The man has an asylum claim pending!'

Priya moves to pick up the voice recorder and again I smother it with my hand.

'Let go of it.' She slaps my hand. 'Let go, I said!'

I take my hand off the device.

'Thank you.' She presses record. 'Time: 15:12. Resuming

interview. Now, where were we? Ah yes. Who do you work for?'

I shoot forward and stop the recording again.

'I'll have you for assault!' she shouts, then rocks back on her chair and scowls at me. 'You are a journalist, aren't you? Come on, out with it. The sooner you come clean, the sooner you can start preparing your mitigation.'

My attention is drawn momentarily to a noisy bluebottle buzzing in and out of the lampshade overhead.

'Are you always so astute?' I ask. And I mean it. She is wrong, of course. Appealing as it sounds, I am not a journalist. But she has destroyed me in argument, and in record time. I study her more closely and – can't be helped – I am drawn in. In the glow of the bright lamp, those round brown eyes seem almost olive-coloured, and – what is that? – there's a small hole on the side of her left nostril. A piercing perhaps? Once again, I find myself wondering who the person is behind the uniform.

'What do you want?' she asks, and I am back in the room.

'A few things, I guess: information, the truth, justice...'

'Stop dodging my questions, prick! You know there are serious criminal sanctions for the shit you're pulling?'

'There are worse sanctions for the shit you're pulling.'

'Oh really?' she says aghast.

'Breaching international law...'

'What?'

'Tell me, how many of those selected for onward transfer are represented by lawyers?'

She frowns. 'All our detainees have access to a lawyer.'

'Not what I asked.'

'I'm not playing this game.'

'It's no game, Priya!' I reply, gripping her arm in desperation, then letting go again. 'How many were given a full asylum interview?'

'As I feel sure you know,' she retorts, 'not everyone in here claims asylum. And of those who do, many choose not to have a lawyer – yourself, for example.'

I press on, unabashed. 'What do you know of their whereabouts? The transferees' I mean?'

She pauses. 'Once transferred, a detainee is no longer our responsibility.'

'You don't have a clue where they are, do you?'

'My colleagues will,' she says.

'Well, De Rossi must,' I probe.

'All right Columbo, where are you going with all this? If you're insinuating that he's doing something dodgy, I can safely tell you there is no chance. The man wouldn't break a bylaw, he's so clean.'

I allow her words to settle a moment.

'Too clean?' I ask.

She rolls her eyes.

'Humour me for a moment? He's the manager here, right? So, why's he doing menial tasks?'

'He isn't.'

'He is conducting screening interviews, for Christ's sake – that's chumps' work!'

'Steady! He is supervising the new staff – totally normal.'

'Does he also organise transfers by any chance?'

She laughs. 'Oh, wow, we have a genius in our midst. Of course, he bloody does. He is the manager!'

I sigh.

'Worn out, are we?' she asks. 'Go on, please, make me laugh some more. What is it you think he's doing?'

'No,' I reply flatly, and now nobody is laughing. 'You tell me where he is transferring them to.'

She gives no ground. 'Where are detainees normally transferred to? Other removal centres, medical facilities...'

'In other words, you don't know?'

'Well...'

'Well, you are going to help me find out.'

'Don't be ridiculous, I have more urgent things to do than pursue some half-baked conspiracy theory.' She places a finger on the record button of the voice recorder.

I stand up to leave. 'You're going to shaft me, aren't you?'

'Yes,' she replies.

'Very well. But ten quid says you can't find a trace of Abay. Nor of Tapa, for that matter.'

\#

I let the door slam behind me and keep walking, braced for a tap on the shoulder at any minute, or a shove to the floor, or worse. They'll escort me to De Rossi first, presumably, then to the police. And what will I tell them? My pulse accelerates – I don't even have a coherent idea of what the thugs are doing, let alone proof! How in god's name could I have been so foolish as to trust an immigration officer? And how many vulnerable people could suffer as a result? It occurs to me to hide.

11

Halfway down the corridor, I duck into the TV room where five men are sitting on tatty sofas watching the cricket in silence. The walls are adorned with grubby fingerprints, a broken light switch and stock photographs of Home Secretaries past and present, getting in and out of big flashy cars.

I walk in and introduce myself.

'Fahad,' one of the men responds. He points to a small space in the middle of one of the sofas. 'Come. Sit, sit.'

I squeeze in and sink myself as low as I can, like a young child shutting his eyes so as not to be seen. Then I see that the man to my right is crying. I catch his eye; he looks away.

'Who is winning?' I ask tentatively, and the men look at me like I have just desecrated the graves of their ancestors.

Fahad swallows. 'India,' he confirms.

'Ah no!' I reply. 'Still, not over yet, gentlemen.'

Just at that moment the TV commentator's voice rises several decibels and the cameras shoot to the pitch being invaded by hordes of screaming, jubilant fans in light blue shirts. Three of the men in the room stand up and walk out, leaving me with Fahad and a slender man in his thirties, wearing a fitted shirt and a cloth cap.

Fahad asks me where I am from and I lie, of course.

'We are all from Lahore,' he says, 'except Salim here. He is from Karachi.'

The man fidgets, plainly not understanding what we are saying. 'Poor Salim,' Fahad continues. 'He is...gay, you know?'

'OK,' I reply, unsure how I am expected to react.

Apparently unsatisfied with my response, Fahad expands: 'I know what you are thinking. But no, he is not like the fakes, all right? He really is' – he grasps my arm – 'a homosexual.'

'Yes,' affirms Salim.

'OK…' I reply again. 'He is happy?'

'Does he look happy to you? The man is dying.'

'What?' I examine him more closely. The man really is excruciatingly thin, and indeed, slumped motionless in his chair, he looks far from well. 'You are right,' I respond. 'This man needs help, urgently.'

'Don't worry, the officer said he will be taken somewhere else soon, where he can get treatment.'

'No!' I react, causing both men to jump. 'Does he have a lawyer?'

Fahad relays that he has asked his own lawyer to see him, a certain Mr Abassi, 'Expensive, but top notch.'

Never heard of him. 'Does he have the money?' I ask.

'He has nothing, but it's OK. We have had – what do you call it? – a whip around?'

'Salim could see a solicitor for free,' I explain.

'Not a proper one, though.'

'Yes, a proper one.' I tell them about the advice surgeries my firm runs in the centre, by which I mean 'next to' the centre, of course – they wouldn't knowingly let us lawyers inside. 'What day is it? Wednesday. There is one tomorrow.'

Fahad shakes his head. 'Mr Abassi is a highly reputable gentleman…' he begins again.

'Fine,' I interrupt, 'but…'

'But what? You don't know anything about him!'

I take a deep breath. 'I know an excellent firm of solicitors – number two in the country – who can help Salim *for free*.'

Fahad begins to look more interested, and I convince him to let me ask Salim some questions, while he translates.

Getting to grips with Salim's account is a challenge. He is timid and less than coherent a lot of the time. I focus on what seems most urgent, namely his health, and soon learn he has been experiencing multiple problems: breathlessness, extreme tiredness, nausea, cramps, trouble swallowing and something akin to a seizure.

I stress that he must refuse to be transferred anywhere – at the very least, until after he sees a solicitor – and when I see them both nodding, I breathe a sigh of relief. Mr Abassi may be perfectly competent for all I know, but who wants to risk finding out? The difference between landing a good lawyer and a dud can be, quite literally, the difference between life and death.

#

The men leave and with no sign yet of anyone coming to arrest me, I return to my cell. If the fuckers had wanted to find me, they would have come looking by now. And that might be a relief, I reflect. But it doesn't answer what they plan to do with me.

12

Not a peep from Priya all day and it's hard to know whether to be grateful or alarmed. Working around the one-hour midday lock-in, I do a couple of rounds of the centre, looking for clues, trying to dream up arguments to elicit her help, et cetera, but aside from the odd vague anecdote from the rollie smokers in the courtyard, it proves fruitless. A good proportion of the detainees I approach appear either unwilling or unable to talk. One bloke I come across, who is foaming at the mouth, even tries to take a swing at me.

'Spice!' a passer-by shouts over his shoulder, referring, presumably, to the psychoactive substance. 'Turning everyone into thugs, man.'

Of those who do engage with me, it's the limbo they want to talk about. One poor Yemeni woman I spoke to said she had been in here three years and counting, despite her lawyers' best efforts to get her out. She rolled up her sleeve to reveal multiple lacerations on her forearm.

'What else can I do?' she said.

But another person, a Chinese dissident who spoke good English and flinched every time an immigration officer came close, summed it up best: 'Can't stand the waiting; same time don't want it to end...'

Deeply distressing as these accounts are, I have to remind myself that there is precious little I can do about it right now. It's hard enough to challenge the indefinite detention policy in court and I focus my efforts, instead, on why it is that those I spoke to haven't been 'dispersed' themselves. And it's not easy, this: while a pattern of sorts is emerging, the deeper I dig the less I seem to uncover. Talk about cognitive dissonance – half of me is screaming for answers, while the other is whispering calmly that there are none. And all this in the knowledge that at any second, I could be seized and the whole investigation rendered academic.

#

Back in my cell for the night, awaiting the clunk, there is a faint knock on the door, followed by a whisper.

'Just you in here, Guerrero?'

Priya?

'Guerrero?' she repeats, a little louder this time.

'Yes, just me,' I say.

'Shhh!' She shuts the door behind her and turns off the light. 'They catch me in here, I'm screwed, you understand? Listen, I've found virtually nothing on the OTT.'

'Didn't think you would,' I whisper back.

'Listen, please. OK, I'm going to make a decision on your asylum claim.'

'OK.'

'I'm going to dismiss it, obviously. But I'm going to accept your nationality as Argentinian, understand?'

Smart: they cannot send me to Argentina without an emergency travel document, and for that, they need my consent.

'You're buying me more time,' I say.

'I wouldn't put it quite like that. I'm buying *us* enough time to complete our investigation.'

'Oh, I see it's *our* investigation now.'

'I'm 95% sure there's no malpractice here. But for peace of mind…'

I feel my shoulders dropping. 'You need to rule it out.'

'Exactly. I'm going to need your co-operation.'

'Of course. Look, for what it's worth, you're doing the right thing.'

'We'll see about that. I'm not at all convinced.'

'You don't have to be. With stakes this high, suspicion is enough.'

'To get me fired.'

'No.' I try to reassure her. 'Something's awry. Trust me, I've seen this shit before.'

'Oh yes?'

'Confession time. My name is Alex, and before this – OK, until very recently – I was…'

'Go on.' She clasps her hands together.

'…an immigration and asylum solicitor.'

'Ha! I knew it!'

'No.'

'No, what?'

'No, you didn't,' I tell her. 'Or you would have said.'

'Well, all right, I suspected it. Subliminally at least, I knew you were one of them.'

'Explain?'

'A lefty, do-gooder, no-borders type with little better to do than hamper our government's efforts to control immigration in a safe, regulated way.'

I laugh, but it's triggering.

'You sound like a fucking politician!' I snap. 'Don't believe all the tripe you're fed in this place. Trust me, if your people controlled immigration safely, mine would be out of a job.'

'Ah yes,' she says wryly. 'You mean the job the government contracts you to do properly.'

'Which we do! It's our job to hold them to account!'

She checks the time on her phone.

'Help me with something,' she says. 'What made you suspect the OTT is dodgy?'

'The evidence,' I say. 'And precedent, I suppose.'

'What precedent?'

'All right. Before I began my little sojourn here, I was often struck by how opaque you lot could be, but never more so than in the case of a certain Congolese client of mine – Zizimia Imani was his name.' I write it down for her. 'One minute he was detained in here, the next he had been "dispersed" to Glasgow without notice or explanation.'

'There will have been a reason.'

'Then why not tell us what it is?' I compose myself. 'I knew something was off, just not *how* off. Incompetence and cover-up seemed the most likely explanation. Not once did I imagine that anything coordinated existed, let alone a so-called "*Onward Transfer Team*"…'

She folds her arms. 'Go on.'

'Well, it got me thinking…'

'Yes?'

'Strictly speaking, it wouldn't be the first time an immigrant was "disappeared", would it?'

'Oh, codswallop – give me one example.'

'Remember that story of a year or so ago about the Yemeni bloke they seized in a dawn raid and refused to name?'

'The terrorist, you mean?'

'That's the one. At least, that's what they labelled him…'

'Honestly, you lot, you're all the same. Everything's a conspiracy, isn't it?'

'Whatever. They never revealed his identity,' I remind her, 'so how was anyone to know who he was, or what he did or didn't do?'

Silence.

'If his neighbours hadn't reported the brutal way he was dragged from his house naked and shoved in a van,' I continue, 'he wouldn't have existed at all, for god's sake.'

'OK, let's not get carried away.'

'Who's getting carried away?' I ask. 'Me? Or your colleagues? Man's probably dead for all we know.'

'Shit…'

'I know, right? Is it any wonder we don't trust you guys?'

'No, I mean "shit" as in, is that really all you're going on – a standard transfer and an unrelated, historic injustice?'

'*Four* unexplained transfers now, in fact. Probably many more. Here, right under your nose. And, of course not. You asked me what raised my suspicion. Since then, there's been more.'

'More what?'

'Evidence,' I tell her, though admittedly it's a big word for it. 'I'm compiling a list of common characteristics among those they choose for onward transfer, vis-à-vis those they don't select.'

'You've hardly met anyone have you?' she replies. 'Can't have been here a week.'

'True, and I'd like to meet more. But you know what? Already, a pattern's emerging. A deeply troubling one too,' I stress. 'Unless I'm wrong, it seems they are profiling people – and it's anyone's guess where they are moving them to.'

I think I hear a short sigh of relief.

'OK, OK, right. Make me a copy of your list, yes?'

'Sure. Wait! How do I know I can trust you?'

'You don't,' she replies.

I hesitate a moment.

'I'll have it for you tomorrow morning.'

13

Five days left

I awake to the sound of a note being stuffed under my door. I hop down from my bunk and find that it is unsigned. Written in bubble writing, it simply reads 'L-183 X'. A locker number?

#

In the canteen, Fahad taps me on the shoulder.

'I need to talk to you. It's Salim. They said he can see someone from Hatton Gardens firm you mentioned.'

'Hatton Taylor? That's great news! Thank you, thank you!'

'No, wait, I haven't finished. He wasn't at breakfast and he's not in his cell either. I'm worried about him. He's not a well man.'

'You have checked the bathrooms?'

'All three of them. I've asked the duty officers on our floor too. No one could tell me where he is. I tried Healthcare, but he's not there either.'

'OK, leave it to me.' I grasp his arm. 'Quickly, though, you know where the lockers are?'

'The lockers are for staff only. I tried to get access to one but…'

'Those ones. Where are they?'

'Outside Rosey's office, isn't it?'

'De Rossi's? OK, great.'

En route to the lockers, who do I bump into but the manager himself.

'Ah, Guerrero, still here I see,' he says. 'Have you not been interviewed yet?'

'Yes sir, I have,' I respond, slipping back into role. 'It was painful to go through all those things that happened to me in *La Argentina*, you know?'

'Oh, I can quite imagine,' he replies, his tone the epitome of earnestness. 'I'll check what's happened to your file – you will be wanting a swift resolution of your case, no doubt.'

Once De Rossi is out of sight, I find the lockers, pull out the list I have copied for Priya and scribble furiously on the other side of the paper: '*Urgent: Salim is missing – v. ill – concerned he's being transferred – needs a lawyer asap – needs proper medical attention*'. I stuff the note through the locker's mailslot.

#

On returning, I pass Priya in the corridor who, professional as ever, barely registers me. I too keep walking, pausing only for a fraction of a second to register her scent – *Escape*, couldn't make it up.

I find Fahad still in the canteen.

'Any more about Salim?' I ask.

'Yes, good news,' he says. 'I asked to see De Rossi, who confirmed he has been transferred to a place with better facilities to manage his health.'

I freeze. 'Did they give a name?'

'Trout House. It's near...'

I run off to find Priya.

#

Too late. As I hurtle down the corridor towards the lockers, I see

Priya enter De Rossi's office and shut the perspex door behind her. I glance over my shoulder to see the coast is clear, then crouch down to listen. It seems she got my message.

'...the Indian chap?'

'Pakistani, sir. His name's Salim Khan?'

'I've told you before, it's Gian to you, darling, OK?'

'Yes, sorry Gian.'

Just then, I am interrupted by footsteps in the corridor. An officer. Novak.

'Well, well, well – what do we have here?'

Caught in the act, I clutch my ankle and roll onto my back. 'My ankle, my ankle!' I cry. 'Please. Take me to Healthcare.'

It's not a bad performance, I feel, but Novak is having none of it.

'Sure I will, chap, just as soon as you have explained to the manager what you were doing snooping in on his conversation.'

'*Perdón?*'

He grabs me by the mohican and pulls me to my feet.

'*Qué cojones haces?*' I yelp.

'Well, your ankle seems to have made a miraculous recovery,' he sneers, getting right up in my personal space. 'No issues with load bearing, I see.'

'You ill?' I ask – well, there are limits...

'Eh?'

'Your breath, it stinks of garlic.'

He punches me square on the nose, knocking me to the ground, then jumps on me, snarling, unsparing, a hungry little bulldog unleashed. More blows. I use my arms to protect my head but he grabs my neck, he starts to squeeze and – Jesus! – I'm choking. I grab his forearms to try to prise them off but...no...use...passing out...

'If you die, you die,' he whispers and I feel my eyes rolling back before, by some miracle, a passing detainee rushes in to stop him and a second calls out for help. The door is flung open and out storms De Rossi.

'What in god's name is going on here?' he growls.

Sheepishly, the thug gets up and dusts himself off.

'I caught this man listening in on your conversation, sir.'

'I see. Thank you, Novak. I'll take this from here.'

De Rossi ushers me into his room and shuts the door. Now, if I learnt one thing from my internment at boarding school it was that you get your excuse in early. Yet before I can even open my mouth, the manager pulls a paisley handkerchief from his pocket and hands it to me.

'Here, mop yourself up,' he says. 'Extremely sorry about old Novak, he's so…irascible.'

'It's really not your fault,' I reply, and De Rossi pauses.

'You should know that a Pakistani gentleman – erm, Faizal was it? – came to see me earlier.'

'Fahad?'

'Yes,' Priya interrupts.

'He mentioned your joint concern for a friend. Salim, correct?'

'Mr De Rossi wants to reassure you,' Priya interrupts, 'Salim's been transferred to another detention centre, where he'll receive more specialist health care than we can provide here.'

'Which one?' I ask, as if Fahad had not already told me.

'I shall have to check again,' De Rossi answers. 'One of the larger centres, closest to his nearest and dearest, no doubt. Why do you ask?'

'He knows no one. Fahad and I, we want to stay in contact with him.'

'Well, naturally,' he replies. He removes his glasses, pulls out a cloth and begins cleaning them. 'I shall get you the contact details for him at his new address just as soon as I have them. How does that sound?'

'Thank you, I would like them this afternoon please,' I respond. 'Salim, he gets very anxious.'

'Of course he does, that is very understandable. To reassure you, however…'

'I want to reassure *him*,' I interrupt.

'Mr Guerrero, you need to show more respect to Mr De Rossi,' Priya butts in, glaring at me, 'especially if you want his help.'

'No, it's quite all right,' De Rossi responds. 'I do understand the concern. As I say, I'll get those details to you as soon as I can, Mr Guerrero. Now, if you'll excuse me, I have much to be getting on with.'

'Thank you so much for doing this, Gian,' Priya says, sounding almost sycophantic.

'Yeah, thanks Gian,' I say, delivering a fake smile.

'A little familiar, perhaps?' De Rossi asks.

'Sorry.'

'Sorry *sir*,' Priya corrects me, glaring.

'Oh, sorry, yes – sorry sir. Sorry.'

De Rossi smiles broadly. 'Go on,' he says, 'both of you, shoo!'

But I am not quite done. I ask him where Tapa has gone.

He scratches his nose. 'Tapa, you say? Of course. Any others?'

You tell me…

'Mr Guerrero?' he prompts.

'No. Thank you, sir.'

'All right, then be gone,' he says jovially, and ushers me out.

#

Later on, De Rossi finds me and confirms that Salim had been moved to Trout House. He seems less polished than before, and do I detect a faint trace of alcohol on his breath?

'Why Trout House?' I probe. 'Is it a hospital?'

'It is near one. Look, I am afraid I can't tell you very much more without the man's consent.'

I begin to feel sick again. 'But you have his – how you say – "*datos*"?'

'His details, perhaps? Yes,' he replies. 'I ought to be able to get them for you within a day or two.'

Something doesn't stack up.

'You can give me the number for Trout House, no?'

De Rossi laughs. 'I'm afraid there is none. All liaisons with detainees are now done through staff or via regulation mobile telephones. Do not worry, I am sure he will be issued with one very soon and when he is, they will let me know.'

I thank him for going to the trouble and his shoulders drop.

'And…'

'Tapa?' he interrupts, then bows his head. 'Not such good news there, I'm afraid.'

'What happened?' I ask.

'Heart attack, I am told.'

'What? What hospital is he in?'

'No, I am afraid he…he has moved on.'

'Where to?'

'No, I mean he is no longer with us.'

I feel a numbness in my throat. 'Yes, yes,' I answer, unwilling to register what I am hearing, 'who is he with now?'

De Rossi looks me square in the eye. 'We lost him, Mr Guerrero,' he says unflinchingly. 'Tapa is dead.'

14

Later that evening, Priya pays me another clandestine visit.

'You got my list?'

'What? Oh, yes. What was it again? No legal representation, non-white…'

'Yes,' I confirm eagerly, 'and either ill or unskilled. All the transferees I know of so far have met that definition.'

To my bitter disappointment though, Priya seems unimpressed.

'Did you hear about Tapa?' I ask hurriedly.

'Yes, look, hold on a second, OK?' She proceeds to tell me how she waited until De Rossi had clocked out for the day, went back into his office, checked through the paperwork on Salim's file pin and found his transfer papers, correctly addressed to Trout House. 'There was even an email read receipt at the top of the bundle, which proves the documents were duly sent,' she relays.

'Well, that is odd in itself, isn't it?' I suggest. 'I mean, who leaves a read receipt at the top of a bundle?'

'Erm, lots of people? Think we can safely assume you're not an admin person, Mr Guerrero.'

Seriously? I'm back to *Mr Guerrero*? 'OK, but I mean, isn't that a bit anal?'

'Managers *are* anal,' she tells me. 'It's their job to be. They *manage* things, see? Anyway, I hope that assuages your concern about Salim? I'm sure Gian will get his number for you soon.'

'We'll see…'

'You should also know I randomly cross-checked other files

and guess how many of them made reference to the *shady* Onward Transfer Team?'

'Tell me.'

'Many. You are not going to believe this. The reason is simple: each and every file that concerns transfer of any detainee to any other removal centre is, by definition, a matter for the Onward Transfer Team. Don't believe me? Their logo is literally stamped on every such document.'

I try to compose myself. 'Well, I've never once heard of that group. Hey, nor had you before this job, right?'

'This is my first Home Office job.'

'OK, anyway, you know what I mean. As far as we're aware, the onward transfer business doesn't exist in any other removal centre, right?'

'But that's just it, it does – in effect, if not in name. Every removal centre has transfer capabilities.'

'Oh, come on, Priya. You don't think it odd that in a linked network of removal centres, just one has an umbrella group to deal with transfers?'

'No, not especially.'

'Nor that outside Herringsworth, no one seems to have heard of it?'

'Erm, I've just told you it's on all their transfer literature!'

'Exactly! And still no one's heard of it! Can you be sure the email to Trout House was genuinely sent?'

'There was a bloody read receipt on Salim's file. I just told you!'

'A print-out. You know you can manufacture those, just by editing a genuine one, subbing in different details and pressing "print", right?'

'Whoa, this is conspiracy theory on a whole new level.'

'Is it?' I am getting desperate. 'Tell me – these files. Are they not normally locked away in filing cabinets?'

'Not always.'

'You said the bloke was anal…'

'All right, yes.'

'So, you had a key?'

'To the office, for emergencies. Not to the cabinets.'

'Then, how…'

'He had forgotten to lock one.'

'Ahhh, I seeee.'

'Oh, god, what now?'

'He wanted you to find them.'

'Oh, please.'

'Did the stamps you saw look fresh? Bet they did.'

'Enough of this craziness. Off the record, I called Ian about Tapa too.'

'Ian…?'

'My fiancé. You know he heads up Removal & Reception for us, right?'

'I heard your colleagues say something to that effect, but I…'

'In a nutshell, he runs a transport logistics company and Herringsworth outsource removals to him. Basically, he charters his planes to us, coordinates the removals, ensures minimum reception standards are met on arrival, and so on.'

'Cosy.'

'Yeah. Point is I asked him about Tapa's story and he confirmed that, often, it proves more cost-effective and less restrictive to fly returnees to Africa first, before flying them on to other states. In other words…'

'I knew Tapa wasn't making it up.'

'No, I doubt he was. They were probably intending to route him via Africa to Chechnya.'

'A touch circuitous, don't you think?'

'A touch, yes. But you know these entrepreneurs – they'll do anything if it's *financially viable*.'

'And never mind the fact that he had an outstanding asylum claim?'

'Did he, though? Had he actually made a claim at that stage? I've found no record of one.'

'He told me he had.' I pause. 'Where is he now?'

'Tapa? Transferred.'

'To?'

'Somewhere he can be better looked after.' She sighs.

I gather myself. 'No.'

'That is what I was told,' she replies.

'You don't know, do you? Tapa is dead.'

'What?'

'De Rossi told me earlier. Heart attack.'

'Oh gosh,' she replies, putting a hand to her mouth.

'Allegedly.'

'Oh, don't start that again.'

'He was on to them. I told you at my interview what he said…' I pause. 'It's a bit odd that you didn't know, isn't it?'

'No, I've had my head down. He's probably sent an email out or something. Oh no, I'm so sorry to hear that,' she says softly, her eyes welling up. 'He seemed a sweet man.'

'Who should not be dead. If he really is…'

'Enough.'

'Check your email.'

Hesitantly, without dropping eye contact, she reaches for her phone, then begins scrolling through her emails. 'There,' she says, looking over her shoulder and passing me the phone. 'He sent it to all staff.'

I read it carefully.

'Satisfied?' she asks me.

'All right, so he sent out a generic email. Wait, give me that a sec,' I continue, reaching out and grabbing the phone. 'Yep, he sent that *after* telling me about it.'

'And?' she asks, shaking her head. 'You're incorrigible, aren't you? That means absolutely nothing.'

She is right. 'Yeah,' I vent. 'Well, the stress he suffered in here can't have helped his condition.'

'They were trying to move him to a better environment.'

With no comeback to this, I change tack. 'Still nothing on Abay? Anything on Imani, my old client?'

She takes a deep breath. 'Nothing on them in the filing cabinet I saw. Must be in another.'

'If there's a record at all.'

She rolls her eyes. 'What will it take to convince you this is legit?'

'Is that what you're trying to do?'

'Only because it plainly is!' she exclaims. 'Seems you want to see abuse where it does not exist.'

I take a moment. 'Or maybe it's because my time as an immigration and asylum solicitor has taught me never to trust you lot? There's always an abuse. The only issues are what type and how big it is!'

Priya makes for the door.

'Where are you going?'

'Oh, come on! I've investigated this fully, indulged your wild conspiracy theory and taken you at your word. Now take me at mine.'

'Love to,' I reply. 'What's the address?'

'That's not even funny.'

'Neither are you.'

'What's that supposed to mean?'

'You're bloody in on this, aren't you?'

15

Four days left

'Not a word, remember? I could lose my job for less.' She is hurrying me out of the health centre.

'Carole, you have my word,' I reply, stuffing the bit of paper with De Rossi's and Priya's email addresses in my pocket.

'Seriously, they're very precious about their details being given out. He'd better never know it was me that gave them to you.'

I thank her again, rush upstairs and catch Amir just in time, packing up his belongings for release.

'That's it, mate, I am outta here!'

'Congratulations again, *amigo*, I am very happy for you! Before you go though, I have a little *favorcito* to ask of you...'

#

It's a hard sell. Amir has been legal in the UK less than five minutes and here I am asking him to hack the manager of the detention centre from which he is finally being released.

'What? King Dandruff himself? Are you joking?' Nope, this is going to require more than goodwill.

I play the flattery card. 'Sorry, *maestro*, I know it's a serious challenge and everything, but, well, you're the only person I've met with the skills, and the *cojones* to pull this off.' Then I throw in some intrigue. 'Listen. Between us, OK? There is something very dodgy

75

going on here.'

'Ooh, spooky!' he grins.

'I'm serious, Amir. People are disappearing, man.'

Still grinning, he leans forward and whispers in my ear. 'I know.'

'You do?'

'Yes. And I know why too.'

'Tell me, please,' I ask anxiously.

'Because – hold on to your seat, man – this is a *removal* centre!'

When he has finished laughing, I try again: 'How long have you been in here?'

'It'd be two months tomorrow.'

'And in that time, have you heard of anyone moving to another detention centre?'

'Have I?' he replies. 'They transfer folk all the time. What's your point?'

'Any of them white?'

He thinks about it and admits that he cannot remember seeing any. 'I couldn't say for sure though,' he adds. 'Most of those transferred stay so little time you barely register their existence before they're gone again.'

'I don't think that's an accident.'

'What do you mean?'

'I mean they only seem to transfer non-white people. Don't you think that's odd?'

I ask him if he still has a copy of his screening interview, and to check if there is capital letter or something written on the first page. My thinking is that the 'W' printed on mine might have referred to my ethnicity. Amir then tells me something new: allegedly, Herringsworth is used as a hub for dispersal to other centres – 'To cut costs', Novak told him. Yet, that is odd in itself, for Novak told *me* he knew nothing about transfers...

'Did he tell you why they are dispersed?' I ask.

'It's to even out numbers, he said, I think. Oh, and to place folk nearer their loved ones, that's right.'

I reflect a moment. 'And you?' I ask. 'Are you near your loved ones here?'

'My girlfriend's in Croydon, so not the closest, but it could be a lot worse. She never visits anyway.'

'No?'

He sighs. 'They banned 'em didn't they?'

'What?'

'No social visits for at least a month now. They *told* us it was to crack down on smuggling, but I reckon it's just because old Dandruff felt like it. He does whatever the fuck he wants, that bloke – gets off on it.'

I nod in agreement, and try a different tack: 'You really don't like him, do you?'

'Do you?'

'But you're not prepared to hack him?'

Silence.

'You told me it was easy,' I press him.

'It is easy.'

'Then…?'

He sighs. 'Look, the issue is this, right: the more connected the person you hack, the more likely you're gonna be tracked, like. And you don't get much more connected than government servants – which is basically what old crusty is.'

'Ah, I get it,' I say all-knowingly. 'You are scared.'

'No!' he retaliates. 'I am…careful.'

'Ha! Is that what you call it?'

#

In the end, it is the lure of heroism that seals it.

'Just imagine, for a moment,' I tell him, 'my instinct is right…'

'Here we go! All right, go on, then.'

77

'You hack him.'

'Yeah…'

'And, you find some *seeerious* shit on him.'

'Such as?'

'I don't know…he is a member of the KKK in Europe…or a massive money-washer or something like that – anything – there must be something on him. Then…'

'Yes…?'

'Then imagine that it was you, Amir, who outed him…'

His eyes flicker.

'…and the number of victims and potential victims you would have helped. Then…'

'Ok, I get the message.'

'No, I am not sure you do yet. Then imagine those victims thanking you, personally and publicly, and the implications for your career. I don't know, they would probably recruit you to secret services or something! Or to some big tech company!'

'No mate.' His eyes light up. 'I'd get the funding to start my own.'

'My point is simple,' I emphasise. 'Yes, it is a risk. But it is a risk worth taking.'

By this stage, the man is nodding along with me. 'Here, take it,' I say, pressing the piece of paper with the email addresses on into his hand. 'I would give you my email too, but I've no access in here.'

'No one does…'

'Which is why I need you, Amir.' He looks down at the paper in his hand. 'Think about it like this,' I insist. 'Why on earth would I take a risk with you, a stranger, if I did not think I was onto something big? You could tell on me, and then what? I would become even more fucked than I am now!'

For a moment he seems convinced, then takes a step back. 'Whoa whoa, who are you?' he asks, waving the paper at me.

'I was wondering when you would ask,' I reply. 'I'll tell you who I am. I am a trained lawyer, with a very good sense of smell. And guess what? I smell a rat in our midst. A rat with dandruff.'

'Fuck it, let's get him!'

'OK, good. Look into anything on the Onward Transfer Team and these four names: Abayomrunkoje, Tapa, Salim and Zizimia Imani.' I write them down for him in order. 'The first three were taken this week; the fourth some months back. Tapa is dead, it seems, and the other three's whereabouts is anyone's guess.'

'I'll need to get him to click on a link to something.'

'Something enticing, no?'

'That's right. Something he really wants.'

'Sure, you said earlier. And, I think I have just the bait...'

16

Three days left

The Refusal Letter arrives promptly, even by the Accelerated Procedures Team's standards. As expected, my claim is carved up into segments, each one either accepted or rejected.

I see that, once again, Priya had been true to her word: my identity and nationality are accepted without question. She has also accepted that I arrived in the UK from Spain on a false passport (as indeed I did – even if the bloke who obtained it for me was not in fact an agent, but a delinquent friend of mine). To my amusement, she has even acknowledged that the cattle herding methods I said I employed were '*not altogether inconsistent with traditional gaucho techniques*'.

But then comes the inevitable. She categorically rejects my claim to have been targeted by the so-called Leafy Path: despite an exhaustive search, not one reference to them has been found, nor has any evidence been adduced by me to substantiate this core part of my claim. And she does not accept, therefore, that I suffered persecution in my native Argentina. Claim refused.

#

I corner her coming out of the Ladies.

'Find anything on anyone yet? Any evidence the OTT is genuinely a transfer team and not a vehicle for…'

'For what?' she snaps back. 'You don't even know what you are accusing them of! Can you not hear how mad you sound?'

I get closer to her so as not to be overheard. 'You promised me you would at least rule out the possibility of any abuse.'

'Yes. And, to my satisfaction, I did. Here, I suggest you look at this.'

She hands me an official print-out of the names of those recently detained at Trout House. And there, at number seven on the list, is a Mr Salim Khan.

On seeing the name there, I feel instantly queasy, hand the note back and ask to sit down. She smuggles me into a breakout room, checks that no one has followed us, and shuts the door.

'You see?'

'I've got to admit,' I say, drawing breath, 'this doesn't help my theory.'

She smiles sympathetically.

Last try: 'De Rossi could have redirected him there when we sounded the alarm, no?'

But she indulges me no further. 'It's time to come clean on your identity.'

'Or what?' I ask.

'Or you will face imminent removal to Buenos Aires!'

'I can think of worse places…'

She balks. 'All right, prison then, when they bust you and return you to the UK.'

'*If* they bust me,' I reply. 'Besides, *Nullum crimen sine lege*.'

She scratches her temple. 'Nope. You are going to have to remind me.'

'The legal principle that a person cannot face punishment except for an act that was criminalised before he performed it…'

'Nice try,' she laughs. 'You've committed enough individual immigration offences to keep a court busy for a week! You need only start with the document offence…'

'Humour me,' I swagger, but I fear I have overlooked something.

'Let's see – using a false instrument?' Shit... 'That alone can earn you up to ten years...you did know that, right?'

'In extreme cases...' I retort. But the truth, I reflect, is that I have barely, if ever, had to think about tariffs. While many of my former clients came to the UK on false passports, refugees are protected from punishment for such things and in practice, not even my least credible asylum seeker clients were ever prosecuted. The difference between them and me, however, is that I am not, in fact, an asylum seeker of any description. Quite the contrary. I am a British citizen, with a right of abode...

'True...' she replies. 'But you're looking at 12 months minimum if you fess up now. I mean – let them remove you to Argentina first and...'

'They'll double it?'

'At the very least, I'd imagine. The courts will want to make an example of you.'

I feel sick.

'Look on the bright side,' she tries to console me. 'At least you won't be charged with impersonating an asylum seeker in your own country of origin. *That* offence, as far as I know, does not exist yet...'

I laugh, but I can barely breathe. For the first time, perhaps, I am conscious of the sheer extent of the mess I am in.

'You know, this may surprise you to hear but, on reflection, I'm not entirely sure this mole thing was such a great idea after all...'

'Don't be so harsh on yourself,' she says sarcastically, though with more than a hint of compassion. 'You might have at least planned it a bit though...'

A kerfuffle breaks out the other side of the door, and I hear someone saying, 'Couldn't keep away, could you, Romeo!'

There is a knock and in comes Ian, doffing his Panama hat, the brilliant white of its toquilla straw accentuating his sunburnt skin.

'Not disturbing you, I hope?'

'Bunny, you're back! I've missed you,' Priya says, removing the label from the hat.

'Bunny?' I repeat under my breath, appalled.

'Yeah, that's right,' he replies, still staring lovingly into her eyes. 'People often have cute names for each other…when they are in love.'

She blushes, but again I kill the moment. 'What is yours for her, then? Is it Bunny too?'

He coughs. 'It is actually. Any more questions?' he asks with a bemused smile. 'Come grab me when you're finished, my love.'

'Oh, we're done here anyway, thanks. Mr Guerrero was just querying his Refusal Letter.'

'There's an appeals system for that, isn't there?' Ian quips. He takes Priya's hand and ushers her out. 'You staying here, Mr Guerrero?'

'As long as I can,' I reply, which elicits a chuckle.

'You know, I rather like this guy,' I hear him say as the door closes behind them.

#

Alone in the breakout room, I flick off the light, lie on the floor and contemplate my fate. Amir might still come up trumps, I muse. But that depends on how far his technical ability is real and not embellished. Even then, there is a good chance he will find nothing. There is even a strong possibility, I have to concede, that De Rossi is legit (albeit, still a dick).

I pull out the appeal form, fold it, rip it into shreds and throw it up in the air. Interesting as an appeal might be, the risk of stumbling across a barrister or judge who knows me is too great. I would be bound to get one of the really nice ones too – those dyed-in-the-wool heroes, who give their all for little reward but a periodic besmirching in the gutter press. I couldn't handle the shame.

I have run out of road. And, with a growing acceptance that my instinct about the transfers was unfounded, I confront my choice: fess up and face national humiliation, jail and a criminal record, or embrace my removal.

Either way, I ridicule myself, there'll be plenty of time to reflect on how the fuck it all went wrong, to pen that disaster memoir. At the same time, something weird is going on. For the first time in god-knows-how-long, there is no discernible tension in my neck and shoulders, and my breathing feels deep and steady. It hits me that in spite of the spectacular mess that I find myself in – or because of it, even – I no longer feel scared.

I let myself imagine what would happen if I were actually to write the stupid thing, and allow myself a wry smile. It would be slow-build, naturally, but well worth the reward at the end. In fact, such is the sheer idiocy of what I have done, publishers would probably be all over it. They'd go all out – turn it into a feature film. You can just picture the trailer, complete with Redd Pepper-style voiceover: *'FAIL: the full story behind what caused a man to sink to the very depths of stupidity and claim asylum in his own country...'*

FAIL

17

Two years before I lost the plot

Is there anything people won't do for money, I wonder, staring out over the City of London from a top-floor conference room at Wallis Grunt commercial law firm. Today marks the end of my solicitor's training, and the panel sitting across the table from me is offering to keep me on and to double my (already generous) salary. Tempting? It's a no-brainer. But something is holding me back.

It's funny how we tend to focus on whether others want us, to the exclusion of the bigger question, namely whether we want them. I'm embarrassed to admit that since starting here two years ago, this is the first time I have genuinely considered whether I want to work here. And the answer, awkwardly, is not what I expected.

'Mr Donovan? Can we assume that's a "yes"?'

It is dawning on me that there may be a limit to the number of corporate softball matches I am willing to sacrifice my summer evenings for. I should be less frivolous. At risk of sounding idealistic or ungrateful, even, I studied law to make a difference to people's lives, not to be holed up in a data room all day, compiling disclosure bundles for some ethically challenged energy giant – I know, which begs the question: why come here in the first place?

'Mr Donovan?'

Easy. Dad's idea. And the small incentive of a free legal training, settlement of ALL my student debt, paid employment for two years and the chance I'd take to it, and multiple opportunities to do *pro bono* work (few of which have materialised, I notice…).

'Mr Donovan?'

'Yes, I…I was just…'

'Giving us an answer?'

'Yes.'

'Wonderful!' The panel members rise to their feet.

'No. Sorry, I meant yes, I was giving you an answer…'

As they hover above their seats, I confirm that I wish to decline their offer. And after a cringingly inarticulate attempt to explain myself, I return to ground level with a bump. Seconds later, however, moving through the giant revolving doors to the street, a lightness returns to my step.

#

A week passes, and with no plan and bills to pay, the novelty of being unemployed is wearing off fast. I've done some searches for law firms specialising in human rights work, but any that do seem to demand a wealth of related experience, of which I have precisely none. Did you not consider this before you resigned, my late father might have asked, and it crosses my mind that I have made a terrible mistake. 'Law is one of the noble professions,' he told me. And to a greater or lesser extent he was right. Questionable morality aside, we held ourselves to high professional standards at Wallis Grunt which is more than could be said of, say, certain firms of estate agents.

Just then an advert I spot on LinkedIn grabs my attention. *Do you have a passion for justice and holding the government to account?* it reads, and I click on the link. The job is for a solicitor/caseworker at Hatton Taylor, a firm specialising in immigration and asylum law. I read on with interest but do a double take when I see the pay – one-sixth of what I would be on if I had stayed at Wallis Grunt. Still, I tell myself, everything's a trade-off, and a quick look at my outgoings suggests it's just about feasible – the advantages of being a bachelor. They seem legit too – ranked second in Chambers & Partners – and so what if they're based in South London? I tart up my CV, download an application form to peruse and resolve to think on it.

An hour or two later, I'm halfway into a special-offer bottle of *crianza* and thinking about drunk-dialling my ex – she'd say I was a fool for leaving the job, I imagine – when a news item about refugees appears on the television. It features a dapper KC with a floppy fringe – I don't catch his name – lamenting the loss of a boatload of some 70+ asylum seekers off the coast of Dover.

'Unless and until proper safe routes exist for these people,' he says, 'we are going to see many more casualties of this nature, and on a much larger scale.'

The camera then crosses fleetingly to a woman whom the KC introduces as his junior.

'Each and every one of these deaths was preventable,' she agrees, and I am ashamed to admit that I miss what she says after that, struck instead by the subtle lilt of her accent and the compassion in her bright eyes. I don't believe in fate as such, but seeing these two standing up for the vulnerable gives me the shot in the arm I need. I fill out the application form and send it off.

#

I go a month without hearing back from Hatton Taylor and by now I have contemplated pretty much any and every form of gainful employment I can imagine: internships with NGOs – fat lot of good as they're all unpaid; freelance journalism –similar issues; skilled apprenticeships – I'm 'overqualified' apparently. Shit, I've even toyed with returning to Wallis Grunt and begging for my job back. Honestly, if it weren't for supportive friends like Danso in situations like this, I don't know what I'd do.

'Alex, chill,' he told me a week ago, in typical Danso style. 'Worst case scenario, the sofa's yours – in fact, hold up, Hemingway, you can write your memoirs from it!'

Anyway, enough prattle. The news just in is that finally – wait for it – Hatton Taylor have offered me an interview. And call me woefully naïve but my sense is that, if I can just get a foot in the door here, a new world awaits on the other side. Perhaps, even, a world where people really care.

18

Warm Friday afternoon in June, and I'm haring down Peckham Road, one eye on my phone. I turn right down Rye Lane and slow to a brisk walk.

#

Hatton Taylor's offices are set back from the road in a converted Edwardian villa. I ring the bell and the receptionist shows me to a large conference room. A 1950s juke box sits in one corner. Otherwise the furnishings are sparse and less swanky than my old city firm's and the coffee and biscuits are conspicuous by their absence.

I take the liberty of opening a sash window. Above it, chipped cornicing runs around the high dusty ceiling like an antique picture frame. Just then, there's a knock on the door and in come my interviewers.

They introduce themselves by their first names: Marina, Karl and Kenan. None of them are wearing a suit, and Marina has on a chunky, multi-coloured necklace and bright yellow blouse.

'And you must be Alex Donovan.' She smiles. 'Please, take a seat. Right, why the switch from corporate law?'

'Jesus! Why don't you just ask him direct?' says Karl and all four of us laugh.

'Well?' she says.

'I want to help people,' I reply. 'And it's the closest I can think of to being a priest, without having to believe or be celibate...'

Kenan leans forward. 'So, you are OK with obedience?' he quips, and we are away.

#

Thirty minutes later and we're standing up and shaking hands: I am going to be an immigration and asylum lawyer. Marina makes a phone call and a drinks trolley arrives. I brace myself to meet my new colleagues.

First to arrive is the firm's Senior Partner.

'Jedrek, hi,' he says. 'Welcome aboard.' He shakes my hand and explains that he will be supervising me. The rest, comprising lawyers and support staff, turn up in dribs and drabs, some making a beeline for me, others heading straight for the trolley. There's not a briefcase in sight and no one attempts to engage me in chat about banal reality TV shows. And when someone puts on some old-school hip hop, I find myself beaming inside. The corporates can keep their biscuits.

#

When enough people have left and it seems polite, I steal quietly away. Or so I think. On the way to the bus stop, Marina comes into view. She is standing outside a pub called Stormbird, cigarette in one hand, Martini in the other.

'Not so fast!' she calls out, and I recognise half the people I have just met. 'There are two types of legal aid lawyer.' She laughs, brushing her fringe out of her eye with the back of her hand, and gesturing for me to join them. 'You're either a fitness nut, or a boozer.'

#

I stay until the bitter end – well, you would, wouldn't you? – and I'm heading home when I see a 24/7 and remember something. I grab a six-pack of Stella, take a bus across town and leg it down Bermondsey Street, looking out for a dingy loft and loud music: my friend Danso is DJing at a squat party.

#

Up six flights of rickety stairs, and I'm in, engulfed in smoke and dancing. It's heaving. I find the makeshift bar and trade in my beers for some cold ones from an ice bucket on the floor. As I turn around, I clash heads with someone and apologise.

'No, you're all right,' she replies, and we lock eyes.

'Why, thank you...' I offer her my beer.

She smiles and holds up hers. 'Have one, thanks.' And with that, she disappears back into the party, leaving me with the sensation that I have seen her before somewhere.

#

There's a sort of landing at the back of the building and some stairs out onto a roof terrace. There I find her, looking out over the cityscape towards The Shard. She is fairer than she looked inside and her eyes sparkle with the city lights around her. As I approach, she tosses her cigarette on the floor and stamps on it.

'Filthy habit,' she says.

'There are worse, trust me.'

'Oh yes?'

'Talking to strange men on dingy rooftops.'

'Who says it's dingy?' She lights up another and offers me one. We do names – hers is Amy – and in no time we are on to, 'I'm curious, what do you do with yourself, Alex?'

I've been waiting to say this to someone, and today I kind of can: 'Actually I'm a human rights lawyer.'

She tilts her head and asks what type of human rights work I do, and I tell her, adding that I am, in fact, ehm, 'yet to start'.

I'm dying to ask her about herself, but her questions come thick and fast. Which firm am I joining? What do I make of them? Why the move from corporate? I'm talking too much, but it's so easy.

'You wanted to help people...' she prompts me.

'That's right,' I say, cringing at how earnest I must sound.

'So, you decided you would become a noble defender of human rights.' She smiles.

'That's right,' I say again, puffing out my chest. 'A fearless apologist for a secular religion I can call my own.'

'Good for you.' She laughs. 'Seriously, we need more people like you.'

Blushing, I concede that I don't suppose I'll solve all the world's ills... 'But if I can help vulnerable people to navigate our complex immigration and asylum laws and keep them safe, I'll be a happy man.'

'Ahh,' she says, 'that's really lovely. Well, well, well.'

'Well, well, well...what?' I reply, and seize my opportunity. 'And you, Amy? Can I ask what you do?'

She smiles. 'OK. Erm, how to put this? Your firm instructs us. I am a barrister at Ascham Chambers.'

Oh god – I fan my face with my hand – I knew I recognised her. Still, faint heart never won fair lady. 'Another beer, perhaps?'

She politely declines and I'm resigning myself to take the hint when a couple of long seconds later, to my delight, she asks if I know anywhere round here to grab a bite.

#

You can always rely on the Spanish. It takes us less than two minutes to reach Jose's Tapas Bar and though the place is officially closed, the waiter and I remember each other from a long lunch I had there with my old man. He clears us a space at the white marble bar and goes to fetch a cloth to wipe it down. The whole room is candle-lit, and every so often, when there's a gap in the chatter, you can hear the broken cry of flamenco guitar.

Amy's phone buzzes. 'The boss,' she mouths to me. 'Anton, hi, yes, sorry, I was famished. Yes, I'm absolutely fine.' She rolls her eyes. 'Yes, not to worry, I'll get a taxi. I said I'm fine! Cool, see you Monday after court.'

'Your boss was at the party?'

'I say "boss". He's my head of chambers. But, yes, some of the clerks invited us along. You know, I'm quite glad they did...' she blushes, and diverts her gaze to the serviette-strewn floor.

'You refer to the music?' I ask.

She laughs. 'Actually, I did enjoy it. He's good that DJ.'

The waiter appears. I order a couple of glasses of *Rioja* and we chat about his family while my new acquaintance squints at the menu chalked on the wall behind the bar. She invites me to choose, and when the waiter's gone again, she turns to me.

'A Spanish speaker I see...*hombre*!'

'You too?' I ask.

'No.' She laughs. 'I did a case with Marina Perez. She's at your...'

'She interviewed me,' I interrupt. 'Seemed lovely.'

'Amazing lawyer too. Anyway, she told me if you ever want to appear like you've understood something, you just say *'hombre'* – works for everything.'

'*Hombre.*'

The waiter appears and fills her glass. I thank him again for letting us in and he shushes me.

'This man is a gentleman,' he tells Amy to my embarrassment. 'Last time he was here, he invited everyone a drink.'

Was my late father actually, a while ago, but no need to disabuse her of this version. The conversation moves to Spain and to Andalusia. She raves about Seville and I wonder, could she go any higher in my estimation? OK, marginally perhaps: she hasn't seen Cádiz...

Oops, I'm off. I tell her about the *pueblos blancos* of the Costa de la Luz, about the remote fishing village of Zahara de los Atunes and its wild and infinite beach, about its night life and its picaresque population.

'Oh, and it is home to the most beautiful restaurant in the world,' I add.

'Big claim…'

'*El Refugio.*'

'No,' she says. 'You're pulling my leg?'

'Kid you not. It's a terrace by the sea, with a beautiful sprawling fig tree in the middle.'

'Yum, figs are my favourite,' she whispers, and I start to question whether any of this is real.

It is. When the bill comes, my card is declined. She instantly offers hers but the waiter again comes to my aid.

'Loyal customers rule,' he declares. 'You pay twice next time.' At last, I remember his name.

'*Mil gracias*, Rogelio.'

'*A ustedes*, Don Sanz.' He laughs and opens the door for us.

'Sanz?' Amy asks on the way out. 'Your surname?' And I am forced to confess that the last time I was here, I may have attempted to introduce myself as the Spanish music sensation, Alejandro Sanz.

#

On the walk to the bus stop, I discover that Amy lives in Kilburn. I offer to get her a cab, but she reminds me I have no money. I press my Oyster card into her hand. 'Here, at least have this.'

'I have money.' She smiles, handing it back. 'Not much, but enough for the bus.'

We walk straight past the first bus stop. And the second. I learn of her upbringing in Connemara, how her father passed away when she was 12 and how her mother turfed her out four years later. 'Bless her, poor thing, it wasn't her fault. No space. I was the eldest and she had five younger mouths to feed.' She found some work, she continues, her tone lifting, front of house in a fancy hotel, then finished school and applied to Oxford to read Jurisprudence. 'To my astonishment, they offered me a full scholarship.'

'Always wanted to be lawyer, then?' I ask.

'I'm one of the precocious ones who knew when they were like… four,' she replies. 'I had my own wig by eight…'

'You serious?'

'I had you there.' She laughs.

I stop counting the bus stops.

#

It must be, what, two in the morning? Three? Anyway, we're passing the Globe Theatre and I offer her my arm. She hesitates, then takes it and I feel a shudder. I never want this night to end.

#

It doesn't. On we drift, past the Tate, down the South Bank as far as the Festival Hall, then up the steps to Hungerford Bridge. Halfway across, Amy stops to let some noisy revellers pass, and we peer down at the obsidian-black river beneath, rolling silently on.

'*Tamesas*,' her voice is gentle. 'The old Celtic word that gave the river its name. It means "dark".' It is quiet now, just the wave-like swoosh of distant traffic, and the slosh and slap of the water on the piers below. I want to bottle this moment and keep it somewhere safe.

When I look up, she is pointing back across the river, the tips of her hair lifting in the gentle breeze.

'Sublime isn't it?' she says, and we watch, mesmerised for a moment, as The National Theatre morphs from shamrock green to warm sunset red, majestic like a Rothko monochrome, tightly framed by the night sky.

'You know, you just don't get that in the west of Ireland.' She laughs. Our eyes meet again, the lights and the water behind her softening and eliding like *bokeh* effect behind a subject in sharp focus. I move closer to her, and she to me. Then a shout.

'Amy!'

She looks to her left as we are hit by a waft of marijuana.

'He's here, come!' I feel her arm tightening in mine.

A few paces down, on the Embankment side of the bridge, we stop and listen as an elderly-looking man in a red, black and white rastacap, strikes up a tune on a steel drum. On his t-shirt are the words 'Peter Pans'.

'Trini,' she whispers in my ear, as he throws her a knowing nod. I reach into my pocket and drop the little change I have left on his music case. He stops.

'Yes, yes, my emerald empress. Where you been?' He points at her and looks at me. 'This wonderful lady got me a gig at her work Christmas party.' He smiles. 'Jus' imagine. A big-ass hall full to the brim with fancy attorneys. I telling you, I cleaned up that night!' Just then, his expression drops.

'Tell me, dear.' He puts a hand on her shoulder. 'How is she?'

'My sister?'

He nods.

She looks down and affects a long intake of breath. 'She is in the clear!'

'Yes, child!' He shuts his eyes, all smiles and reaches forward for a fist-pump. 'Now that is some proper good news!'

#

Amy gives the man a fuller update: her mum's moved over and is renting a two-bed with her sister somewhere in Woodside Park.

'Only problem to address now is her much-revived sense of humour if you can call it that. Seriously, growing up, I couldn't decide which was worse – Claire's jokes or mum's soft rock ballads!' And when he has relayed to her his own news, he declares himself done for the night and starts packing up his kit.

'Look after yourself, Pete.'

'Always,' he replies. 'Later, gal. Good to meet you...'

'Alex.'

'Alex, cool. Take care of her, you hear? Precious cargo you have there.'

'Scouts honour,' I reply. She puts her arm in mine again.

#

Boundless beautiful night. We wend our way through Covent Garden, past Trafalgar Square and on up Charing Cross Road. Then it's north to Euston Station, the pretty way, via Bloomsbury, taking in all the squares and gardens we can along the way. It is still and warm and almost the only people about now are the street cleaners and a passing ambulance crew. But the sun is rising and it's home time. Almost. In the empty station, she buys us each a tea and we find a spot outside to sit and drink it.

#

Her cup is still half-full when she stands and dusts off her jeans.

'Thank you for a really wonderful night,' she says and holds out her hand. I smile and shake my head, then move to kiss her, but sense she is hesitant.

'Safe journey home,' I tell her. 'I'll be seeing you around, I guess?'

'Yes please,' she says. 'I mean, I hope so.'

#

I walk home through Regent's Park with a spring in my step,

taking in Avenue Gardens, the tiered fountains, the roses, those towering ash trees. I can feel myself smiling as memories of the night return, one after the other, each as happy as the last. 'Amy,' I say aloud, and hatch a plan.

19

I start by finding her on Google. Turns out there are a disproportionate number of barristers called Amy, but I get there in the end. Next, I ask Danso to email her the playlist of his set last night – copying me in – and to sign off the email: 'With compliments from Señor Sanz'. Then, I wait. And wait…

#

Three days later, Danso and I receive a 'Reply All' message, in which she thanks us for the music and a 'good night'. She signs off 'Best wishes'. Oh. We chew it over and conclude that it is going to take more than an edgy playlist to win her affections. Challenge accepted.

#

The job begins well and in week three I get my first opportunity to instruct a barrister. It's a Somali refugee appeal and my supervisor, Jedrek, is holding my hand throughout the process. When I mention Amy's name he nods with approval: turns out that not only is she kind and funny and gorgeous, she is a 'very promising young junior' too. Time to get to work on that evidence bundle.

#

A week later, I show up for a conference at her chambers in Gray's

Inn. I've chosen a late slot on Friday afternoon for it and I am antici-
pating some sort of reference to that sublime night to kick us off, but I
have underestimated her professionalism.

'Absolute fuckers,' she says on collecting me from Reception. And
with good reason: not only did the Home Office refuse our client's
asylum claim, his interviewer essentially tried to bully him into con-
ceding his case. It is all on tape, however, and Amy is confident we can
win the appeal. She also says we have grounds to lodge a complaint
on our client's behalf.

There is a short pause.

'Yes, absolutely,' I respond, decoding that 'we' in barrister-speak
appears to mean 'you', as in, me.

The client arrives late and in a state. Amy sits him down with the
interpreter and offers us all a tea or coffee.

'*Maya, mahadsandid,*' the client says, and makes a prayer-like gesture. He is white-haired and thin, and his shiny grey double-breasted
suit is at least two sizes too big for him. He has a kind, gentle face,
though he looks older than his 61 years – testament, perhaps, to his
having endured two decades of civil war.

'Mohamed is fasting today,' the interpreter explains. 'He says to
me he needs all the help he can get.'

Amy whisks him through his statement. She knows it backwards
already, even down to the individual paragraph numbers, and finishes
up by offering him some advice on giving evidence – try to answer the
question clearly; ask them to repeat it if you don't understand; if you
don't know the answer, that's OK; be courteous; how you come across
is as important as what you say, and so on.

When they leave, she signals for me to stay back and my heart
leaps.

'Was that really the first asylum statement you have drafted?' she
asks. 'It made me cry.'

'That bad?' I ask, and she snorts with laughter. In this field, I'm
discovering, you take your light relief where you can get it.

'It was beautiful, Alex. It read less like a statement and more like – I don't know – a poem!'

My heart is singing now, and before leaving chambers, I chance my arm: 'Don't suppose you fancy a swifty?'

'I'm sorry?'

Oh god! 'A drink?' I clarify.

'Oh, erm, that's very sweet of you. It's just, um, I've got a lot on and…'

'No worries.' I retreat as fast as I ran in. 'Another time, perhaps.'

'Yes, sure.' A poorly exposed screensaver of a couple on a moped appears on her desktop. 'I mean, maybe when I've cleared some of this work.'

I thank her for the conference, turn and walk out the door, but she follows me.

'Alex?'

'Yes?'

'Thank you.'

#

I would say I am disappointed, but crushed is a better word. When I check my email later though, there is a message from her. The first part is a formal note of the conference with some follow-up thoughts about case strategy. But at the end, she asks if I have a non-work email address that she could send something to. I sit up, and reply.

#

When her message arrives, it reads as follows:

Dear Alex/Alejandro(!),
I am sorry about what just happened. It was rude, and I feel I owe you
an explanation. I'd be really grateful if you would keep this message

to yourself.

That night, it was magical. I won't forget it – couldn't forget it – though it might be easier if I could. You came from nowhere, charming, gallant, funny...gorgeous. Tender. Within two minutes, I felt I knew you. And within five, I knew I didn't want to leave you. I honestly cannot believe I am writing this.

What I failed to tell you, Alex, is that I have a good man who loves me, who cares for me, who tolerates me. I couldn't bear to hurt him, and I would not be being true to myself if I did not tell you. I can't be sure if you felt the same thing that I felt that night, but it scared me. And forgive me if this seems melodramatic, but it can't happen again, Alex. It was wrong of me not to mention him, I make no excuses for it. But I need you to understand why I didn't, and that I am sorry. It is presumptuous of me, but I know you will understand. You're a perceptive bastard, aren't you? A rare, rare find. And I'd... But I can't. I'll stop there.

Take great care, Alex.
Xx

#

A month later, I receive a call from reception. 'Alex, I've got Amy Phelan on the line for you.'

I manage to put my tea down without spilling it. 'Thanks, could you put her through?'

She is calling to tell me about our client's hearing, and – YES! – his appeal has been allowed on the spot. She doesn't think the Home Office will attempt to appeal the Decision either, which means they will grant him refugee status. I stand up and punch the air.

When I have recovered my composure, I promise to inform the

client, then ask Amy how she is. As expected, she gives little away and I am going to hang up, but I surprise myself.

'I want you to know I do understand, Amy,' I say. 'I should have replied to your message. I just…'

'Please, no need to apologise,' she tells me. 'Thank you, Alex. Means a lot.'

That gentle voice.

'If ever there were a rare find, Amy, it is you.' I close my eyes. 'But I respect your situation. What can I say? I respect you.'

There is a muffled sound, then the line goes dead.

20

Days become weeks, weeks become months and today marks a full year since I started at Hatton Taylor. Alas, it's almost as long since I last saw Amy. Time flies when you're a legal aid lawyer. The work never stops, and neither do we. We're contracted to record seven chargeable hours a day, which means putting in at least another three for everything else – often many more. No complaints, of course. As Jedrek reminded us only today, it's a privilege to get to do this work. Indeed, at risk of sounding conceited, how many of us outside the medical profession can say we save lives every day? Speaking of which, two of my favourite clients were granted asylum today, I've booked tomorrow off, and tonight, at long last, I am going out!

#

It's nine-thirty when I emerge at Tottenham Court Road tube station, and still just about light. I walk briskly through Soho Square and down Frith Street to Little Italy. I'm due to meet some old City mates for dinner, and I am praying they don't do me over with one of those 'Shall we just split it five ways?' tricks. I know it sounds tight, but some of us have to think about these things, and besides, it's always the ones who have consumed the most who suggest it. Bruno, typically – the bastard couldn't eat a fish finger without pairing it with some fancy wine. I rehearse my after-dinner speech: 'Lads, what part of legal aid lawyer do you not get?' Right, I'm here.

Once inside, I cross the dimly lit dance floor, past the long mosaic-tiled bar, to the restaurant section at the back, where a tuxe-doed man with a clipboard greets me and shows me upstairs to our ta-ble. They're playing *Music to Watch Girls Go By* and my lot are already half-cut. Jesus, was it always so loud in here?

'Thursday is the new Friday!' shouts Bruno, passing me a shot of flaming sambuca. Well, this was inevitable, I suppose. I bite the bullet. And – who'd have thought? – it turns out to be quite fun. There's lots of drinking, reminiscing, more drinking, dancing on the tables (they actively encourage it in here), then news reaches us of a hen do on the floor below.

'On a Thursday?' I query, and promptly remember Bruno's stag, a couple of years back – he strung it out a whole week. Ay, those were the days when I had money… He's now yanking my arm: someone has to go down and invite them up, and as fate would have it, that honour has fallen to me…

#

At a glance, two of the women are in their sixties and the rest, like us, are late twenties/early thirties. But the striking thing is the atmos-phere: it's alarmingly sedate. That won't last, I pledge. But it is just as I am introducing myself as 'Tony Stagioni: a man for all seasons', when whose eye should I meet? Only Amy's…

Running on instinct (and a full tank of embarrassment), I keep up the act and ask for a volunteer to come upstairs to meet the boys and report back to the hen. There is some polite laughter – damn, this lot are serious! – then Amy puts up her hand.

'Your name?' I ask, my pulse racing.

'Lorraine,' she replies. 'Like the quiche?'

#

'Well, thank god for that,' she says under her breath as I escort her out of the room and past the dance floor. 'Love her to bits and everything, but I was dying of boredom!'

The place is rammed but we find some quietish stairs to perch on and she relays how, late as ever, she downed a couple of ready-mixed G&Ts on the way from the tube to the restaurant, 'Then I arrive and they're like, "Did you have any trouble getting here?" Kill me now!'

'My lot are the other extreme,' I laugh. 'They're probably setting fire to the table cloth by now, they're so wasted.'

Tuxedo man reappears and we stand up.

'Can't sit there,' he says, and Amy pulls out her cigarettes.

'Keep me company?'

#

'True friendship', said Isabel Allende, 'resists time, distance and silence', and the same is true, it seems, of whatever this is. Outside the venue, in a small cordoned-off space near the front of the queue, we trade stories with the same ease as before. I learn of a daunting, high-profile Iraqi appeal that her head of chambers has got her involved in, and of her summary removal from the chambers' pupillage committee for failing to score any aspiring applicant below a 17 out of 20, 'they were all magnificent, I tell you'.

In exchange, I fill her in on life at Hatton Taylor, and watch her blush as I share some comments I've heard about her 'top-notch' legal drafting. Amy. It truly feels like I've known her for years. And for a moment, I forget that I haven't.

'How's Claire?' I ask.

As the words leave my mouth, I get that sick sensation you feel when you make yourself vulnerable. While it seemed obvious to me that night that Amy's sister had recovered from a serious illness of some sort, she and I never actually spoke about Claire ourselves – what if she's not all right and I've just put my foot in it?

'Claire, my sister?'

'I'm sorry, it's none of my…'

'No, no, you're all right. Claire has…' – sharp intake of breath – 'sorry, "had", ovarian cancer. Still early days, but she is in remission. Her oncologist says there's not a trace of it left.' There is a pause. 'God, it's just…you never *really* know, do you? If it's gone for good, I mean?'

No, I suppose you don't, I reflect. And, just like that, we are right back there on Hungerford Bridge, watching the water and whiling away the small hours. Or anywhere, in fact. Talking to Amy is like listening to a beautiful, evocative piece of music through headphones: in an instant, your surroundings fall away, taking with them any ambient sound, and there you find yourself, weightless, suspended in that liminal space between thought and feeling.

Amy describes the ordeal – how bloody tough it all was on her mother and on her younger siblings, how she put Claire up in her small flat and looked after her between treatments, the sheer impotence she felt at not being able to take away her sister's suffering. 'Then there was the sickness itself,' she adds, stubbing her cigarette out. 'And – my god! – the uncertainty, the disorientation the poor girl had to contend with – I mean, can you imagine? You are trying to summon the strength to fight the damn thing and, at the same time, confront your own mortality.'

Out it pours, her eyes well up, and it is as if she were living it all for the first time. I picture her sitting tenderly at her sister's side, and it is too much.

'She is lucky to have you,' I whisper, as we embrace.

#

'I'd make a terrible witness,' she says a moment or two later. 'To answer your actual question, Claire is doing well, if a bit lonely. Needs a man in her life, if you ask me, but she says she's not ready. Meanwhile' – Amy opens her clutch bag and pulls out a tissue for her eyes – 'mum has gone and joined a rock choir and is in her fricking element.' She chuckles. 'Honestly, I don't think I can remember her happier. She might get herself a job, mind – the woman's bleeding me dry! Uh-oh' – she grabs my arm and pretends to hide behind me – 'Mr Charming's back…'

'Can't stand there all night.' The six-foot penguin lowers his clipboard. 'Staying or leaving?'

She looks at me, then towards her feet. 'Actually, we should probably…'

'Dance?' I reply, and lead her back in, past the bar to the dance floor.

'Alex, what are you like?' she shrieks, but moments later we are dancing, her arms loosely around my neck, her scent soft and sweet like jasmine. In the middle of the floor, camouflaged by drunks, she looks up at me, unflinching. I am distracted a second by the music – unbelievable. Dean Martin, 'That's Amore'.

'Bells will ring
Ting-a-ling-a-ling
Ting-a-ling-a-ling
And you'll sing Vita Bella!'

I step closer, I'm lifted off the ground…and fall badly on my leg.

\#

Who takes an espresso saucer onto a dance floor anyway? What did they imagine it was, a fucking private view?

'Not your night by the looks of things,' says a kindly paramedic as she and a colleague bundle me into the ambulance and begin plying me with painkillers. 'Gonna be a while before you walk on this, I'm afraid.'

'When the world seems to shine
Like you've had too much wine, that's amore.'

The last thing I see before I pass out is Amy's tearful eyes.

21

Two months pass and before I know it, I am hobbling about back at work, caseload ratcheting up again. Aside from a brief exchange about my recovery, I've not heard a peep from Amy. Nor do I feel able to contact her. As far as I know, she's still with the bloke – 'Jon', I gather – and that fleeting chance of an impulsive, blameless kiss feels firmly in the past.

'Everything happens for a reason,' Kenan says, passing me in the corridor.

Sure, I scold myself, everything except that shit decision I made – or did we have to dance?

I am back to full-time pleading with the Home Office: for better access to my clients, for action on their cases, for proper healthcare for them, for their release from detention, for cancellation of their removal directions, and so on. This is the battle that never ends. Just when you sense that you might be making ground, you are called back to the Home Office removal centre for new clients, many of whom are chronically unwell, most of whom will be living in fear of imminent return to lands they have left. On it goes.

The job has its glamour too, mind. Today, for instance, I get to have my first case conference with Amy's head of chambers whom I now know to be the eminent Anton Fletcher KC. The client this time is an apostate who fears harm if returned to Pakistan. She also alleges that on arrival in the UK, the Home Office detained her for two days without food or drink.

I've been looking forward to working with Anton Fletcher. My colleagues are always waxing lyrical about him. They say he possesses an extraordinary legal mind and a silver tongue; indeed, according to Marina, 'He could literally charm the birds from the trees'. Dr Doolittle eat your heart out.

#

In the end, the conference is short. Really short. I mean, we have barely sat down when he delivers his verdict: I, Mr Donovan, have grossly inflated my client's prospects of success on appeal, and we would be well-advised not to pursue it; without evidence, her abuse claim is equally hopeless. Ouch.

#

When he is gone and the dust settles, I recover a bit of perspective. After all, is it not the role of a barrister to make these kinds of decisions? I tell myself not to worry about my client either: however genuinely felt her fears may be, literally thousands of refugees owe their lives to this KC; it is safe to assume that he would not have negatively advised her if she were truly at risk of harm. And who could dispute that the man has judgement? It was he, after all, who offered Amy a tenancy in his left-wing chambers, despite objections that she had once represented the Home Office. O Amy – could anyone in their right mind ever let you go?

22

The skies get colder and darker, and now any word from you-know-who is reduced to the odd safe, helpful comment I see her make on the online refugee advice forums, or to second-hand tales I hear of brilliant things she has achieved in court. I didn't even see her at the Immigration Lawyers Practitioners' Association AGM this year. I scoured the room while an NGO person showed grisly slides of abuse in a removal centre, but not a trace of her.

Meanwhile, the Home Office continues to amaze – and not in a good way. Take this morning. I get in to find out they have effectively kidnapped my client – Congolese, bullet wounds, PTSD, the works – and moved him from our local removal centre to another in...Glasgow. The result? He is no longer in our legal aid procurement area, and I can no longer represent him. I mean, what the fuck?

\#

Sometimes, the only thing for it is to step out of the office, take a deep breath and remind yourself of why you're in the job – renew your faith in it, if you will. And for this, Peckham is the perfect place.

A case in point: the brightly coloured little café I'm sitting in is owned by a Nigerian couple, run by an Ethiopian woman and the waiter who just brought me my cinnamon coffee is Polish. Incredible when you think about it. And beautiful – all these cultures under one roof, each informing the other like multiple narrative voices. Whatever horrors and dreams push and pull people to settle on our shores, I muse, whatever challenges arise thereafter, who could seriously deny the benefit they bring?

'Ka-ching!' goes the cash register, a customer leaves and my eyes fix on a poster above the door; it shows a row of yellow minibuses and has the words 'WELCOME TO LAGOS' emblazoned across the top. Immigration – I cup my hands around my warm coffee mug – without it, there'd be none of this richness. That alone might justify the work we do. But this job, it's about more than that. Every day, people walk through our door, often straight off a plane from some horror they've managed to escape, with little to their names but the clothes they are wearing. And thanks to the job, we get to help keep them safe.

An anxious glance at my watch reveals it's time to go back. I'm about to stand up when the warm, aspirate flow of Arabic drifts into my consciousness and two men in flowing white jilbabs glide past my table on their way up to pay. One of them is holding a set of prayer beads, my thoughts elide, and it occurs that the reason I do what I do is actually very simple: I believe in it.

For most of my life, it seems, the fear has been of just passing through obliviously, not believing in anything. From a young age, in fact, the only thing I truly believed in was doubt. And who wants to believe in that?

I start to feel light-headed and right on cue, in comes the nausea. Curious how, still, years on, even the briefest meditation on the past takes me back to that bare brick classroom. I never enter, never want to. That is, not until now…

For all its privilege, boarding school was a shitty place to find oneself, even for an only child like me. There was this goodly monk, though, called Father Ryan, who was kind to me and made those first weeks and months easier. He took the older boys for Theology and taught us Religious Studies. Being silver-haired, clever and softly spoken, I think he reminded me of my father. He even made the same tired groaning sound when you asked him a tricky question, and as with Dad, you felt you could ask him literally anything.

I was ten years old when I started at the school and he told me twice in the first term that I was 'Theology A-level material'. I took encouragement from this and felt special. Alas, it didn't last.

We must have been halfway into the Lent Term. Father Ryan was explaining the concept of Original Sin.

'We were all born bearing its curse,' he told us, 'paying for the misdeeds of Adam and Eve,' and so on.

Odd what the brain chooses to fix on. In this instance, it was the rhyme. Round and round the words tumbled in my head like a slow-spin wash cycle until something jarred and I was right back in the British Museum, where we had gone with the school the previous week, staring at the Rosetta Stone.

196 BC, the object label said. And I must have been doing that spaced-out, gaping thing Dad had warned me against, as next thing I knew, the guide was standing at my side.

'There's even older writing than that, young man,' he whispered, and told me about the Kish tablet, '...thought to have been written in 3500BC.'

Mind-blowing. But it wasn't so much the date itself that dumb-founded me. I was anxiously trying to square it with what Mr Karl had told us in Biology about the Omo Bones, 'thought to be 233,000 years old', and the fact, therefore, that humans had existed for literally hundreds of thousands of years longer than writing.

All that time without reading or writing, I wrote in my diary that night before lights-out.

#

When I raised my hand in class the next day, Father Ryan recip-rocated with a smile.

'Ah,' he said. 'Alex. Not like you to have a question.'

I remember my cheeks flushing and feeling for a passing moment like the teacher's pet. And while that was the last thing any of us would have wished to be – no one liked a 'suck' – there was a strange comfort in feeling seen.

'OK, this might seem crazy…' I began, prompting some sniggers from classmates in the rows behind. 'But, well, you know how the first writing we know of dates back to 3500BC…?'

'I'll take your word for it.' Father Ryan smiled.

'And that humans have been around longer than that – I mean, *much* longer?'

He blinked. 'Alex, is this relevant?'

The sniggers turned into laughter, my palms began sweating and I remember wishing I'd never embarked on the dumb question. To his credit, though, the learned monk kept a straight face and invited me to finish the question.

'Oh…just that…if Adam and Eve were the first humans… Then who saw what happened to them?' Father Ryan glanced at his watch. 'I mean, if writing hadn't been invented yet, then who wrote it down?'

A silence came over the room and for the first time, the gentle man lost his temper with me.

'Alex, are you quite done with being facetious?' he asked, locking me in a stare, then got on with the rest of the class. Lesson learnt, I thought: when it comes to questions of religion, keep them to yourself.

Father Ryan never asked me again about my A-level choices and to be fair, I didn't blame him – who, in his shoes, trying to teach a syllabus, would want a pesky gadfly like me buzzing around his ear with off-topic questions? At the same time, I couldn't forget my school report for that year, in which Father Ryan described me as having 'a propensity to be flippant'. It was the first time anyone had ever called me that; I had to look both words up. It felt like a label, and it really bothered me.

\#

Gratefully, it was soon time again to return to my other life. Dad did the pick-up from school that summer. A sitting judge in the High Court, he would get decent holidays like me, and we stopped off at the 'boozer' for a refreshment on the drive home. 'Pint of Harveys and a shandy for the lad,' he said.

Things were back to how they always were, it seemed. But the following morning in mass, I remember my pulse racing when I knelt down in the pew next to Dad. I can't have been more than 10 inches from him, but it was as though he were in another place altogether. And when I shut my eyes to pray and nothing came, my eyes welled up.

When the priest came in and we all stood up my father must have noticed my tears.

'You OK, Alex?' he whispered.

'Itchy eye,' I said, whereupon I felt sick to the pit of my stomach: this was the first time I had ever consciously lied to him.

'Well, for heaven's sake, don't rub it,' came the response.

And that was that, I hoped. But the second reading that day was *Matthew 14:22-33*, in which Jesus walks on the water. It began to trouble me and I later mumbled through the creed like, well, like a person without a creed.

I struggled to eat my lunch that day and while Mum was making some of her delicious fresh mint tea, I took a seat next to Dad on the porch and summoned the courage to ask him about the parable. His response was reassuring.

'Does it matter if it really happened? I mean, it's possible, isn't it?' He put a hand on my shoulder and gestured towards the hills. 'If God could make all this – the entire universe – then surely it is not beyond the bounds of possibility that he could walk on water?' I hesitated. 'If he felt like it?' he pushed.

'I guess…'

'Well then' – he grabbed a ping-pong bat – 'what are you worried about? First to 11?'

That night, though, lying in bed, I reflected on our conversation and I couldn't sleep. Something was still niggling. On my father's reasoning, anything in the past could have happened at any time, right? So why believe anything? I wasn't sure how Dad would respond to this question. I only knew I couldn't risk asking him. There was this sense, somehow, that he'd been trying to protect me. But if so, from what? I shut my eyes and prayed that there was a God...

The Arabic-speakers must have left a good few minutes ago. I glance again at my watch and – crap – that's now 30 chargeable minutes to make up tonight. Still, I tell myself, only a few months and I'll get some respite: I've booked some annual leave – Spain – and without wishing to sound desperate, it couldn't come a moment too soon.

23

Spain comes and goes in a flash, of course, but the days length-en out to full stretch, and London basks in birdsong and barbecues. Bliss! I mean, sure, it's a shame to have lost another weekend to work. I am not exactly brimming with excitement about my six-monthly appraisal with Jedrek tomorrow either. But it is an honour to do what I do, and what is a year of radio silence from Amy to a man with my general good looks and gumption? Am I protesting too much?

Elegant, dimly lit and tucked away behind Camden Road, the Lord Stanley has become my Sunday night refuge. With no sign of Danso yet, I plonk my case papers down on the horseshoe bar, order an IPA and check my Twitter – sorry, 'X' – account.

My news feed is awash with tributes to Anton Fletcher KC, who, it becomes clear, has won that big Iraqi asylum appeal Amy mentioned to me. He has retweeted a link to the Decision, which has attracted 613 likes in 7 minutes. His comment reads, '*Court finds new, vulnerable class of asylum seekers worthy of protection. Couldn't have done it without my Amy*😊 *@AmyPhelan #IndispensableJunior*'. I hesitate, then click on the link.

The case concerns asylum seekers from Iraq and provides guid-ance for all future Iraqi asylum determinations – serious stuff. The tribunal has also defined a new class of asylum seekers at risk of harm, namely '*High net worth professionals between the ages of 20 and 45 hailing from Iraq*'. Catchy… I take a slug of ale and gaze up at the emerald lincrusta ceiling. No, fair play to them.

I am interrupted by the loud screeching sound of a bar stool being dragged across the floor, and a familiar, raspy voice in my ear. 'Hey Alex, sorry I'm late.'

#

'What time do you call this?' I reply, feigning irritation, and watch with fondness as Danso sets about disentangling his headphones from his dreadlocks.

Straightaway, he launches into a tirade of how his boss had been pestering him all day about a new live streaming platform he has built. 'I was like, I can't tweak this anymore, it's Sunday night, it's done – let me go!'

'You finished it?' I reply, laughing. 'Congratulations!'

'Meh, thanks,' he replies. 'Maybe save the praise till it gets off the ground. In this market, that's going to take some serious publicity... Anyway, boring, boring. So, tell me, how was it?'

My mind draws a blank.

'Spain? Your holiday?'

'Shit, sorry,' I reply. 'Seems an age ago already.'

He looks hard at me. 'Ever thought of going anywhere else?'

'Don't you start.' I laugh. 'I went to South America one year, remember?'

'Still Spain, basically. Anyway, it was good, right?'

'It was,' I tell him. 'A real tonic, thanks.'

Silence.

'Seriously? That's all you're going to tell me? Let me help you. What. Did. You. Do. There?'

'Right, yes.' What is wrong with me? 'Let's see... I ate, drank, swam, saw some friends, scored some weed, had a crazy idea, took a date to the Lemon Fish...that sort of thing.'

'Awesome!' he enthuses, then puts on his Poirot voice. 'A date you say? Or a dalliance?'

'Well...'

'Knew it! He's back.' He laughs. 'You know, for a time there, I feared you'd lost your mojo? I was like – DUDE – just join Tinder like the rest of humanity.' He clasps his hands together. 'So, does she have a name?'

I nod. 'And a bloke. Saw them out together the next day.'

'Nooooo!' He steers us back to the Lemon Fish.

I explain that it's a *chiringuito* – a pop-up restaurant on the beach. Then I proceed to describe it: its intimate open-air stage, its makeshift cocktail bar, its unparalleled position between the sea and the foothills of the Sierra del Retín. I am not doing a bad job either, I think, but Danso must hear the lugubriousness in my voice.

'All right, out with it,' he says, rocking back on his bar stool. 'It's not still…'

I bow my head.

'Oh buddy.' He facepalms. 'Hang on.' He swivels on his seat and orders himself an alcoholic ginger beer.

I can't help myself: 'You still drinking that shit?'

#

Outside, dusk is giving way to night. A steady flow of patrons begins moving inside, bringing with them a chorus of clinking glasses and warm, gentle chatter.

Danso doesn't hold back:

'She was always going to stick to the secure option.'

'See that's the bit I don't get,' I reply. 'Why is *Jon* considered the secure option?'

'Seriously? OK, let's see.' Danso draws breath. 'He's committed, mates with her mates, good job, well off…'

'Good job? He works for the bloody Home Office!'

'Exactly. And, guess what? Unlike some, he gets *paid* properly…'

'OK, but Amy's not like that.'

Danso laughs. 'Ay, Alex, my boy, everyone's "like that", at least to a degree.'

'She said…'

'Go on.'

'She said she wanted to be with me.'

His eyes narrow.

'All right, not in so many words,' I concede.

'Ha! I thought you lawyers were meant to be all about "attention to detail"? Look, even if she did say that, what did she ever *do* about it? I've met her type, man. She wants to keep you just where you are, chomping at the bit, her adoring My Little Pony.'

'Are you *trying* to wind me up?'

Danso raises his hand. 'I'm just trying to…'

'Yeah, I know. Look, I'm sorry. You're a good friend to me, Danso.'

'Good?' he replies, 'I'm the best! Watch this.' He ushers over the barman and orders another round.

#

When the drinks arrive, Danso raises his alcopop aloft. 'A toast to moving on,' he announces, prematurely as it happens.

'I blame Anton Fletcher KC for introducing them.'

'The human rights lawyer?'

'Yes,' I confirm, then clarify that *anyone* who works in immigration and asylum law is essentially a human rights lawyer, including me.

My friend looks puzzled. 'But you're a solicitor?' he says, and I can feel us slipping into the stagnant swamp that is legalese. 'Solicitors *are* lawyers,' I confirm hastily. 'We meet the clients, prepare their cases et cetera, then hand them over to barristers to do the work in court. Got it?' He nods, and – breathe – we're out.

Back to Jon.

'Here.' I reach for my phone, bring up Instagram and flick through the man's recent posts. 'OK, check this out. Does this man really look to you like the secure option?'

Danso drags his bar stool closer and has a good look. The picture shows a bearded man in his late 40s, wearing a llama-print poncho and holding his lips to a set of panpipes. Behind him, you can just make out the ancient Incan citadel of Machu Picchu, and beneath the photograph, there is a caption that reads 'Michu Pingu'.

'That him? Well, he can't spell, can he?'

I release an involuntary growl. 'Afraid it's deliberate. Pingu is his nickname for her – git says she waddles.'

'And she takes that shit?'

'There's worse. Here…' I show him some more posts. One is a picture of Jon in a vest, pistol in hand at a shooting arcade. Caption reads, 'Getting my guns out'. Another is a sort of homage in which he succeeds in lavishing Amy with so much effusive praise, he all but canonises the woman.

'Whoa…' exclaims Danso.

'I know, right? How does she fall for it?'

'Search me, pal. Why do cheeses succeed? Maybe she's not as clever as you think?'

'Oxford double first in Jurisprudence? She's no slouch, mate…'

'OK, so, maybe she just loves him, then? Cheese and all?'

'Or maybe she *wants to believe* he is genuine,' I reply, conscious that I am starting to sound like a stubborn client who won't accept that his case is shit, 'and her heart leads her head?'

'Or…'

We both laugh. 'Go on.'

'…maybe he *is* genuine?'

I pause and point at the alcopop. 'If that man's genuine, I'll drink one of those.'

#

By the time the bell rings for last orders, everything seems a little rosier. Standing over the pub's trusty upright piano, I listen as Danso plays me the melody of his latest composition. It is strangely beautiful.

'Now,' he says, 'just imagine the same melody played on an electric violin. Yep, found a super-talented young Afghan fellow busking under the arches. Crappy pick-up mic sellotaped to the sound post, barely spoke a word of English, but the sound…! And you haven't heard the best part yet, my friend. I want you to do the lyrics and vocals.'

'Seriously? Wait, let me think about it… Done!'

'Awesome! Oh, should've said. I'm on a tight deadline with this one. Pop round tomorrow after work and we'll lay 'em down?'

'Ah…'

Danso rolls his eyes. '…I've got this case…' he mocks.

It unlocks something.

'You don't get it, do you?' I snap. 'Just you try running asylum cases, we'll see how chilled you are. It's h…'

'High stakes stuff? Yes. I do get it, mate. Really I do.'

'I…'

'It's cool. I'll get someone else in.' He picks up his drink and swishes around the remnants. 'Look, I didn't come here to make things worse. Just wish you could get a bit more balance, that's all, do more of your singing and writing and stuff, hang out with us lot more, find some…'

'Don't say perspective,' I hiss, then bow my head in shame. 'I'm so sorry.' I reach for my pint and see my case papers staring up at me from the bar. 'It's just impossible.'

And just like that, the seal is broken.

'If I could only rely on the bastard Home Office to be above board, I wouldn't need to worry about my clients 24/7. I could sleep!' I feel my posture deflating like an unplugged bouncy castle. 'Maybe it's just the nature of the job?'

'Go on…'

'I mean there's no let up. Ever. Every day it's the same story – crisis upon crisis, instantly yours to resolve. And each nightmare as dreadful as the last: unaccompanied children at risk of removal to violent hellholes, women facing 'honour killings' at the hands of their own families…shit, the last client I signed up on Friday, a Peruvian woman, had escaped the bloody *pandillas*…'

'Pandillas?'

'Criminal gangs so brutal I could barely listen to her account. And after years of intimidation and abuse, she summons the strength to go to the police, and guess what they do?'

'They ignore her?'

'Worse, I believe. Anyway, I should stop. Probably told you too much already.'

'Lips sealed,' he replies, fiddling with a beer mat. He looks up and our eyes meet. 'I just wish I could help you somehow.'

'You already are.' I grab a serviette and discreetly dry my eyes.

#

We gather our stuff together and make for the door.

'Hey, maybe the Home Office will reduce your workload for you again,' Danso says, play punching my arm. 'Remember that time they effectively kidnapped your client and moved him to the other side of the country?'

'Oh, fuck yeah.'

'What hilarious word did they use again?'

'Dispersed,' I tut. 'Months acting for the bloke. Congolese, vulnerable as they come. Then, just like that, "We write to inform you that we have dispersed your client to Glasgow".'

'And the reason?'

'I forget exactly. "Logistical" I think, or something equally nondescript. I put in a Freedom of Information request to find out more, but so far they haven't so much as dignified me with a response.'

'Tossers.'

'You said it. For all I know they could have removed him from the bloody country!'

'Don't even joke…'

#

Outside, the night is now still and quiet. We part ways on Camden Road. Straight and wide and lined with street lights, it could almost be a runway.

24

Monday morning and it's back on the treadmill. I stuff a half-eaten croissant in my pocket, jump on my push bike and check my phone. 07:15 already. With a fair wind I'll be in Peckham and at my desk by 08:00. A diary reminder pings up on the screen: *Appraisal with Jedrek.* Wobbling, I try to check what else the day holds in store – HONK! – a lorry brushes past me. Impossible.

I thread my way through the traffic on York Way, pelt down Gray's Inn Road, into Legal London and shoot out the other side. The sun is already gathering height over Blackfriars Bridge, transforming the murky waters below into pools of swirling silver. 07:43. I pedal harder.

By the time I reach Peckham, I am drenched in sweat. Rye Lane is already bustling with butchers, fishmongers and grocers preparing to open, arty types, take-away coffees, suits, overalls, bins, buckets, mops, phones and loud marketeers setting out their stalls. At intervals, the aromas are overpowering. Who needs smelling salts, I muse, as a large freezer door opens into my path, damn near knocking me off my bike.

'Hey, watch where you going!' yells a man in a bold, red and gold *dashiki*. 'Oh my god, you cyclists have a death wish.'

I come to a stop outside the office, disconnect my seat and wheels and chain the frame to the railings. En route to the shower, I pass my supervisor doing up his tie in the mirror and try to slide past unnoticed. No such luck.

'All set, then, Alex?'

'Yes, more or less,' I reply.

'Good stuff. I took the liberty of selecting some files from your desk for auditing.'

I sort of half nod. 'Are we still on for 08:15, Jedrek?' I ask. 'Obviously, if you want to make it a little later for any reason…'

'We'll make it 08:30.' He shakes his head and skips off up the spiral staircase to his office.

#

The shower floor is a carpet of half-used and empty toiletries, dumped by colleagues old and new. I clear a space with my foot, pick up a smart-looking bottle of Pantene Pro-V and massage it through my hair. 'Here's the science part,' I mutter to myself as the warm water trickles over my hands and down my back to the ground. In an instant, I feel my shoulders dropping and my neck muscles releasing, though the sensation proves short-lived.

A knock on the door and an unfamiliar voice:

'You gonna be long in there, please?'

'Just a sec!' I call out, putting the shampoo back carefully where I found it.

I dry myself, sling on my trusty jeans and a t-shirt and make for the open-plan area. Once there, I dump my stuff on my chair and nip back to the bathroom.

'Yep, still there, you bastard,' I whisper, applying cream to a spot on my nose.

The pesky intruder returns and shoves past me to the shower, knocking the spot cream to the floor.

'I didn't have you down as the make-up type,' he says.

'Sorry, have we…?'

'Oh, do excuse me, I should have made your acquaintance before teasing you. I am one of the new solicitors here.' He holds out his hand. 'Toby.'

Before I go to meet my fate, I ping off a terse letter to the Home Office, demanding an urgent response to that Freedom of Information request I told Danso about, and threatening to sue them if they don't disclose my old Congolese client's file. 'Logistical reasons', my arse! I give them three days.

#

Jedrek's office is an unimposing little room, poorly lit, set on a wonky floor and decorated with rows of parallel shelves, each piled high with paper wallet files, yellow and sideways-on like a cartoon stack of pancakes.

On entering, I try a new approach. 'Have you seen the state of this?' I ask, showing him an article headed '*Health Tourists Swamp British Hospitals*', together with a picture of a huge crowd, presumably sourced from some random picture archive. A busy man at the best of times, Jedrek acknowledges my gesture with a sort of backwards jerk of the head and whips out a steel pocket comb.

'Punctuality, file hygiene, efficiency,' he begins, running the comb through his lank red hair.

'Yes, right…' I reply, pulling up a chair.

'I'm just focusing on these three things today. That way you'll remember them.'

'I'll do my best,' I reply, and watch as he rips open one of my wallet files and takes out a wad of messy case papers.

'Now, we're piloting our new clocking-in system next week, so we'll skip straight to file hygiene.' Jedrek reaches into his desk drawer, pulls out a box of treasury tags and a single hole punch, and hands them to me. 'From now on, I want you to think of these boys as your minders. Wherever you go, they go. Go on,' he says, clasping his hands together, 'read the letters on the side.'

I examine the hole punch. 'Oh, gosh, you have initialled it for me…' I don't know whether to laugh or cry but before I can do either,

Jedrek has stood up and stretched out his arms. I stand and brace for impact. Two manly taps on the back later, we are back in our seats.

In the interests of expedience, I try to take the initiative. 'So, that's punctuality and file hygiene covered, which just leaves…'

'We're not done with issue two, old boy,' Jedrek cuts in, then pauses. 'Tell you what, how's this for a scheme: you tell me how you think you could improve your file hygiene?'

Deep breath. 'Let's see. I could ensure that I punch and pin all my work – in reverse chronological order, of course, so that it's easy for my colleagues to pick up and run with in my absence.'

'Great! More ways you could improve?'

'I could…label my files with regulation stickies?'

'Yes!' His frown returns. 'Why?'

'So that they look cleaner and are quickly accessible from a horizontal position in the filing cabinet?'

Jedrek leans back on his chair and folds his arms behind his head. 'You see?' he says. 'You know this stuff.' I nod – well, of course, I know this admin stuff: it comes up every appraisal. I know I should just bloody do it too, but it seems there are always greater priorities. And besides, if anyone else ever did have to work on one of my files, they would find the papers *broadly* in order, and the names written on the file covers, so…

'You did that last time,' Jedrek observes, his tone changing.

'I'm sorry?'

'That little, noddy, shruggy thing. You did that last time.'

'I'm not sure I underst…'

'No, I think you do. You pretend to take my advice on board, to get me off your back, then you carry on exactly as you were.' He may be onto something… 'Truth is, you simply can't be bothered to do the admin properly, can you? Well?'

My phone pings. A new diary entry: *Gema Rodriguez statement: Peruvian asylum claim.* Oh crap. She will be here in a flash if she isn't in reception already. I ask permission to return to my desk.

'No, not this time,' comes the flat reply.

'But, she's in a bad…'

'I'll tend to Ms Rodriguez. You are going to fetch me all your remaining files, and we are going to go through them together, one by one, until each of them is perfectly…'

'Hygienic?' I interrupt.

'Out!'

#

As I pull the files from my shelf, I take stock of the morning's events. The appraisal has not begun brilliantly, my vulnerable client has been kept waiting and, yet again, I shall have to work late to complete my chargeable hours. But against all that, the firm's Senior Partner and founding father is about to do my admin for me. Result.

What follows is hard to watch. Sweating and without even so much as a coffee break, the great man ploughs through each and every one of my 70 active files, filleting them like fresh mackerel in a busy market place.

He is merciless. Snorting and rubbing his chin as he goes, he rips pages out, flags up absent attendance notes, checks that billable work is time-recorded correctly and justified in accordance with the legal aid contract specifications, drafts a contemporaneous note of the appraisal itself and fires off an email to none other than Mr Anton Fletcher KC, requesting an in-house workshop on assessing the merits of potential new instructions. It is, on any analysis, a remarkable spectacle. And, incredibly, it is done by lunchtime too.

Jedrek clicks his mouse, shuts his laptop and looks up for the first time in four hours.

'Tiger? Come on, I'll treat you to lunch.'

#

The Tiger is the partners' go-to venue for casual, confidential chats. It is tatty, dark, and just noisy enough. Hidden away on the left as you walk in is a discreet, roundish cavern. Today, it has been nabbed by the estate agents from across the road, so we keep moving and settle on a torn velvet banquette under a moose head.

'Is this your favourite watering hole round here, then?' I ask.

'Third point: efficiency,' he resumes.

'Yes, of course.'

'Alex, I'm going to level with you.'

I freeze.

'My partners and I see you as someone with genuine potential.'

'Oh…thank you.'

'Let's see. You're bright, well-liked…you clearly care greatly for your clients and you've been here – what? – two years now? So…'

I sit upright.

'…we want to help you get to the next stage.'

'The next stage?'

'I suspect you have a sense where I'm heading with this?' he continues, smiling.

Do I? I think. And then it hits me 'My god!' I exclaim. 'You're preparing to make me a salaried partner.'

Jedrek balks. 'Good one,' he replies laughing. 'Give up? My partners and I want to invest in you becoming AC.'

'Associate…counsel?'

'Erm, no,' he responds. 'Administratively competent.'

#

For a few seconds, all I can do is stare at Jedrek, mouth wide open like a grouper.

'Is there an issue?' he asks, tilting his head.

'Jedrek, I…'

'Look, call me Jed,' he interrupts.

'Yes, OK. The issue, Jed, is that – how to put this? – I win my cases. I mean, I win all of them.'

'Your point being?'

'Well, I kind of *am* competent, aren't I? Some might even say more than competent.'

He smiles sympathetically. 'Alex, you should know by now. We all win all our cases here; we are the Number Two Immigration Firm in the country for a reason.'

'Fine,' I reply. 'We are *all* competent, then.'

'No, Alex. To be competent, you first need to be…' he stops himself. 'No, you tell me. Go on.'

My pocket vibrates. Furtively I check my phone, and see it is a message from Danso. '*Al son, I'm freaking out. Think I just met one of the ones...*' One of the ones?

'I'm waiting…' says Jedrek.

'Efficient?' I suggest.

'Precisely! In all seriousness,' he says, 'how do you expect to become a solicitor if you can't keep your house in order?'

ENOUGH! shouts a voice inside me.

'Erm, actually, Jed, I already am a solicitor.'

'Not in this field, you're not.'

'I am literally on the roll of solicitors.'

There's a pause.

'You are not on our website,' he replies. 'And – let me be clear – you won't be until we deem you to have the requisite experience.'

'Is two years not enough?' I ask.

But rather than answer me directly, he simply pulls out a handkerchief, blows his nose, and carefully folds the tissue into his inside pocket.

A young, bored-looking member of the bar staff brushes past and I motion for him to stop.

'Sparkling water, please.'

'Drinking at lunch time?' the barman quips. 'You have to order at the bar, mate, sorry.'

Jedrek produces a debit card, asks the barman to put it behind the bar and bring them a couple of menus. 'Look, Alex,' he says, putting a fatherly hand on my shoulder. 'I wouldn't be bothering with any of this if I didn't believe you had a future here. Don't you see? I am investing in you.'

I look up and meet his eye. It can't be easy managing me. 'Yes. Yes, I get it,' I reply. 'Thank you.'

'I mean it,' he stresses, eyes unblinking. 'I really want you to understand this. Few if any of us at the firm enjoy the admin part, but it is a necessary evil, you see. It enables us to stay afloat financially, and it allows us to maintain the excellent service we provide, to the people in our community who need it most.'

As he says this, I begin remembering some of my most cherished clients: Fadouma, the enchanting Somali grandmother beaten to within an inch of her life by Al-Shabaab extremists for not wearing their regulation *abaya*; Nomore, the characterful, Zimbabwean MDC activist whose name was owed to her mother's desire to stop at her, her eighth child; Najeebullah, the young Pakistani boy thrown out by his father for falling for another boy; Blessings, the brave Jamaican 30-something who found the strength to flee a life of systematic domestic abuse.

'Alex? Were you listening to what I just said?'

'Absolutely,' I answer, snapping out of my trance. 'Look, for what it's worth, Jed, I think it is remarkable what you have created – the firm, I mean. I understand your determination to protect it.'

Jedrek stretches his fingers out on the table in front of him and smiles. 'Well, you must include yourself in that generous appraisal, Alex,' he says. 'You have always been one of us. It is why we took you on.' He pauses and ties his hair back in a ponytail. 'But there is a limit to what any of us can achieve without…'

'The grunt work,' I interrupt.

'Exactly.'

We race through 'efficiency' over scampi and chips as though it were an afterthought, though it becomes clear it is anything but. Essentially, I am to improve my time-management and stop taking on 'hopeless' asylum cases.

'I mean, this last matter I see you've taken on, Gema Rodriguez,' explains Jedrek. 'You must have read the government's latest Country Policy and Information Note on Peru, right? Then, you know it's a non-starter – why pursue it?'

In fact, the only other example he gives me is of that case I instructed Anton Fletcher on (or tried to). I remember the details – the apostate from Pakistan – and it was true, the esteemed KC advised me to drop it. But I confess, I never properly understood why. Indeed, it still troubles me to this day. I dare say the evidence was thin, but then – how could an apostate *not* have been at risk of harm in Pakistan, where even blasphemy is punishable by death?

Anyway, at the end of the appraisal, Jedrek drops his bombshell:

'I'm taking you off asylum cases.'

'What?'

'Don't panic, it's not permanent, necessarily. Just until you learn to better evaluate whether or not a case has merit.'

'Seriously? Can you even do that? What about my clients?'

'Worry not. I'll give your cases a safe home. Meanwhile, for the foreseeable, you will be focusing strictly on immigration cases – you know, skilled migrant workers, that sort of stuff.'

'No! I do not know that sort of stuff.' I lift my eyes to the heavens; the moose stares back. 'Are you demoting me?'

'No, of course not.' He coughs. 'Immigration cases are just as important as asylum cases.'

'Oh, come off it, you know that's not true!'

'All right, there is no need to shout.'

'I'm not shouting!'

25

On return to the office, Jedrek instructs me to read up on the case of a ballet dancer applying to come and work in the UK, while he dictates an apology to Gema Rodriguez, on my behalf, for having given her false hope.

Upstairs in the open-plan, my colleagues are fizzing around like effervescent energy pills. Before doing anything else, however, I go straight to the Home Office website to check the Country Policy and Information Note on Peru that Jedrek cited.

As anyone in the field knows, these notes tend to be shrouded in pro-government bias. They play down the risk of harm faced by asylum seekers in their country of origin, and often contrast sharply with the advice the Foreign Office gives its own UK citizens considering travel to the same place. Even so, this one seems particularly categorical.

Updated a couple of days ago, each and every point it contains appears to be substantiated by independent evidence and sources, including a local NGO and multiple grassroots organisations, none of which I have heard of. Added to that, it presents the police as spotless, guardian angel figures. Not only does this seem unlikely, it is difficult to square with what I believe they did to Gema. Rubbing my neck, I scan down to the end of the report where, in error no doubt, they have published the author's name: *J Price*. I go to make myself a coffee.

Waiting for the water to boil, I fret about my chargeable hours. So far today, I have time-recorded precisely nothing. My pocket vibrates, I take out my phone and see my diary has been wiped clean already and some 20 or so new appointments entered, all no doubt deathly, run-of-the-mill skilled worker cases. A body shoves past me to the mug cupboard. Toby.

'Playing truant, are we?' he asks.

'You tell me,' I reply, and he puts his mug down and looks me in the eye.

'Me? Ha! I've done my chargeable hours for the day.'

'You can't have been here more than six.'

He grins and affects a patronising sort of faux-dumb voice. 'That's right. But six minutes is the minimum unit isn't it? Hence, if I do two separate things – yeah? – within six minutes – yeah? – then I can charge 12 minutes, can't I?'

I laugh. 'You're very sure of yourself for a novice, aren't you, Toby? Stick around a bit and you'll see the non-chargeable work consumes just as much time as the chargeable. Let's see: attendance notes, time-recording, file audits, funding dispute appeals, know-how updates, Continuing Professional Development training, diary meetings. Take it from me, it's a job in itself just staying on top of it all.'

Toby rests a languid elbow on the work surface, as if he were some seasoned criminal hack leaning on a lectern to address the jury. 'OK, thanks for the unsolicited tips,' he says. 'If I hadn't been recruited from Bradford Shields, I might have needed them.'

'Head-hunted? You can't have been in practice more than a year!'

'Three.'

'You look like you've barely left school.'

'Well OK, I took A-levels a year early (4A*), graduated in Law three years later (1st), obtained a Master of Laws degree from LSE the year after that, nailed the Legal Practice Course (Distinction), began my training contract at Bradford Shields and qualified as a solicitor two years later. Anything else I need to clear up or can I get back to work?'

'Two things actually.' I clear my throat. 'First – what went wrong at LSE?'

'Meaning?'

'It's the only grade you didn't mention…'

He takes a moment. 'If you must know, I missed out by one per-cent. Ignorant apes refused me a re-mark too. Now if you'll excuse me.'

'Wait.'

'Quickly.'

'Were you really head-hunted?'

'Yes. Very recently, in fact. I am to take over the caseload of some-one in your asylum team. Hang on…' He leans into my space and gives a short, deliberate, double sniff. 'Yep, thought it was you. Ask next time you want to borrow my shampoo, OK?'

#

Defeated for now, I retreat to my desk and begin reading into the ballet dancer file as I have been told to. To my surprise, these artists are considered in short supply in the UK and benefit from a relatively easy route in. What is more, the evidence needed is already on the file, so the case will essentially win itself. Well, that was thrilling… Arms in the air, I spin around on my swivel chair.

Toby passes the open doorway, then back-steps to make an ironic little cap-doffing gesture.

'I thought you were getting back to work, Toby?'

'I was. But I am told we have to do our *own* photocopying. Hey, how's life down there in the world of skilled workers?' On delivering this blow, he strikes a sort of cheek-sucking pose, like a child imitating a goldfish.

'How do you know what I'm working on?'

He leans forward and prods the papers on my desk. 'I can read,' he whispers, and off he goes.

A flurry of coughs, grunts and shuffling breaks the tension. Toby darts off like a cuttlefish as Jedrek bobs into view. He is clutching so many wallet files it's almost more like they are carrying him. Slowly, carefully, he attempts to put them down, and drops the lot.

'Fiddle! Sorry, Alex, these are for you. Your new caseload – or some of it.'

'Thanks Jed.' I crouch down to pick up the files.

'Don't mention it. Oh, bother! I knew I should have removed your asylum caseload first…'

'Not to worry. Where are they going? I can transfer them for you.'

He thinks about it. 'That's kind, but, no, I'd like you to get to work. I've found a good home for the files with one of our new solicitors: I'll send him over now.'

#

'Oh, hello again.' Toby beams. 'Fancy giving me a hand carrying your old files to my office?'

'You have an office?'

'It was part of the deal I negotiated. Can't hear myself think in open-plan and with 120+ files active at any given time, believe me I don't need distractions.'

I start to feel short of breath.

#

Late that evening, I receive a text from Jedrek.

Alex, you're going to court. I need you at Field House Upper Tribunal tomorrow to take a note of the hearing for me – case number AA-243908. Shouldn't take long but take some other work with you in case there's a wait to get on. And don't forget to charge waiting time on your attendance note, and to enter it into the system.

'Sure thing,' I reply. *'I'll make sure I'm there before 10.'*

'You need to be there for 08:30 latest to meet the client,' comes the instant reply. *'File's on my desk.'*

I pour myself a nightcap to steady the nerves. In other circumstances, the early start tomorrow might have been a blow, but for reasons best kept to myself, I'll be up and out the door a good two hours before then anyway...

26

I get to Peckham for 07:15 and go directly to the billing room. There, I retrieve Gema's file from the "For Storage" pile, take a photo of her contact details and carefully put the file back where I found it. Then it's a quick shower, I grab the file Jedrek left out for me and jump on the number 12 bus back into town.

#

From the upper deck, I text Gema. I apologise for yesterday, confirm that I cannot be her lawyer and tell her that I want to help her anyway. I remind her that she needs to get her asylum claim in urgently (for credibility reasons), and ask when and where I can meet her to take her statement. Gema replies that she is in Stockwell and can meet me anytime today before 10pm, when she heads to the City for her cleaning job. Sorted.

#

Field House Upper Tribunal lies just off Chancery Lane. With time to spare, I choose to have a wander round the Inns of Court; and on reaching Fountain Court, I sit down on an empty bench, opposite the vast Elizabethan Middle Temple Hall.

A bold little finch blows past me like a warning shot, skims over the low, circular fountain and swoops down into the gardens below. Time is ticking. I open the file to see it concerns a 19-year-old Afghan asylum seeker who, to protect his anonymity, is referred to only by his initials, *NA*. The Home Office refused his claim, he appealed the refusal and lost, and the issue for the Upper Tribunal today is whether the lower tribunal was right to dismiss that appeal.

I find the Grounds of Appeal and pull them off the file pin for inspection. They argue that the lower tribunal ignored evidence of a rise in indiscriminate violence in the man's native Kabul, ignored evidence that he tried, unsuccessfully, to trace his family, and ignored evidence that he is penniless, in poor mental health and will have no support if returned. The Home Office Response states that the lower tribunal '…considered all the evidence, found it wanting, and was entitled to dismiss the appeal.' Right then.

On cramming the papers back into his file, I spot the name of our barrister – Anton Fletcher KC – and an instant queasiness sets in. I stand up slowly and tuck my shirt in. At least it will probably be over by lunchtime.

#

The secure entrance to Field House is an inconspicuous double doorway at the top of some steps and a sloping access ramp. Outside, there is already a buzz of activity: barristers emptying their pockets of scuffed post-it notes, loose change and lighters before facing the metal detectors; clerks trailing trolleys laden with lever-arch files; clients of all creeds, colours and tongues bracing themselves to meet their destiny.

Despite the promising start, I have managed to arrive late. Ahead of me in the queue, a man in a black turban, three-piece suit and shiny, brown brogues is being frisked by all three security staff. 'This is absurd,' he is saying, and, albeit sheepishly, others are beginning to show him support. Seeing an opening, I slide around the metal detector and make for the foyer.

With no sign of Fletcher, I check the conference rooms. No joy there either. Eventually, an usher on the listings desk takes pity on me and shows me the way to Court 9, where I receive a tap on the shoulder and hear a soft, familiar voice in my ear. 'Hello you.'

'Amy, hi!' Be cool, be cool. 'You covering for Fletcher, then?' Damn, she scrubs up well...

'Yep. You know what Anton's like,' she replies. 'Seriously, I don't think he's left chambers all week. Says he's got enough on for a whole department! Anyway, where were we?'

'Oh, ah, finding our client, I guess. Seen him yet?'

'No, but then I've only seen a poor copy of his passport photo page. Any idea what he looks like?'

'Search me...'

Using a process of elimination, we whittle down the possible suspects to just two, whereupon one of them, a humble-looking young man in jeans and a smart grey cardigan, stands up and addresses me.

'Mr Anton, sir? I am Nasir.'

'My god, Anton didn't tell him he wasn't doing the hearing,' she whispers.

I pretend not to hear and hold out my hand. 'Right, yes. I mean, no. I am Alex. I'm standing in for Jedrek, and this is your barrister for today, Amy. She is a better version of Fletcher.'

'You can't say that!' Gratefully, our client understands little English.

'You are in safe hands,' I reassure him, while Amy looks around frantically.

'He's never here on time,' she says under her breath.

'Who?'

'Ahmed, the interpreter. Here...' She unlocks her phone and passes it to me. 'He's in my contacts. Would you mind chasing him while I sign myself in?'

#

As it turns out, Ahmed has been 'double-booked'. Or, more accurately, the KC has borrowed him for a client conference in chambers.

'Wait,' I say. 'So Fletcher decides to hold a conference in chambers and you are left stranded in court without an interpreter?'

'There will be a reason for it,' she replies, taking her phone back. 'Look, depending on who it is, the judge may let us use the court interpreter.'

She disappears to call the clerks and returns with a relaxed smile on her face. 'Told you Anton wouldn't let me down. We shan't be needing an interpreter today after all. Our hearing has been adjourned.'

'Eh?'

'Parked behind *ZA (Afghanistan)*, along with a handful of others.'

My mind draws a blank.

'You know, Anton's big Afghan appeal? The 18-year-old violinist from Kabul? In fairness, I ought to have guessed this would happen. *ZA* was heard a few months ago and the tribunal is yet to publish its Decision. When it does, it will contain new guidance on Afghan cases, based on the evidence it heard, and until then, all similar cases have been stayed.'

'I see...'

'What?'

'Nothing, it's just...well, couldn't he have told you? You know, to save you the stress of prepping, coming down here et cetera?'

She shakes her head. 'He probably expected me to twig. Plus, he's got a lot on at the moment – poor guy's drowning in instructions.'

I am confused. 'I thought barristers were supposed to turn work down if they physically couldn't do it?'

Amy chuckles, and reminds me whom we are discussing. 'Physically couldn't do it? You don't know Anton very well, do you?'

Groan. 'Yes, yes,' I snap. 'I know, "The man's a machine", "Never sleeps", bla-di-bla-di-bla.'

'Whoa, I barely mention his name and you're all...triggered!'

'Look, he might have warned us, that's all.'

'Why?' she retorts. 'It's the clerks' duty to communicate these things to us, not Anton's.'

'He couldn't have just called one of us?'

She averts her gaze. 'I am sure he would have done, had he had time to.'

'You mean, had he been physically able to?' I mock. It's a step too far.

'Christ, Alex, you have a problem with Anton, don't you?'

'No.'

'Well?'

'It's just…'

'Yeees?'

I don't believe anyone is *that* wonderful, I want to say. He might have explained to me how I was so wide of the mark in the Pakistani apostate appeal too, rather than complaining about me to Jedrek.

She looks coyly at me. 'Oh, I get it. You're jealous.' She laughs, clutching her brief to her chest.

'That's absurd.'

'Is it?'

'He is an esteemed KC and I am, well…I am but a fledgling.'

'Perhaps, Alex,' Amy responds, changing down a gear, 'but you are no sap, that's for sure.'

I feel my head nod forward and notice I have odd shoes on. Also staring at my feet, Amy moves closer and rests a hand on my shoulder. 'I know this job can be shitty,' she says. 'But you are good, Alex. And it's obvious to anyone you care deeply for your clients. I've seen your work first-hand and for what it's worth, I believe you'll make an excellent solicitor.'

'I already am a s…'

'Yes, shit, sorry. Look, bottom line. Anton is in a class of his own, even amongst his fellow KCs – you just have to look at his track record…' Do I? 'Seriously, I've been three feet behind him in court, the man wipes the floor with Treasury counsel so hard it's a wonder they ever get up again.' As she says this, the corners of her mouth twitch and quiver into an excited half-smile.

This is hopeless, I reflect. I do not suppose Fletcher has time for relationships, nor that Amy has a romantic interest in him as such. And yet, in a strange way it feels as if I have been competing with him all this time – more than with Jon, even. It is almost like he has set this impossible standard, and in Amy's eyes, nothing could ever demystify his allure.

'You OK?' she asks.

I open my mouth to respond, but her tender hand on my shoulder has decommissioned my vocal cords. I shut my eyes to savour the moment, then feel a second hand on my other shoulder. In an instant, my mind flashes back to Little Italy, dancing, her arms around my neck, the way she had looked at me, how close we came. Transfixed, I touch the hand, only to note that it is hairier than I remembered. I open my eyes.

'Nasir, I'm so sorry! We're just discussing, your barrister and I...'

'Toilet please.'

'This way, follow me.'

#

There are four hearings listed in Court 9 today. Out of courtesy, Amy explains, and in case news of the adjournment has not filtered through to the judge, she should show her face.

Bright and carpeted, the hearing room itself looks more like a small hotel conference room than a court. Amy finds somewhere to sit at the back with some other advocates, dumps her files on the identical electric blue chair next to her own and waits for the judge to arrive.

Through a small square window in the top of the door, I watch her pull a pencil from behind her head, let her hair unfurl, and put it up again. There ought to be a term for this look: impeccable, but with a hint of non-conformism.

Two seconds later, I am unceremoniously shoved out of the way by a woman pulling two leather wheelie bags, bursting with files. She collapses on the seat at a table marked 'Respondent', stacks the files up in front of her, rips one open and begins flapping through the pages inside.

The other advocates rise in unison and race over to her, jostling for poll position.

'I'll take *Zambedi* first,' says the Home Office presenting officer, her voice monotone, eyes still fixed on the file in front of her.

Intrigued, I keep the door ajar.

'Yes, thank you. I also appear in the second case of *Appiah*,' one of them begins.

'I said I'll take *Zambedi* first.'

'Yes. Good. Well, we haven't received a Response to our Grounds of Appeal from you – could I see your copy?'

'Name?' the presenting officer asks him.

'I'm sorry?'

'Your name? What is your name?' she shouts.

'Mercer... Arthur Mercer,' the advocate replies, sounding a little bewildered. 'And you can drop that tone with me this minute, understood?'

There is a loud bang on the door and the usher walks in, closely followed by the judge, who pauses momentarily to acknowledge the room with a scowl worthy of a pantomime villain. The only thing missing is the dry ice.

'All rise!' the usher yells, pulling out the judge's chair for him, then stepping down from the bench to take his position at a little formica side table by the door.

Amy catches my eye and gestures for me to come in. Hesitantly, I oblige. She clears the files from the chair next to her and whispers to me to hold them for her.

'Sure,' I whisper back.

'Ahm, whoever it is chatting away at the back there, can I kindly ask you to stop? Good. I'll hear the cases in list order. That means, Mr Mercer, I believe you're up first?'

The young man stands up, makes his way over to the desk marked 'Appellant' and begins spreading his documents out in front of him. Meanwhile, Amy stands up and addresses the bench.

'Sir, if I may, the third case on your list today has been…'

'I haven't got to the third case, yet, Miss…?' he says, glancing down at his papers.

She steadies herself and tries again. 'Indeed, sir. It's just that, if I may, the third case has been…'

'Again, Ms…' he interrupts.

'Phelan, sir.'

'I'm only on the *first* matter. Now, where are we? Ten past ten… Mr Mercer, I see you appear in both the first and second matters. Do you have a time estimate for me?'

'An hour at a pinch, sir,' he replies, eyes widening, dimples deepening.

'Good. Ms Phelan, may I suggest you return a little before 11 to gauge where we have got to?'

'I…'

'But don't go too far, understood? If previous occasions are anything to go by, Mr Mercer will exhibit merciful concision. You will need to be on hand and ready to present your appeal the moment he utters his last word, understood?'

'Forgive me, sir,' Mercer pipes up bashfully, 'but that sounds a little ominous…'

'Yes, very good, Mercer,' the judge acknowledges. 'Indeed, may you live to speak *beyond* today's submissions and, ah, continue to regale us with pithy submissions for many years thereafter.'

'I'm grateful,' Mercer replies, standing up and sitting down again in what looked like a sort of inverted curtsey.

This tribunal mating ritual now in full flow, the judge looks at

Amy as if to say, 'Why are you still here?'

'My case has been adjourned, sir,' she squeaks.

But either he doesn't hear her or he doesn't want to. She signals to me and we leave.

#

'Concise? Him?' Amy whispers as the door shuts behind us. 'Mercer is a human waffle, for fuck's sake, and a syrupy one at that. You know he's Treasury counsel really, a Home Office poodle. He only very occasionally represents asylum seekers, he told me, "to keep abreast of the arguments", basically so he can flatten them. What a jerk! No wonder Proudfoot loves him so much.'

'Proudfoot?'

'The judge you just saw. Big "refuser". Rumour has it when he was a First-tier Tribunal judge, he didn't even know *how* to allow an appeal.'

'You mean…?'

'Yep. Refused everything.'

'Bloody hell!'

'I know, right? Apparently, though, he mellowed a bit after his promotion to the Upper Tribunal. Some of my chambers colleagues even seem to get along with him – all right, one…'

I sigh wearily. 'Anton?'

'Who else?' she blushes. 'Says the man's a softie at heart. And, well, he did find for Anton's client in *KO (Somalia)* – you know that big Decision protecting entirely unsupported Somali women?'

I nod, but I have lost interest.

'Of course, he was also on the panel in last week's Iraqi win,' she adds. 'The young professionals at risk case?'

'Oh right, yes. Congratulations on that, by the way.'

#

It proves near impossible to explain to Nasir what has happened this morning and, after twenty minutes or so of trying, it is plain he has had enough.

'Now I go?' he asks and I assent making a telephone gesture.

'I'll get our interpreter to call him and explain everything,' I suggest to Amy.

'Would you? Thanks Alex. Well, time to kill. Coffee?'

27

'I see the leg's better.' Amy smiles as we stroll down Chancery Lane, and soon she is sharing the wonderful news that her sister, Claire, is bouncing back, going out more, internet dating, and so on. I hold out my arms and in she comes for the hug. I shudder – how I have missed this scent.

#

A stone's throw from the tribunal and directly opposite the Royal Courts of Justice, the neat, urban style Fleet Street Press Café is a firm favourite with barristers. And this morning is no exception – awash with waistcoats, collar studs and wig tins, the chatter is deafening.

A table becomes free by the window, away from the hubbub. 'I'll get these,' I tell Amy.

'Absolutely not. It's my fault we're still waiting to go on.'

'Looked impossible from where I was sitting,' I say. 'Besides, time with you is never wasted.'

Her eyelids flutter. 'Flat white?'

'How did you guess?'

#

She returns with the coffees and points out my dog-eared A4 note-pad. 'Cripes, I see someone needs a new notebook!' She glances at her phone. 'OK, we've got twenty minutes tops.'

'Forty by my watch.'

'You haven't done much advocacy, have you?' she remarks.

I pick up my coffee cup and put it down again. 'All right, no.'

'When a judge says be back in an hour, be back in thirty minutes.'

'Makes sense.'

She rocks back on her chair. 'You know, I love that about you, Alex. Always willing to take advice, admit when you're wrong.'

I look at her quizzically.

'Not like our lot,' she elaborates. 'You won't get an admission out of one of us barristers, not without a qualification of some sort. *"Sorry I went to entirely the wrong court, but the Notice of Hearing was buried in the middle of the Brief..."'*

I laugh. 'Thanks...I think. Or are you really saying that I am a mug?'

Amy takes my hands in hers across the table and, away from the exigencies of the tribunal, she fixes her eyes on me. 'No, Alex. I am saying...you're lovely.' She blushes. And just like that, it seems, she is back in my life.

I look around me to check that no one is watching us, then berate myself. So what if anyone were? I worry for her sake, of course. It is her privacy and reputation I want to protect. Even so, I sense it is wrong of me to pre-empt her reactions to things, before they have even had a chance to form. I love her. And love demands trust.

Perhaps risk even? As we talk, it occurs that maybe what Amy wanted from me all along was not to bow out chivalrously, but to persist – do something radical, even, to win her heart. Looking at her sitting there, elegant in her white ruffle shirt and discreet gold earrings, I remember a line from the Duchess of Malfi: *'The misery of us that are born great! We are forc'd to woo, because none dare woo us.'* None except Jon, I reflect... How foolish I have been.

'You all right?' Amy asks, tilting her head towards me.

'Yes.' I snap out of my trance. 'Yes, sorry.'

She withdraws her hands and smiles kindly at me before checking her phone and frowning.

'Weird,' she says.

'What's up?'

'Nothing. I think. Any idea about techy things?'

'Not really, alas. Can ask Danso, though. The guy who emailed you that playlist I made you, remember?'

'How could I forget that?' she blushes. 'Yes, I think I've still got his email somewhere.'

'Message him. He read Electronics with Music at the Guildhall, and trust me – there is nothing he doesn't know about either.'

'Bah, it's just an email from the clerks I received. Reads as 'read' but I haven't clicked on it…'

'Odd. Does anyone else have access to your account who could have read it?'

'Only IT, but I asked them last time and they were clueless.'

'Last time?'

'It's happened a couple of times before. Anton says it was most likely a 'glitch' or something, but what would he know? Doesn't really matter, I guess. Only, the clerks will think I've seen something when I haven't.'

'Nightmare.'

'Yeah, last thing I need is the clerks thinking I'm ignoring them. It's hard enough keeping them sweet as it is.'

I chuckle. 'Is that all true, then? Do you really need to butter up the clerks?'

'How do you think I get all these meaty asylum instructions?' she laughs.

'Erm, could your ability have something to do with it?'

'I love you,' she says.

'I know,' I say back, deflecting the compliment. 'I'm serious though. Our firm instructs you, not the clerks.'

'Sure,' she says, tucking her hair behind her ear. 'You call the clerks, email them or whatever, but when the barrister you want isn't available for any reason, they tell you who is, don't they? Speaking of which...'

'Yes?'

'You never instructed me again...'

I fidget with the doily between my cup and its saucer. 'No. No, I wasn't sure it was really appropriate, given, you know...'

'You are probably right,' she replies, dropping her gaze then looking at me again. 'I wish you weren't though. I miss that time, our chats...the dancing.'

I laugh. 'Yeah, the dancing ended well, didn't it?'

She places a hand delicately on my knee. 'I miss you.'

I feel my face flush. 'I'm here now,' I answer mechanically, while a voice in my head screams JUST TELL HER HOW YOU FEEL! and she moves the conversation on.

'Hey, I'll never forget that phenomenal bit of forensic work you did for our appeal.'

'Too kind. You mean on the Home Office interviewer's ever-so-slightly repressive questioning?' I tut. 'Officer 31, if memory serves.'

'Yes! Let me see. *"The Sheikhal clan to which you belong enjoy protection from the Hawiye clan, don't they? Well? That's right, isn't it? Yes or no? I can't hear you!"*'

'Hideous, wasn't she?' I chuckle, as it comes back to me. This was the first asylum case I had done. The interviewer, a native Somali-speaker herself, pressurised our client into saying, in effect, that he would be safe in Somalia. And had it not been for the interpreter's outrage and our request for disclosure of the interview record, we might never have known the truth of what happened. In fact, the whole thing was quite extraordinary. At one point on the recording, we discovered, she even tried to speak to our client in Swahili, presumably with a view to claiming he was from a different African country.

'Do you know what happened to her in the end?' Amy asks.

'Suspended, wasn't she?'

'Yeah, I mean after that?' she takes a sip of coffee.

I shrug. 'Promoted?'

Amy nearly spits out her coffee. 'Wouldn't put it past them. Done any more recently?'

'Somali cases? Nah.' I sigh deeply. 'Not likely to any time soon either, I'm afraid. I have been demoted.'

'What?'

'Yep, they've taken me off asylum claims. I am now doing exclusively business immigration.'

As ever, she is quick to reply. 'That's where the money is, isn't it? Could be a compliment, right?'

'Nice try. And, thank you.' I am now struggling to meet her eye.

'Did they give you any reasons?'

'I take ages on my cases, my files are a mess and allegedly I am incapable of turning away clients, however weak their cases. Other than that...'

'Oh bollocks, I'm sorry to hear that, sweetheart. It is temporary though, right?'

'Yes, I think so. So I'm told.'

'Look, for what it's worth – off the record, OK? – I often wish some of your colleagues took longer over their work. You know, to get the detail right? It'd save us a lot of mental gymnastics and embarrassment in court... Awww.' She sighs. 'I'm gutted we're losing you for a bit.'

'Thanks Amy. You needn't worry though. I can always instruct you in a skilled worker appeal?'

'Thanks...' she replies in her over-enthusiastic work voice. 'That would be great!'

I smile. 'Don't worry, I wouldn't do that to you. They are spirit-snipingly boring, aren't they?'

'Not always.' Amy's tone is unconvincing. She glances at her watch again and moves a bit closer to me. 'OK, five minutes to tell me how you are otherwise, Alex?'

Much to my own surprise, I take the leap. 'I miss you,' I declare unequivocally, and it feels good.

'I'm here now,' she parrots my earlier response.

'Haha.' I try again. 'It's not the same, is it? And, yet, somehow it is. Does that even make sense?'

She swallows, glances at her phone again and stands up abruptly.

'Actually, Alex… Proudfoot. Mind if we head back?'

#

We scurry back up Chancery Lane to the tribunal. On arrival, she shoots through the security gate and flies up the stairs to court. I try to stay with her, but to no avail. Off goes the barrier alarm. Back I go. Off it goes again. And so on.

'Please, it's no good, I'm telling you,' I insist, raising my left leg. 'One seven-inch metal plate and 13 screws. It'll ping all pinging day!'

The older of the two security guards saunters over and, frisking me, identifies the rogue mini-bulldog clip in the lining of my suit jacket.

'Well, that'll make all the difference.' I roll my eyes. 'Hey, can you be gentler, please?'

Ping goes the machine again.

'How many times, man? What part of metal in leg do you not get?'

'All right – you can pass now,' the officer announces.

'I'm so very grateful,' I hiss, rushing through the barrier.

Ping.

'But don't do it again.'

I stop in my tracks.

'Did you really just say that?' I ask, incredulous.

'You heard me.'

'Listen pal, if I leave and return, I'll still have the same sodding leg, OK?'

'You are getting aggressive.'

'Just…!' I take a deep breath and make for the stairs.

'Your bag, sir?'

'F'fffuck!' I stammer, run back and grab the file.

#

I arrive at the hearing room as Amy is walking in and tag along behind her. We make for the seats at the back and politely wait to be called on.

Pretty much everything Amy has said about Mercer proves accurate. He seems to blather on *ad nauseam* until interrupted, at which point he will simply concede the point – whatever it is – and move on to the next one.

Happily for us, he is soon on closing submissions.

'This appeal concerns the lower judge's failure to take account of a material part of Mr Appia's protection claim, namely that he was kidnapped from his native Ghana and taken to Libya where he was detained, ill-treated, sold to Albanian mafia and trafficked on to the UK.'

Judge Proudfoot has a leisurely sip of water. 'For clarity,' he asks, 'you are not maintaining that your client was kidnapped, trafficked and so on, are you? I mean, there's no evidence of any of that, is there?'

'Well, sir, there is his account of the same…'

'Yes, indeed. Let's try this another way, shall we? There is no evidence to corroborate his statement to that effect, is there?'

'Sir, if I may, his evidence was unchallenged by the Home Office.'

'His statement.'

Mercer pauses.

'I shall, of course, defer to your better view, sir, but a statement *is* evidence, is it not?

The judge huffs.

'Very well, Mr Mercer, very well. In the interests of procedural propriety, however, I shall say that I am inclined to treat the Appellant's statement evidence as holding very little, if any, probative value.'

'Sir, if I may, the Secretary of State for the Home Office accepted the Appellant's account as true.'

'Mr Mercer,' the judge interrupts. 'I fear you are repeating yourself. I have read the papers and I am aware of the case history.'

'Indeed, sir, but I would hate for the tribunal to fall into error because I failed to direct it to the appropriate guidance…'

'Ooh, that was creepy…but effective,' whispers Amy in my ear.

'Go on.'

'The UNHCR Guidance indicates clearly that witness testimony can be sufficient evidence in and of its own, such are the difficulties asylum applicants can have in obtaining documentation and other evidence. Of course, I am paraphrasing.'

The judge smiles and leans forward. 'Can you take me to the relevant passage you cite, please?'

'I can certainly dig it up, sir, I…'

'Mr Mercer, are you inferring that your instructing solicitors have not served said document?'

At this point, the barrister begins rifling through the papers, thus betraying that he hasn't read them properly – or perhaps at all.

'I'll assist you, Mr Mercer. There is no reference to the UNHCR Guidance in the bundle. *Nullus*. None.'

Mercer finds the index, scans down and quickly concurs. 'You are quite right, my lord. Lamentably, it does not appear to have been served.'

'A simple "sir" will do.'

'Mercer always does that,' Amy whispers again. 'Never misses a chance to ingratiate himself with the bench, especially when he's on the ropes. Slime ball.'

'And they don't see through it?'

'Some must do. I suspect the majority don't want to, though. Just look at him, lapping it up. Look at both of them. 21st Century and our justice system is still clogged up with these grotesque gammon gargoyles – makes you want to retch.'

'Hey, maybe keep your voice down,' I whisper back, nervously, pointing at the table microphones.

'Oh, don't worry about them,' Amy replies. 'You can barely ever hear the advocates' voices on the recordings, let alone anyone further away.'

I glance up at Proudfoot and watch his ruddy, blubber-face wobbling in all directions in tune with each emphatic delivery. Every now and then a piece of his shooting spittle lights up against the window light.

'Is that right, sir?' Mercer asks.

I tune back in.

'Yes, of course it is.' Proudfoot huffs. 'All right, I'm going to rule on this now. Can we just double check the tape's rolling, as it were?'

'I can confirm that you are indeed being recorded, sir,' replies the usher from below the bench, sounding like a prompter propping up a floundering actor.

'He delivers all his decisions *ex tempore* – you know, orally, there and then,' Amy whispers.

'Fancy,' I reply.

'Means he doesn't have to type it up later.'

'Ultimately, the fact of the matter is this,' the judge concludes, 'even if your client were a victim of trafficking – even if he had been abducted by Albanians in North Africa and brought to the United Kingdom for exploitation – the issue was not material to the decision of the first-tier judge.'

Mercer nods in deference.

'That is to say' he continues, 'it was irrelevant to the issue of whether his removal to Accra would be safe and proportionate. To the extent that the judge overlooked the trafficking issue, he was entitled to do so. It follows that the decision of the lower court contains no error of law.'

'What?' I whisper involuntarily, a little louder than I had meant to.

'I am grateful,' Mercer responds briskly, shuffling his papers back into his file and rising to leave.

But Proudfoot is not finished. 'Just a minute,' he says, putting his pen down and locking eyes with me. 'It appears our chatterbox is back.'

28

'It was you blathering earlier too, wasn't it?' the judge barks.

I take one for the team.

'Yes, sir.'

'Stand up when you are addressing the bench. And straighten your tie if you want to be heard.'

'Yes sir, sorry sir,' I reply, only to feel a hand on my shoulder pushing me down again. Amy rises to her feet.

'Ms?'

'May it please you, sir, my name is Ms Phelan.'

He looks up towards the ceiling a moment, then smiles.

'Ah, yes. You are Anton's pupil, are you not?'

'I was, sir, yes,' she replies diplomatically, omitting the fact that it was some five years ago.

'Good stuff. Do send him my warmest regards, will you?'

'Certainly, sir. Sir, I wish to beg your pardon.'

'Whatever for good lady?'

'For talking earlier.' She gulps. 'It was me, not Mr Donovan.'

'I see. Thank you, Ms Phelan. So, just now, when Mr Donovan said he was the individual talking earlier, he was lying to the court, was he?'

'Sir, I...'

'I shall make a note of that. No doubt the Solicitors Regulation Authority will be interested. Tell me, how do you spell his surname?'

'I am still here, sir,' I say, attempting to stand only to find Amy's hand pushing me down again.

'No, let him stand, Ms Phelan. It appears he wants to incriminate himself further.'

He turns to address me directly. 'You do understand contempt, don't you?'

I nod submissively.

'Yes? They told you about not misleading the court at...' he consults the court file, '...ah, Hatton Taylor Solicitors. I might have guessed.'

'They did, sir.'

'And you'll know that in this profession honesty is regarded very highly indeed?'

'Yes sir.'

'That it's paramount, in fact.'

'Indeed, sir.'

'Very well. I'm in a good mood and do not wish any further embarrassment on your esteemed counsel, Ms Phelan.'

'I'm grateful, sir,' I reply, copying Amy's language and sitting down.

'Not so fast, boy. You will apologise for lying to the court. First to Ms Phelan, then to me and, finally, to those of your friends and learned friends here present. Once you have done that, we shall draw a line under this sorry episode. Apart from anything else, we're getting dangerously close to lunch and still have your case to hear.'

'Sir, as regards our case...'

'In a moment, please Ms Phelan. First, the apology.'

I take a moment to rise.

'I'm afraid not, sir,' I respond, now on my feet.

'Excuse me?'

'I won't confess to telling a lie.'

Shocked silence.

'Are you being impudent, boy?'

'Man, sir. And, no, I am not being impudent. It is you who insists on relegating me to the status of a minor.' I draw breath and fire

163

again. 'This is not school, you are not my teacher and besides, I *was* talking earlier.'

By now the judge's face is beginning to turn purple. 'I cannot quite believe I am hearing this,' he utters.

The usher looks up anxiously and offers to remove me.

'Certainly not! I'm not finished with him yet…'

He sits back, clasps his hands together and settles them on his button-bursting paunch. 'Either your counsel is lying,' he resumes, pausing gleefully like a reality TV host about to expel a contestant, 'or *you* are, Mr Donovan. Tell me, which is it?'

'Respectfully, neither, sir.'

On hearing this, his fury intensifies still further. 'You had better explain yourself,' he snaps. 'And quickly.'

'Sir, if I may?' interjects Amy, rallying to the rescue again.

'Sit down, Ms Phelan.'

I resume. 'My learned friend, Ms Phelan, did indeed speak earlier as she has confessed.'

'Aha!' he roars.

'And I responded to her,' I add.

Proudfoot rocks back on his chair with excitement, then composes himself.

'So, it's her word against yours. She said categorically it was not you talking, but her!' he exclaims.

'I hadn't finished,' I reply soberly.

'What do you mean?'

'As I was saying, I responded to her…so quietly there is every chance she did not hear me, so that's possibly why she said I hadn't spoken.'

A look of intense irritation crosses the man's face. I ignore it.

'I'll summarise. I know I spoke, albeit very quietly. I know Ms Phelan also spoke. I admitted I spoke. I never said Ms Phelan did not speak. And I shall not, therefore, confess to a lie I did not tell. For that would be a lie. Got it?'

By now, suppressed laughter is beginning and the judge, fuming, scratches his shiny head.

'You do realise, do you, I am taking a note of everything you are saying?'

'I would expect nothing less, sir, and formally request a copy at your earliest convenience. I should also be grateful for a copy of the recording and a transcript of the same.'

'Well that's not much good,' the judge quips. 'They're virtually inaudible.'

'Which means there is no case against me to answer.'

'Excuse me?'

'There is no evidence.'

'Eh?'

'We are both officers of the court, bound by our ethical duty to tell the truth, are we not?'

'Get to the point, cretin.'

'I say I spoke. You, sir, infer that I did not. You say I was impudent. I say you were discourteous. It is one lawyer's word against another's. Full stop.'

Proudfoot removes, then replaces his glasses, sniffs, and addresses me again. His manner is casual now, like that of an old cowboy contemplating all the spats and hustles he has survived.

'You know, in all my time at the bench, I don't think anyone – anyone – has had the temerity to talk to me the way you just have. This won't be the last you hear of this, Mr Donovan. Understood?'

I turn to look at Amy who has her head in her hands, with one eye peeping through at the judge. But in for a penny, in for a pound.

'Yes, it will be, sir. I am sorry for speaking out of turn, genuinely. But the first time I spoke so discreetly it appears no one heard me. And the second time, well, I spoke involuntarily.'

'What do you mean, you spoke involuntarily?' he asks, raising his voice again.

'I mean I was in shock. I simply could not imagine a situation in which being a victim of trafficking could not be material to a protection claim. Sorry.'

'And you feel that was justification for interrupting a hearing, using up valuable court time and mounting this…bizarre display, do you? Well, we'll just have to see if the Solicitors Regulation Authority agrees with you, won't we?'

I glance at Amy again and consider apologising, but it is too late for that. Instead, I go for the jugular.

'That is fine, of course, sir. But if you choose to pursue disciplinary action against me, bear in mind that the *context* in which I questioned your judgement – your erroneous interpretation of the law – will be a matter of public record, for all to read, from north to south, east to west.'

'Have you quite finished?'

'Nearly. Consider this too. Even if you did manage to stitch me up on this absurd dishonesty charge you are mounting, any rational body would find my noble, alleged attempt to defend counsel's minor misconduct a mitigating feature. At worst, I'd receive a slap on the wrist.'

'Right, that's enough of…'

'Then imagine the consequences for you, sir, were it to be found that the conduct you chose to pursue against me was vexatious…'

'Enough!'

'Spiteful…'

'I'm warning you!'

'And unethical.'

'Out!'

29

Downstairs is much quieter than before. Not an advocate in sight, bar, perhaps, a frowning figure outside with fag in one hand, mobile in the other. Even the officious security officer at the scanner seems to have switched off. I prod him gently to see if he is still breathing.

'Hey, what do you think you're doing?' he asks.

'Just checking you're still alive,' I reply cheerily.

'Get out,' the officer says.

'You know, you're the second person who's said that to me today?'

'Yeah? Maybe you should take a hint then, pal?'

I step out onto the pavement and breathe in the traffic fumes. I consider hanging about for Amy. Ah, what's the point, I tell myself and make for Chancery Lane tube. Before descending, I call Gema Rodriguez and arrange to meet her in the Oval Café and Snack Bar.

#

On emerging at Oval, I see I have three voicemails, all from Amy. The first is along the lines of, 'What the fuck did you just do?' The second is to apologise for the first. And the last to express concern for me and to ask me to call her.

I poke my head around the corner to find Gema is already there, waiting patiently for me in the café. No time to waste, I order us coffees, pull out a wad of A4 and a half-chewed biro, and as inconspicuously and carefully as possible, begin taking her statement. It feels entirely wrong to be rushing this. Complex cases such as hers require hours of work, care and sensitivity to get the statement right, but what other option is there? One saving grace is that I don't need an interpreter.

Gema describes her impoverished upbringing in a Lima slum, how she met a young Salvadorian who took her under his wing, and how she began to suspect he had gang affiliations – the tattoo on his back, late night visits from random people, the expensive gifts, the incremental violence. By the time she confronted him, however, it was too late.

As anticipated it is her account of the police abuse that she finds hardest to relay, though not for want of trying.

'One after the other the men put themselves on top of me,' she begins, before breaking down in tears.

I find her a clean tissue and she soldiers on, but, again, this is so far from right. For one, it should be a senior female solicitor interviewing her about the rape, not a junior male with no resources and a half-baked Spanish accent. When I've got the bare minimum I need, I move on to her escape from Peru and arrival in the UK, and wrap the session up as quickly as I comfortably can without compromising the quality of her evidence. She then signs the statement and I brief her. Assuming the Home Office refuses her claim, she will need to provide more detail of what happened to her and of her fear of being returned to Peru. In the meantime, I will do all I can to find her a suitable legal representative, and, if at all possible, an expert or two to provide evidence in support of her claim. I warn her that given the unhelpful Country Policy Information Note on Peru, and the expense involved in instructing experts, none of this will be easy. But she must not, I insist, give up hope.

#

I will be expected back in the office by now. With one eye on my watch, I give her some brief advice about the asylum interview and

encourage her to see a GP as soon as she can – any problems register-
ing, to get in touch. I see her out, wave her off, and she is almost out of
sight when – what's this? – her dwindling image begins to blur. I stop,
lower my bags to the ground and wipe my eyes.

#

From the upper deck of the number 36, I email a few friends at
other firms to see if they will consider taking Gema on, selling it to
them as best as, ethically, I can. One can but hope…

#

Back at the office, little if anything has changed since the previous day. It is the usual cacophony of cabinet-sliding, paper-rustling,
chit-chatting and door-slamming.

Yet another message from Amy. *'Had to tell Anton, before Proudfoot
did.'*

'OK. What did he say?'

*'Not much, he's livid. Says it may even affect the decision in his Afghan
violinist case, the big one that's pending: Proudfoot's on the panel…'*

'Yeah?'

'Yeah? Is that all?'

'I'm very sorry. Better?'

No response.

I put my earplugs in and begin a steady trawl through the new
business immigration files on my desk, stopping only occasionally to
answer the phone or a generic question from a colleague: 'Are you
able to open Folders on your Outlook?'; 'Do you know what code
we're meant to time-record waiting time under?'; 'Have you seen
Jedrek, he's not at his desk?'

The only vaguely colourful case I find concerns an investor applicant from Equatorial Guinea, a character who calls himself 'Sisco

Money' and whose savings exceed – wait for it – 228 million US dollars. But as luck would have it, he has already been promised entry clearance to the country, and the application is therefore but a mere formality. Next.

#

228 million, I reflect again. It's been a long day but before I log off for the night, I pull up a form and assess myself. Yup – were I ever to need it, I am officially broke enough to qualify for legal aid.

I turn off my desktop, the whirring ceases and now all that can be heard are the muted sounds from the street outside: cars passing, dogs barking, laughter, indiscernible voices. It's nearly 9pm and the pubs will be in full flow. Tempting to see if anyone's around, or it would be if I weren't so exhausted.

Unplugging my phone from its charger, I get an urge to call my dad. Were he still around, he might invite me to meet him in the nearest 'watering hole'. We drank a lot together, he and I. Often, that is to say – birthdays and celebrations aside, of course, the whole 'pub' thing was more a euphemism for talking than a place for any serious drinking. He was always so attentive; it sounds borderline blasphemous to say aloud, but it sometimes felt there was almost a spiritual dimension to those sessions. And the most memorable of all was the first…

It was summer holidays time again. My trusty father arrived for the happy ride home from school, only this time it was, 'Here,' – he passed me the dog lead – 'you find a table out the back.'

A few moments later, Dad reappeared holding not one but two full pints of Harveys. I can't have been more than 14 years old but he worried little about breaking 'arbitrary' laws such as that defining the legal drinking age; they were an insult to discretion.

'Well?' he asked, leaning forward across the rickety moss-covered table. 'Bit bitter?'

'Bit...' I nodded. 'But nice.'

'That's my boy!' Dad exclaimed, thumping the table. I had another sip, and another, the woes of school began drifting away and then it was just Dad and me, together, warm in the midday sun, with not a care in the world. He went in to use the loo, I thought, but reappeared with another round.

'One for the road.' He winked and slung some peanuts on the table. The feeling, a deep indescribable happiness, lasted the whole way home where Mum was waiting to greet us.

'You chaps took your time,' she said, one hand on her hip, the other on the door frame.

'Scarcely,' Dad replied, flinching like a rescue puppy as he passed under the human arch and disappeared into the hall. I remember grabbing my stuff from the boot and hoping, praying, that the Eden of the last couple of hours would stay with me forever; for the first time since losing my religious faith, it felt once more almost like there was nothing in the way, nothing separating us.

Sure enough, 'going for a drink' became synonymous with connecting, transcending the mundanity of daily life and talking about things of 'greater moment', as he would put it. It was an unmitigated joy – or very nearly. Thoughts and stories, reflections, worries and dreams would pass between us, as if by osmosis. 'Another cheeky half?' he'd say, and return with two full pints and two packets of salted peanuts.

The issue was that, inevitably, the deeper our conversation went, the closer we got to God. Indeed, whether or not Dad expressly mentioned Him, you felt that He was always there in the wings. Not that this came as a surprise. Dad's faith was the lens through which he saw the world, and in happier times, it had been mine too. I wanted it back more than anything in the world. But for me, it was gone. And with it, my ability to talk to him about religion honestly, without fear of offending him or, worse still, infecting him with my lonely irreverence.

We found a way through: we settled on Love – to his mind, a synonym for God; to mine, a term for the indescribable force that made life worth living. I'm no theologian – I missed that boat – but perhaps our beliefs weren't so far apart after all.

#

Then along came Law. I must have been all of 17 years old, and I was back home for Christmas, doing the whole what-am-I-gonna-do-with-my-life thing. Until then, Dad had always steered me away from Law.

'Do something worthwhile,' he would say. 'Become a surgeon or something.'

'And what you do isn't?' I would reply, desperate to assuage any doubt he might have had about the utility of his life. 'Or is justice not important?'

It became something of a game.

Then one evening, it all changed. We were collapsed on the sofa, watching a news item on the UK's involvement in so-called 'extraordinary rendition' of wanted persons from one country to another – state-sponsored kidnapping, essentially.

'Disgraceful,' I muttered, at which point Dad sat up a bit. 'What was it you always said?' I asked him, swishing the last of some red wine around in my glass.

'No one…'

'…is above the law,' I said before he could, and looked him straight in the eye. 'What would you say if I told you I'd been thinking about reading…'

'Law?' he laughed. 'I'd say, could any Donovan ever choose anything else?' His turn to eyeball me. 'And I'd want to know why.'

'To…' I pointed at the television and wagged my finger at the then Home Secretary. 'To challenge shitty things like that.'

'More specific.'

'Evil,' I replied, remembering too late that Dad didn't believe in 'evil' as such, only in 'an absence of good'.

Glass resting on his stomach, he exhaled slowly. 'You want to be a public lawyer, yes? Human rights, that sort of thing?'

'I guess...'

'Well?'

'I want to help people,' I blurted.

It was surreal. No sooner had the words left my mouth, it seemed, than my fate was sealed. Alex Donovan, perhaps the least conventional Donovan in living memory, that 'flippant', 'zany' boychild who stood for, well, nothing definitive that he could think of, that sceptical, reluctant altar boy, since destined, he had thought, to remain in a perpetual void of terrifying uncertainty, had just talked himself into being – wait for it – a LAWYER. Ha!

And all on a whim, essentially.

Or had I just had a 'vocation'? Either way, it didn't much matter. Why not?

Because Dad was beaming. He saw, I suspect, that for the first time in years, I had seized on something I could truly believe in. And not only did it align with his own beliefs, of course, it endorsed his noble influence in my life. We were home...

Just then a light flickers behind me and – absurd as it sounds – I can't help wondering if it's him, Dad, showing me he's still with me. The light goes off again, as do others. It's one of the billers.

'Anyone up there?' he yells.

It's a good question.

30

The following morning, I get in early and fire up my desktop. And there, waiting for me, is a message from UTJ Proudfoot, forwarded from Jedrek and headed 'judicial complaint'.

'That didn't take long,' I mutter. I open the message and begin scrolling through the prattle before simply skipping to the end: '... *which is why, on this occasion I do not propose to take the matter further. I do expect, however, a full, written apology from the legal assistant in question*'.

'Solicitor,' I growl.

I glance at Jedrek's covering note, which is as angry-sounding as it is curt: *'We had better have a chat about this – 10am in my office.'* Christ...

Predictably, the rest of the complaint email is inaccurate. Allegedly, *'Master'* Donovan had made multiple interruptions, failed to address the bench appropriately, conducted himself in a petulant and aggressive manner and *'bore a dishevelled appearance unbefitting of an aspiring lawyer'*.

'For fuck's sake!' I shout at my screen, then laugh at myself.

'Language,' comes a weedy voice from down the corridor (Toby).

I try to get my head down, but as the minutes pass, I begin to worry about the implications of what I have done and my mouth becomes dry. Amy was right. I crossed a line. I have prejudiced relations between the firm, her chambers and the judiciary. Jedrek could fire me for this.

I leave the office, walk twice round the block, and brace myself for a flaying.

'Shut the door, please.'

'Jedrek, I'm so sor…'

'Don't apologise to me. Apologise to that blubbery ponce.'

'Excuse me?'

'But keep it short and sweet, OK? And, don't send it without showing it to me first.'

'Erm, sure. You…you're not going to fire me, then?

'Why would I do that? For standing up to one of *them*? You have to be kidding. I've had the lowdown from counsel.'

'Amy?'

'Indeed. She said Proudfoot was throwing his weight around again and that you tried to defend her and didn't back down. Well, do you know what? Sometimes needs must. Good for you, Alex.'

'Crikey…thanks?' I have never seen Jedrek so animated.

'He is loathsome, isn't he?' His face changes. 'But you still need to apologise, OK? We rely on goodwill between us and the courts. Much of the added value we provide to clients is, you know, intangible?'

'Sure.'

'I mean our credibility as a firm is our second-best asset. So, we need to nip this in the bud, yep?'

'Sure.'

'Do you say anything but "sure"?' He reaches into his desk drawer, pulls out a packet of peanut M&Ms and throws them over. 'Here. That's for sticking up for counsel.'

'Thank you…'

'Our best asset, of course, is our relationship with the specialist Immigration Bar: you protect it, you protect us.'

'Yes.' Discombobulated, I stand up, tuck my chair under the desk and make for the exit. 'Thank you, Jedrek – I'll have that email drafted by lunch.'

'No. You'll get it to me by 11.'

'Yes sir.'

'Shut the door behind you, would you?' he says, picking up the phone and dialling. 'Anton's going to *love* hearing about this.'

#

I listen outside as Jedrek recounts the story on speakerphone amid bursts of laughter, at times verging on hysterics when it comes to conveying my put-downs and the judge's wrath.

Ah well, I think, at least they are amused. I call Amy. She doesn't pick up – probably in court.

I'd be more relieved – happy even? – but something is niggling. According to Amy's earlier messages, Fletcher was less than impressed by my conduct, and quick to defend Proudfoot. Quite different, then, from the impression he seemed to give to Jed over the phone.

I text her.

'Has the KC calmed down yet?'

'Nope,' comes the reply. *'Blames me, primarily: should have known better etc. Xx.'*

'What? Than to whisper very quietly at the back of court, once? Xx,' I text back.

'No – than to bring you into court with me. You know, given your lack of advocacy experience. Actually, he said something else too. But you may not want to hear it... Xx'

'Go on.'

'Says I should give you a wide berth from now on, that you're a player and a liability to chambers' relationship with Hatton Taylor.'

'Fucking hell, the man's barely even met me!'

'Just reporting back, Alex – don't shoot the messenger.'

I manage to control my anger: *'From what I could glean from his chat with Jedrek just now, he sounded fine about it.'*

'Well, he would, wouldn't he? Don't bite the hand that feeds you, and all that?'

For all her wonderful qualities, Amy can be so annoying! She's right though, as ever. Emotionally exhausted, I put the phone down and set to writing my 'apology'.

#

'Come in!'

'Jed, you asked to see me. Presumably about the…'

'Yes, take a seat,' he replies. 'This is…well, it's a work of art!'

'Thank you!'

He slides his spectacles up the bridge of his nose. 'Now, let's see this again.'

Dear Judge, I apologise unreservedly for each and every offence listed in your email to my senior partner of said date and respectfully thank you for exercising your discretion on this occasion. The insolence you describe – my insolence – will not be repeated under any circumstances. It remains for me to thank you for this learning experience and to add, if I may, that if I were to develop half the great legal mind you have developed, I would die a happy man.

'That last part.' He exhales noisily, suppressing his laughter. 'Don't you think it is a touch OTT?'

'Maybe a touch…'

'Oh, sod it!' he exclaims. 'Ego's so inflated he'll probably love it!' He clicks on 'send'.

Before I go, Jed spares me another minute to ask how the migrant casework is going. I do my best to sound upbeat about it while he sits back on his chair, rubs the stubble on his chin and looks generally unpersuaded. I want to believe that he'll return me to the Refugee Team soon, but how can I prove to him that I can assess the merits of an asylum case when I no longer have any to assess? A dark thought crosses my mind that he and the partners might secretly wish to keep me right where I am, working on formulaic skilled migrant cases forever more… But were that so, they would surely just tell me? My head hurts.

As fortuitously as events have unfolded this morning, it is now 11:15 and I have completed precisely zero chargeable hours. I check my emails and see that Marina has won some long-standing battle with the Home Office over the interpretation of 'benefits' in the immigration rules. No time to look at the details, of course, but it is a high-profile win in the Court of Appeal, everyone is delighted and Jedrek has issued a press statement on the implications it ought to have for impecunious applicants.

Deep breath, I open one of the new skilled worker files I have inherited. What the hell is a 'high integrity pipe welder' when he's at home? With little other choice, I get my head down.

#

By six o'clock, I have zipped through four files and clocked up a good five chargeable hours. Unable to face any more, I clock off: tomorrow is another day. On the way out, I see Marina in her office and pop in to congratulate her on the win.

'Have you not heard?' she barely looks up. 'The Home Office just issued a Statement of Changes and redefined the rule in their favour. It renders the judgment – my whole case – obsolete.'

'Oh Christ…'

'Actually, could you…'

'Of course, I'll leave you in peace.' Poor Marina…trust me to go and make it worse.

'Alex?'

'Yes?'

'You're still here.'

I shut the door on my way out.

#

On the ride home, I try to make sense of my day but the answers elude me. What kind of immigration system lumps together a speech therapist, a welder and a ballet dancer in the same category? And by what strange logic is it OK for us to help Sisco and not Gema? Is this what I signed up for?

HONK! A large SUV beeps a mother and child over a zebra crossing; I pull my cycle helmet strap tighter under my chin and try to imagine I am somewhere else. Something is changing in me. I am ashamed to admit that for the first time since I began at Hatton Taylor, I find myself longing for an escape.

#

Later that evening, I check my emails. It seems that Jedrek may have had a point about Gema's case. Precisely none of my solicitor friends at other firms have responded to my message, let alone offered to help her. And if it presents to them as a lost cause, who, in fairness, can blame them?

A text from Gema: she's had the interview and – thank god! – they've chosen not to detain her. Now she must await a decision on her claim. I sigh with relief, then it occurs to me to text Professor Tait.

'Dear Prof. Tait, I am sorry to text so late. Do you, by any chance, have capacity to prepare a psych report for a vulnerable asylum seeker, victim of torture? Erm, also, I know neither you nor any of your esteemed colleagues do reports "pro bono" – nor should you be expected to – but might you consider doing a one-off?'

Won't work, I tell myself and send if off anyway. The reply comes in instantly:

'Hi Alex, Good to hear from you. My fee is 500 plus VAT. Best, R.'
'Can I call you? Promise I'll be brief?'
'You said that last time...'

#

Professor Tait's kindness is her weakness – she holds out all of two minutes before slashing the fee to 200 quid plus VAT. No time to waste, I examine my online current account – seriously? I switch to savings, make the transfer, text Gema with Tait's details, and advise her to request an urgent appointment.

#

Just as I am getting off to sleep, I receive a text. Amy! I sit up, and open it.

'Hey Alex, I just wanted to say sorry to you for how I've handled this whole Proudfoot debacle, and that whatever Anton says, I understand why you did what you did. Thank you for having my back. Xxx'

I hold the phone away from my face and squint. Three kisses.

31

The annual Human Rights Lawyers Awards are a little like the Oscars, only with less glamour, more alcohol and longer acceptance speeches.

'It's important to support these things,' Jedrek briefs us, his plea further weakening my will to attend, 'and they're at the Law Society this year so nice and central.'

In the end it is Cheryl, the receptionist, who persuades me. I bump into her on the porch outside the office, sucking the life out of a rolly.

'Go on,' she says between drags. 'Free booze, innit?'

I make for the bike shed.

#

One near-miss with a bus and a rolling spat with a cabby later, I arrive at Chancery Lane. I fix my bike to the railings, pull my crumpled jacket out of my rucksack and run up the Law Society's front steps, through the imposing, custodial columns that stand either side of the entrance.

Once inside, I hurtle across the carpet to the reception desk.

'You are late,' the receptionist is withering.

I bite my tongue.

'And, you might want to take that off,' he adds, pointing at my cycle helmet. 'First floor, turn right, straight ahead.'

#

The auditorium is packed. I find standing room at the back and scout for Amy in the audience. I have just picked up a glass of red from the trestle table when an usher takes my arm and shows me to one of the last two remaining seats – in the front row, naturally.

By the time I spot Fletcher approaching the podium, it is too late to turn around. The main lights dim and a spotlight floor lamp in the centre aisle lights up the lectern, adorning the KC's head with a giant halo.

On the projector screen is a slide, setting out the 1951 Convention definition of a refugee. It reads, simply:

'...someone who is unable or unwilling to return to their country of origin owing to a well-founded fear of being persecuted for reasons of race, religion, nationality, <u>membership of a particular social group</u>, or political opinion...'

I stash my wine under my chair as Fletcher begins.

'I am most grateful for that very kind introduction.'

'You deserve it,' calls a middle-aged woman with ginger dread-locks, a couple of rows behind me. 'We love you, Fletch!' cries another, and a burst of applause, whistles and whooping ensues.

'You are all too kind,' he responds. He combs his hand through his fair, floppy fringe, pauses and does that trick of looking directly at several people in different parts of the room.

'Your Lordships, my learned friends, supporters, critics and – last but by no means least – my instructing solicitors,' he says, eliciting a chortle. 'I wish to open with a quote from a mentor of mine and – on any serious view – the greatest authority on Refugee Law, the late Professor John Medway:

"There is a growing movement to expand the legal definition of a refugee. This is understandable: the number of those in need in the world far exceeds the number of legal refugees. Yet, such campaigns must be resisted. For to expand the definition would not only dilute our cherished refugee framework, it would

destroy it.

"Moreover, if we work innovatively – within the definition – we can extend protection to classes of refugees even the Convention drafters themselves could not have envisaged."'

He lowers his half-frame glasses and projects his voice to the back of the room. 'Of course, Medway was absolutely right. If you will permit me, I should like to explain why.'

'Top class, isn't he?' I hear someone say.

On he goes.

'Some of you may have noticed the words *membership of a particular social group* highlighted in the definition behind me,' he says with a knowing smile.

Nods in the audience.

'This, the nebulous fourth refugee ground, is where the Convention can do the most work.'

There are a couple of confused looks among some of the junior attendees, but he soon has them nodding along again.

'As the refugee lawyers among you will know, it is possible – and perfectly ethical – to argue that more and more groups of people fall within this fourth ground and are, as such, entitled to protection. Indeed, all that is required is a case-by-case approach and a little creativity.'

He takes a sip of water.

'Take the recent landmark case of *FA and others (Iraq)*, for example – a case I was fortunate enough to run...'

Again, a volley of applause interrupts his flow. He lets it ring out for a few seconds then, head down, raises a hand aloft like a rock star bowing out at Wembley. Quiet returns.

'The reason the appellants in *FA* anticipated persecution was because of their group status as young, wealthy professionals. Rightly then, the Upper Tribunal recognised them as a Particular Social Group, entitled to refugee protection.'

He takes another, slow sip of water. I look around. The eyes of the elderly man on my right are beginning to glaze over and one or two of the more daring attendees on the end of our row have surreptitiously pulled out their smartphones. I pick up my wine glass from under my seat, lift it to my mouth and take as big a gulp as I dare. On looking up again, I am skewered with Fletcher's eagle-eyed stare; his face is flushed.

'I'd like to break with tradition, if I may,' he improvises, 'and wrap up this acceptance speech in record time.'

There is relief in the room. Backs straighten in their chairs, smiles return, while some of the more experienced listeners tilt their heads, demonstrating their sustained, intellectual engagement for all to see.

'I am truly humbled to have been named Human Rights Lawyer of the Year. It is a wonderful boost for me, for my practice and for my chambers.'

More applause.

'I pledge that I shall continue to take the fight to the Home Office, day in, day out and with one simple aim: that any asylum seeker who may conceivably fall within the refugee definition be recognised as such and protected from serious harm.'

Before the audience members have time to clap again, he swiftly adds, 'I have a request before the merriment resumes.'

He holds up his trophy and nods to a man in a sash at the back, who is brandishing a little briefcase. The man walks ceremoniously up to the podium, takes the trophy and sits at the front of the stage. He opens up the box, takes out an engraving kit and begins inscribing something on the trophy. It is quite a spectacle. Fletcher adds some commentary. 'The guild has kindly granted my request that this award be shared with my brilliant junior, whose name will appear just below mine on the trophy. Ladies and gentlemen, please be upstanding for Miss Amy Phelan.'

Blushing, Amy half stands, half curtseys, then drops again into her seat. She does not get off that lightly though.

'Speech!' the room cries, and she is up on her feet before all her peers and less prepared than a witness to a car crash.

Then, as if in slow motion, she clambers over a portly guest to the centre aisle, inches forward and steps over the uplighter as elegantly as she can. Alas, however, there is no step up to the podium from where she is standing. A murmur ensues and a bossy bloke several rows back begins waving his arms and mouthing, 'Move back and let her round.' It is no good – they are packed in like passengers on a low-cost airline.

With nowhere to go, Amy looks up at Fletcher, helpless as a lamb in a ditch, appealing to be rescued. He rises to the challenge. Theatrically, he lifts up his foot, pulls off a loafer and points at Amy's feet, whereupon she bends down and removes her heels while he extends an arm and then pulls her onto the podium with him. She tries to put her heels back on but he advises against it.

'Don't bother,' he whispers, 'just thank everyone.'

I pull out my notebook in anticipation.

'Gosh. Well, that was easy!' she exclaims, receiving one or two half-hearted laughs. 'Erm… I just want to say thank you so much to all those who support our work, from our loyal clerks, to our support staff, to the solicitors who instruct us, to the judges who listen to us so…patiently.'

She pauses.

'Gosh, gosh…obviously, I wasn't expecting this…' She looks to Fletcher again, who is looking down at his feet and lightly rocking back and forward on his heels. 'Of course, I also want to thank the man standing here next to me, to whom I owe not only this accolade, but – let's face it – my entire career.'

'Nonsense,' he retorts with his bright, trademark smile, following which she seems a little more confident.

'I quickly also want to thank our brave lay clients, a couple of whom are in the audience and whose harrowing plight few of us could ever even imagine, let alone withstand.'

More applause.

'And, I want to endorse what Anton said. It is imperative that we continue to work together, with the Home Office where possible, to ensure that those who warrant protection are recognised as such. And, yes, that means interpreting the Convention definition of refugee imaginatively and fearlessly.'

At this point, the whooping returns and a portly, ruddy man at the back whom I recognise as none other than Upper Tribunal Judge Proudfoot, holds aloft his glass and shouts, 'Well, I'll drink to that!'

The caterers arrive with reinforcements, people begin looking round at them and the usher stands up and nods at Amy as if to say, 'wrap up now'. For a moment she appears to oblige. But she's not yet finished.

'Finally, while I have this platform,' pockets of indistinct chatter are beginning to break out, 'I wish to draw attention to those migrants not classed as refugees but who, often, are in similarly dire need of protection: the men, women and children who risk their lives to come here, in search of vital medical treatment, for instance, clean water or simply enough food to feed their families. We must lobby governments to do more to identify, process and protect these people, namely those at risk of harm for reasons *outside* the scope of the Refugee Convention – and whose cases fail to meet the very high threshold for protection under human rights law.'

With the headline act now long gone, the noise levels in the room shift up another notch, and thirsty audience members begin coughing and fidgeting with all the patience of expectant infants on Christmas morning. It is hard to imagine how Amy can keep her train of thought.

'Tell me,' she perseveres, raising her voice, which has become barely audible now. 'Is being tortured any worse than watching your family starve? We need a change in approach. We cannot continue to pick and choose the people we admit, without proper regard for what befalls those we discard.'

A few applaud, while the majority stretch their legs and make for the refreshments.

'Thank you,' she says in a rather wilted voice, and steps down off the podium.

#

I find her crossing between the Reading Room and the foyer, bottle in hand.

'Great speech, Amy.'

'Aw, thanks angel. Ever-so-slightly bloody nerve-racking, but hey. Here, looks like someone needs topping up.' The wine falls, bounces and swirls around my glass. 'I was hoping you'd come.'

'Wouldn't have missed it for the world...'

'Oh, cheer up, it's not that awful!'

I smile. 'Actually, Amy, I was wondering if...'

'Go on.'

'I was hoping we could talk at some point?'

'Sure...'

'It's just, well...' I look her straight in the eye. 'I think you might be making a big m...' A hairy hand appears, takes the bottle and pours its remaining contents into a pint glass.

'No sodding wine glasses left. Hi, I don't think we've met. Jon Price.' I recognise his surname from somewhere.

'Alex Donovan.'

'Ohhh, you're Alex. The caseworker, right?'

'Solicitor actually.'

'Yeah. Hey, it's good to finally put a face to the name.' He engages me in a crushing handshake. 'Oh, sorry mate – don't know my own strength! Anyway, must dash. Proudfoot needs a refill. Coming, Pingu?'

'I'll be along in a minute,' Amy replies, and off he goes.

'Seems they'll let anyone in these days,' I remark.

'This is the Law Society, Alex, not Amnesty.'

'OK sure, no offence, but he works for the Home Office, right?'

'They are not *all* bad.' She huffs. 'Jon regularly volunteers for fact-finding missions, I'll have you know – travels to some of the dodgiest parts of the globe. While we're ordering our Pret A Manger cappuccinos, he's out risking life and limb.'

She moves a little closer and whispers quietly. 'You don't know this, but Jon's work on the ground in Iraq provided crucial evidence for Farouk Ahmed.' It takes me a moment to register that she is talking about '*FA*', the refugee in that big Iraqi appeal she and Fletcher have just won.

'That's not so unusual, is it? Opponents sharing intelligence?' I am clueless, in fact.

'If it's not, it's pretty bloody rare,' she replies. 'Jon saved that man's skin.'

It is as she is saying this that I remember where I have seen Jon's surname. I decide to sound her out.

'I noted the latest country report on Peru is attributed to a J Price – your Jon, I assume?'

'Not *my* Jon,' she says.

'Sorry…'

'No, I am. I didn't mean to snap. Jon was livid about that, you know? Don't blame him either. What kind of monkey leaves the author's name on a country report?'

'You read it?'

'Not yet, I confess.'

She moves closer still and the traces of alcohol on her breath only make me want to kiss her more. I watch as her shiny red lips form different shapes before returning to their perfect repose.

'Hey, did you understand what I said just now?'

'The thing about Jon passing you info?'

Her lips are now touching my ear. 'Jon fed Anton evidence that undermined his own case!' she whispers. 'Point is, he's one of us, really – behind closed doors, he prides himself on it.'

I concentrate. 'What evidence?'

'You know, virtually all the stuff about the heightened risk to wealthy Iraqis – Anton said that without it we'd have had no case.'

'Wow,' I reply, with genuine surprise.

'And…'

'Go on.'

'OK – totally between you and me – it's not the first time he has helped Anton either. Remember Khadija Osman? You know, *KO (Somalia)*, the case on entirely unsupported women? Your friend, Judge Proudfoot's decision?'

'Yeah, sure…' I blag again. 'That was a good while ago, right?'

'2012,' Amy confirms. 'Actually, would you hold this a moment, darling?' She passes me her drink and kisses me on the cheek. 'I'm bursting for the loo!'

\#

I sit on a red velvet chaise longue – there's a first time for everything – and have a sip of her wine. There is hope yet.

Next, I whip out my smartphone, furiously type '*KO Somalia*' into the search engine and scroll down past a series of cage-fighting videos to find the case. I have just begun to read the Headnote when I feel a hand on my shoulder. Amy's.

'Refreshing our memory, are we?' She joins me on the couch. 'It wasn't the most helpful case, with hindsight. You basically have to be *completely alone* to fall within the guidance. How many young Somali women can there be with no family, friends or discernible ties to any existing clans whatsoever?'

'None, I'd wager.'

'Exactly, very few. It had nothing like the far-reaching effect other pioneering cases have had. Still, instructions are instructions. And it saved Ms Osman and a handful of others in her position – credit where credit's due and all that. Anyway, enough legal chat. How are you, lovely?' That word again. 'I feel spoilt seeing you twice in one week.'

Just then, a heavy slap across my back.

Jon.

'What's going on here, then?' he asks. 'You done with hitting on my woman?'

I glare at him.

'All right big fella, only teasing!'

'Jon, do you have to be so...'

'No, it's all good,' I interrupt, forcing a half-smile, then screwing up my nose as a musky, citrusy smell announces the arrival of the man himself.

'Anton Fletcher KC,' he says, extending his hand. 'I think we've met...'

Yes, I want to say, I'm that player, remember? I guess his cologne instead.

'Dior Sauvage?'

'I'm sorry? Oh, erm, yes actually.'

'Alex,' I say.

Fletcher leans in slightly and pushes his fringe out of his eye. 'Alex Donovan?' he asks, like a long-lost acquaintance.

'It seems your reputation precedes you,' Jon mocks.

'Now, now, Jon. Mr Donovan kindly instructed us on a recent Afghan appeal.'

'Well, technically it was Jedrek, but thank...'

'I'm terribly sorry,' Fletcher interrupts me. 'Would you give us a few minutes to discuss a matter?'

'Sure. I'd best be off anyway. Long ride home.'

No one is listening. Amy has already turned towards Fletcher and is waiting attentively for what he has to say. Behind them, Jon has signalled to Proudfoot, who is stumbling over to him, clearly off his face.

I make my way towards the door. As I pass through, I can just make out Fletcher's voice counselling Amy to move on to the water.

Outside it is still light. Loud, lascivious family lawyers flop about on the steps exchanging juicy divorce stories, while a young Eastern European waiter tries to pick up pieces of broken bottle by their feet.

I stuff my jacket back in my rucksack and begin wrestling with my rusty D-lock.

'Bugger,' I growl, barely noticing the receptionist standing over me.

'I am afraid attaching bicycles to the Society's railings is strictly prohibited.'

I try to keep my cool. 'Ah, you're the receptionist who kindly showed me to the Reading Room earlier.'

'Concierge. You need to move your bicycle now, sir, or I'll...'

Enough. 'What? Or you'll what?'

There is a crack as I finally manage to prise my lock open.

'I beg your pardon?'

'Granted,' I yell over my shoulder and bolt back up Chancery Lane.

32

Friday morning and I am back at my desk. For a moment, all is quiet, before the familiar sounds of stairs creaking and metal blinds rolling up herald the advent of a new day. At least I am not hungover, I reflect. Might as well be, though. I can't concentrate, so I make myself a tea. Then a coffee. Nope.

I step outside and take a turn around the block. Bad idea: the usual cacophony of engine noise, shouts, barks and beeps feels particularly oppressive today, and all the while, I can feel that precious chargeable time slipping away. The dull ache in my leg returns and I start to feel disorientated. I stop a moment. Something is happening to my vision too – it is becoming blurred and pixelated. Get a grip, Al, I tell myself, and go back in.

Toby.

'Ah, if it isn't my esteemed colleague,' he chirps, passing me on the stairs. He stops. 'Hey, I meant to say, you know that pre-action letter you sent the Home Office, to release your client's file? Congolese guy they dispersed to Glasgow?' I stop in my tracks. 'Yeah, well they released…'

'They did?' I interrupt. 'And? Anything?'

'No, sorry – or yes – impossible to tell.'

'Eh?'

He chuckles. 'Take it you have never seen one of these disclosures before? File copy was so heavily redacted it could have been morse code! It's the same every time. Damn all we can do about it though, short of breaking in and snatching the files ourselves!'

'Not such a bad idea…' I turn and follow him back down.

'Hey, what are you doing?' he asks, looking over his shoulder.

'Leaving,' I tell him, and walk out the door.

#

I make it back to York Way, roll down North Road to the Goodinge Health Centre and lock my bike up. Then it's not long before I hear my name called.

'Do come in and take a seat.' The GP has kind eyes. 'I am Dr Thomas, the locum here this week. Tell me, what seems to be the problem?'

'Well, I…my…' It's like my throat's seized up or something.

He looks up from his notes. 'Here, grab one of these,' he says, handing me a box of tissues. 'Now, I see you are a solicitor, is that right? Hmm, sounds stressful…'

#

One slightly high blood pressure reading and a normal ECG later, he signs me off for two weeks for stress and anxiety.

I well up with guilt and tell him he can't; he makes it a month.

'But…'

'But nothing. Tell me, Alex, what good will you be to anyone without your health?

To my shame, I feel my eyes filling up.

'Suggestion,' he says as I get up to leave. 'Use this time to do *whatever* you like. Something you're into, something you've always fancied trying – whatever – something *you* want to do, OK?' He smiles and hands me a sick note. 'Any more problems, you know where we are.'

#

Outside, there is an empty space where my bike was. Squinting, I just about make out some youths in puffer jackets, scuttling away towards New Clock Tower Place. And then they are gone. I perch on the surgery wall a moment. A cloud crosses in front of the sun. Is this how it ends, I wonder, my noble dream slipping away from me.

33

It's 10:30 on Saturday morning and yesterday's still sinking in. I head down to Arancini Brothers café on Kentish Town Road, nab a discreet spot in the back corner behind a cheese plant and open my work bag.

I know, in theory, I am not to do any work for a month. But I at least owe it to my clients to have their files in good order so that no deadlines are missed, and so that Toby can hit the ground running.

I start typing up old attendance notes while berating myself for having left them until now to do. 'It's all about contemporaneous notetaking,' Jed emphasised to me, while taking a note of the same. But it is never that easy. For a start, most of my asylum seeker clients suffer from either Post Traumatic Stress Disorder or depression, or both, and taking detailed witness statements from them requires a level of sensitivity psychotherapeutic counsellors would be proud of. Inevitably, then, admin takes second place.

#

When the waiter comes over, I order the breakfast wrap, relax my shoulders and resume typing. But as the place starts filling up, I begin to lose concentration. And by the time my enormous breakfast arrives, I have achieved so little I find myself fretting about how long it is going to take to eat.

My phone pings. A text from Amy.

'Hi sweetie, are you about later?'

I resolve to ignore it.

More people arriving.

This is hopeless.

The waiter returns. 'Everything is OK, sir?'

'Great thanks,' I reply with a fixed smile. 'Could I have the bill, please?'

#

Outside, the streets are beginning to bustle, and with the morning all but written off, I pick up a newspaper from the kiosk and veer off right, along the canal towards Camden, one eye on a piece about this year's Wimbledon, the other on the water.

Ping.

Danso this time. *'Hey Al, have you seen the weather outside? Pint on the lock?'*

#

When I arrive at Lock 17, Danso is sitting on a bench overlooking the water, headphones on, scribbling in a smart little notebook. The midday sun has transformed the filthy canal below into a wavy up-side-down watercolour of the Ice Wharf opposite.

'Writing your memoirs, Danso?'

'Nah, I'm penning the lyrics for that track I mentioned. Hey, this is for you.' He pulls out another identical little notebook.

'Moleskine? You shouldn't have!'

'I didn't. Two for one offer. Now, check this out.' He hands me the headphones. 'Got the violin part laid down – I'm telling you, Zalmai's got it, man!'

'Who?' I ask, lowering the headphones.

'You know, the violinist I mentioned?'

'No. Yes. I mean, what did you say his name was?'

Danso laughs. 'Ah OK, I know my pronunciation's shit. Zalmai, Zalmay...Zalmey?'

'Surname?'

'No idea.'

'Could you find out for me?'

'OK...' Danso scrunches up his face. 'You gonna tell me why? He famous or something?'

'Look, it's probably nothing. Just that Amy recently mentioned a big Afghan asylum appeal involving a young violinist, and I could have sworn the initials were ZA. The result's pending.'

Danso's eyebrows shoot up. 'Oh shit! Could be a coincidence, right?'

'Probably,' I try to reassure him. 'He's as good as you hoped, then?'

'Better! Go on, have a listen,' he says, standing up. 'Pint of...?'

'Beer.'

'Amusing.'

'Oh, I don't know, mate. Anything.'

Danso returns with a satisfied grin on his face and an unduly large tumbler of murky, yellow froth.

'Oh... Hoegaarden.'

He rolls his eyes. 'I'll see if they'll take it back.'

'No, give it here.' I laugh. 'Wait! What in god's holy name is that?'

'What? Never seen cider before?'

'Give me that! *Rhubarb* flavour?'

Danso ignores me. 'So? Come on. What do you think? Good eh?'

'Good? It's stunning!'

'Told you! Shit...if it is him, they'd better let him stay. They will, won't they?'

'Don't know. OK, probably. Will depend on his case.'

'But he's from Afghanistan...'

'Not enough on its own. And, if he is no longer a child...'

'Oh crap.'

'Still winnable, but not clear-cut. Look, there is every chance it is not him. For all I know' – I cough – 'there are lots of violinists in Kabul. Do find out his surname though?'

'Yeah, yeah of course...' Danso has fixed on a woman drifting elegantly past in a straw boater, her suit jacket swung casually over her shoulder.

'Hang on.' I cock my head to one side. 'Weren't you supposed to have met "the one"?'

He laughs. 'Don't you listen? I said *one of the ones*. Ah shit.' He sighs. 'It was looking good. You know, she was ticking the boxes: funny, smart, pretty. You'll like this one: Irish. But then...'

'Yes?'

'So, I get back to hers, right?' he says quietly, looking over his shoulder, then back at me. 'And I'm talking some place *way* up on the Northern Line. Anyway, she opens the door to her bedroom...'

'Bloody hell! You don't waste any time, Danso.'

'Let me finish, let me finish. And, there...' he slows for effect '...on every wall but one, are giant posters of...guess who?'

I laugh. Here I am again, being regaled with yet another nail-biting war story from the man whose charm, it seems, no mortal could ever resist.

'The pope?' I ask.

'You know, I quite like the pope. No. Worse. One more guess. Go!'

'You?'

'Ha! No. Ready?' He fixes his eyes on me. 'Michael Bolton.'

'Shut the front door!' I exclaim. 'Wait. Pre or post-mane?'

'Both!'

A detailed description ensues of how Danso went 'straight into reverse', shut the door in front of him, reopened it clutching his head, rattled off his standard migraine excuse, shut the door again – and ran!

When I ask if he thinks maybe his reaction was a little extreme, I am met with defensiveness. For music men, Danso explains, there is a limit, a line – and Michael *Bolotin* fandom crosses it. She will never understand his own, 'much cooler' music, nor, by extension, him. It is doomed.

'Wait, Bolotin?' I ask.

'His real name.'

'Sorry.' I cough. 'Who did you say the fan was? You know what I think, Dan?'

'Nope, but you're gonna tell me.'

'You're scared of commitment.'

'Tosh.' He scoffs. 'I just cannot abide a Boltonian, that's all. However sweet she seemed...' He takes a long swig of his disgusting drink.

'Give her another chance,' I tell him.

He rocks his head back, gargles, swallows and put his glass down.

'Hmph. OK. Maybe.'

There's a pause.

'Alex?' he says, but I barely hear him. I'm wondering just how many chances I have given Amy. This time, though, Danso is prepared.

'Now come on, mate.' He shakes my shoulder. 'Keep staring at the closed door and you won't see the open one.'

I exhale. 'Real headfuck, Danso. One minute it is as if her bloke didn't exist; the next, she is going home with him.'

'Who?' he jokes, and glances at his watch. 'Eight minutes, 47 seconds. No mention of her for nearly nine full minutes. My boy's making progress...'

#

I am too. Five minutes is all it takes, and I am 'back in the room'.

'Live-streaming platform's fully up and running,' Danso announces.

'Hey, that's excellent!'

'Yeah, thanks. Good to have it done, anyway. Mate, you've

dropped something.'

He reaches down to grab my newspaper for me. Or so I think. In fact, he crosses one leg over the other, opens it out and begins reading it himself.

'Hey, I haven't even read that myself, yet!'

Half-ignoring me, he begins reading out the headlines. Then, 'Wow...'

'All right, what's so interesting?'

'Just the shit that's going on in Libya right now – mental, isn't it?'

'The refugee camps?'

'Exactly. According to this, not even the UN lot are feeding them.'

I snatch the newspaper out of his hands and scan through the article. 'Poor bastards. Released from the detention camps, and now – holy shit...'

'What?'

'Despite growing starvation, they – the UN – are "phasing out" food catering in the relief centres. Here.' I pass the paper back to him and he reads out the passage.

'An aid worker in the camp reports those in charge are deliberately with-holding food aid to motivate them to leave...'

He puts the papers down. 'Fuck me...'

'I know, right? What are we coming to? Someone needs to change the record!'

'You said it...' Danso covers his mouth with his hand.

'Hey, you brought it up.' I scowl, and flick the frothy head off my pint at him.

He laughs. 'First time for everything. I'm just glad you missed the ISIS article. Another one of your obsessions, isn't it?'

'Erm, not really.'

'Oh no? No interest in mind control, cults, radicalisation?'

I snatch the newspaper back and find the headline. *'Secret services warn of risk of jihadist attack against Spaniards in Sahara region'.*

'That's the one. Something about refugees and camp workers

being isolated, vulnerable to attack and stuff.'

'Yeah.' I read on. 'According to this, it's the geography of the place: makes it harder for the international community to police...' I pause a moment or two, deep in thought, then glance at my watch. 'Listen, I'd best be off – work to do.'

'Saturday? You sure?'

I pull a sick face.

'Wait.' Danso grabs my arm. 'I think I know the answer to this, but are you free any evenings next week to give me some feedback on the track I'm assembling?'

'Actually mate...'

He raises his hand. 'Don't tell me, work?'

'No, it's... Oh, it's nothing. GP's signed me off for stress.'

'Shit, sorry mate...' His focus softens. 'Could be a good thing though? You can still come and jam, surely? It can be low key, chilled. I'll make you some grub...'

'Honestly?'

'Yeees?'

'I'd love to.'

'Great!' Danso comes in for a high five.

'First though,' I tell him, 'there is something I need to do.'

34

I arrive at the office to find there is a new sign outside the building, comprising a yellow warning triangle and the words, *Have You Clocked In?* Really…? I ask myself. Next, they'll be holding class assemblies and singing from *Songs of Praise*.

The office itself is virtually empty, but for a couple of poor souls in the billing room and a new junior solicitor in the room next door, whose name, to my shame, I have already forgotten.

'Tea? Coffee?' I enquire.

'Just had one, thanks. Take it I'm not the only one who didn't meet their time-recording target this week?'

'Oh to be at that stage! I'm still writing up old attendance notes. Going to be a long one, I fear…'

My colleague contrives a sort of half-smile. 'My supervisor says…'

'Always time record as you go along?' I interrupt.

'Same supervisor, then.' Her smile is more natural this time.

'The firm's "best practice" policy. Personally, though, I'm damned if I'm going to spend my entire day thinking in 6-minute units. What was it Eliot said again? "I have measured out my life in coffee spoons."'

'Oh, I'm not sure I've met him yet. Which floor is he on?'

I hesitate. Has she really never heard of the poet? Or was she engaging in existentialist banter?

I gamble: 'Hmm, I know what floor he's not on…'

No response.

#

I collect the files I need from Toby's office, lower my mangled Venetian blinds and embrace the drudgery.

#

A couple of hours in, I consider putting on some music and decide against it. Six attendance notes after that, I pop out for some air.

#

On the way back to the office, I pick up a bottle of Pantene from the chemist, then take a detour via Peckham Rye. Everywhere I look, young, healthy-looking people are making the most of the sunny weekend. I lie down on the grass and use my bag as a pillow.

#

It is past six when I wake and see I have missed a message from Amy. A rush of adrenaline. I open it.

'Hi Mr, hope you're enjoying the sun! Can I see you later? In chambers and have the car so can come find you?'

On second thoughts, what is there left to lose?

#

Back in the office, I finish off my attendance notes, stash the files back in Toby's room and write him a little message on a post-it. *'Hey Toby, just to say thanks in advance for looking after my old clients. It's a comfort to know they are in safe hands. Stay sharp. A.'*

I grab the shampoo from my bag – it's only then I see I've bought the anti-dandruff version – stick the note to it and leave it in his desk drawer.

Amy pitches up at 8pm in an MG F convertible. Last person remaining, I lock up and off we speed.

'Nice wheels.' I shut my eyes and let the sensual summer air caress my face.

'Oh god, I hate this car,' she replies. 'So yuppyish, isn't it? In another life I'd have a nice vintage Vespa or something…be more hip.'

'Tattoo?' I humour her.

'Not for me,' she muses. 'Now, a discreet little nose stud, maybe…'

I nod. 'That could work.'

'So, lovely, where do you fancy?'

#

St Paul's gardens are an oasis of calm. We park up, find a bench looking out towards the Thames and take in the sounds of the city.

'Is it just me or is it a bit chilly?' she asks. I put an arm round her.

CONFRONT HER! yells a voice in my head. But she snuggles in closer and delicately places her head on my chest. I stroke her hair and…is this really happening?

She asks after my family with all the warmth of someone who knows them, and we gossip and giggle about our peers with unrestrained freedom. All of it – her laughter, the way we look at each other – everything feels so effortless, so natural.

I tell her about the GP et cetera, and she takes my free hand in hers.

'In this work you'd be inhuman if you *didn't* feel the stress at some point or other,' she says gently. Her touch, her scent, her warmth. Once more it feels as it did that night we first met when, tipsy and unable say goodbye, we wound up arm in arm, wandering the streets of London until the sun rose over the city, exposing us like a silent witness to a crime. It's as if her loyalty to Jon were only ever but a contrivance of my imagination, a myth disproved and all but forgotten.

She speaks openly of her dream to live in the country. The Lakes, perhaps, with animals and children, '...in that order'. I picture myself moving there with her – walks, fires, laughter, love... We talk and talk, minutes become hours, and...

'Shit, look at the time!' It's almost midnight. Amy unzips her wheely bag to reveal four thick lever-arch files. '1,500 pages to get my head round by the end of tomorrow...'

'What?'

'Only received them last night.'

'The fucking nerve! Better not be colleagues of mine,' I tell her.

ASK HER OUT! the voice returns.

'Actually, Amy, are you about over the next month at all? See, there's this flamenco festival on at Sadler's Wells, and...'

'Erm.' She bites her lip. 'I am not actually.'

'No?' I persist. 'You sure?'

She looks directly at me, then far away, through the plane trees on the North Bank, over the water and beyond.

'We're going away.'

'We?'

'Jon and I,' she says, her tone now impatient.

Gently, I take my arm away and stand up.

She looks up at me, her eyes wide and sad. 'I...I can explain...'

But I can no longer hear her.

'Where are you going?' I ask, and she whispers something inaudible. 'I missed that.'

'Barbados,' she says.

Well, there it is, I reflect. Bar-fucking-bados. I turn away to compose myself. A commuter ferry drifts into view and is gone again.

'Good luck, Amy,' I say, turning to her. 'I mean it.'

She stands up and grips my arm. 'Wait, please!' her voice is shaky. 'Can we...can we still be...'

'Friends?' I peel her hand away and she begins to cry. 'Let's see how we fare, shall we? You're right, it's late. Goodnight, Amy.'

'Wait, I'm going north too. I'll drop you home...' She is now on her feet and zipping up her trolley bag.

'No. I mean no, thank you, Amy.'

'I'm so sorry.'

The fading murmur of rubber on cobbles signals her departure.

#

Desperate as the losing side in a relegation battle, I choose to walk home. Some forty minutes or so in, as I drift ghost-like up Hampstead Road towards Mornington Crescent, like a gift from above I am offered the light relief I need. There on my left, floating out from Mestizo Mexican restaurant, come the words:

> '...*So tell me all about it*
> *Tell me 'bout the plans you're makin'*
> *Oh, tell me one thing more before I go...*'

The irony of the lyric alone might have been enough. But it's the fact that it is the hit ballad by Mr Bolton himself that tickles me. I instantly think of Danso's dating story, feel my cheeks lifting and shake my head. And when the chorus duly arrives – *'Tell Me How Am I Supposed To Live Without You'* – I laugh out loud. Like a tortoise on its back, life has a funny way of righting itself.

35

The time off work blows by, of course. True to my word, I fit in a music session with Danso, take a walk on the Heath and so on, but I end up spending most of it writing something for Amy from the heart. *'For your eyes only'*, I type in the email subject header, and off it goes. 'Swoosh'. Last roll of the die, I tell myself. Then I wait…

#

And wait…

#

24 hours and still not a sausage. I pack a bag and book a one way flight to Jerez.

#

When evening comes, I run an early bath and grab my phone and a bottle of *Rioja*. Once I'm in, I reach clumsily over the side of the tub, pick up my phone and press play on Kind of Blue.

Ping.

Her, finally. *'Hey lovely, hope you're OK?'*

That it? I think. Nope – *still typing…*

Ping.

'Listen, Jon wanted to discuss a project with you or something, so I passed

him your number – hope that's cool Xxx'

I stare at the message in disbelief.

'Whatever,' I eventually respond.

Fuck her.

Ping.

A different number: *'Hi Alex, Jon here (Amy's man).'*

Take her!

I read on. *'Fancy meeting to discuss an exciting new project Anton Fletcher KC and I are working on? Where are you exactly? It's time sensitive so we'll need to meet tonight/tomorrow latest.'*

I lob my phone onto the bathmat and sink slowly back into the water, fully submerging my head and holding the wine aloft like the torch of the sunken, drunken statue of liberty.

36

06:47 and back in the office to pick up my stuff. I dump my bag, pull out my phone and check my messages. Still nothing further from Amy. She, like most of the Immigration Bar, will have been up a good hour by now.

I text her. *'Might you at least have acknowledged it?'*

No response.

I gather my belongings and leave.

#

Outside, the rain is sheeting down over Rye Lane. I jump in a cab, take a deep breath and begin composing an email to the firm's 'All Staff' group. *'Dear all, it has been a genuine...'*

Nope.

'Dear colleagues,' I try again. *'It is with a heavy heart...'*

Hilarious: I can't even bloody resign. Don't then, whispers my inner contrarian, and the thought of turning around and walking back in sparks adrenaline and exhaustion in equal measure. I reach into my pocket, double-check the flight departure time on my boarding pass, and shut my eyes. Andalusia awaits...

#

Paddington Station is a dynamic collage of umbrellas, bags, newspapers, coffees and croissants. I jump into an empty-looking carriage on the Heathrow Express and check my phone.

08:45 and not a peep from her.

'Go to hell,' I mutter under my breath.

'Excuse me?'

I look up to see a diminutive, tweed-clad man staring at me from across the aisle. 'Not you, sir.'

The man inches his trousers up a little and shuffles forward on his seat. 'I should think not.'

I examine his face. How could anyone, I wonder, get to seventy plus and not have a single discernible smile line? Fuck him. 'But you can go to hell too,' I say casually, and even I am a little surprised at my rudeness.

'I beg your pardon?' he replies, raising a hand to his heart and jutting his neck forward.

'Well, all right, look at you. Zero awareness. What are you? Seventy? Eighty? Come on,' I appeal, remorse kicking in. 'Here you are, unaccompanied, in an empty carriage, picking a fight with someone half your age…I mean, imagine if I was less of a gentleman?'

'Were.'

'What?'

'If I *were* less of a gentleman. Subjunctive.'

The train begins pulling out of the station and a series of muffled, multilingual welcomes come over the PA system.

The man adjusts his hearing aid, stands up and hobbles over to me like a cross between a wounded Lee Van Cleef and Uncle Bulgaria. He then picks up my bag and tries in vain to put it in the overhead locker.

'What exactly do you think you are doing?' I ask.

'Teaching you to be civilized,' he replies, and sits down in the seat next to me.

\#

We sit in silence for a couple of minutes. Mad fucker, I think to myself and reach into my rucksack for my headphones. The man pulls them off me.

'That is the trouble with your lot,' he says. 'You don't know how to sit still, do you? Perpetually bouncing from one stimulus to the next, you don't know how to…be.'

'Oh, I'm sorry,' I reply. 'Tell you what, I'll take life lessons from you when you learn how to crack a smile.'

The man's face seems to flinch slightly. A very faint twinkle, perhaps? More likely a scowl. Whatever. I dig out my water bottle and take a swig.

'Botox,' the man says, eventually.

I spit the water out onto the empty seats in front of us. 'What?'

'The reason I can't smile.'

'Seriously?' This is too much for me.

'No. Not seriously. But it made you laugh, didn't it?'

#

Ping, a message.

I step off the Express and open it. Her. *'Morning Alex,'* it reads. *'I don't understand. Could have acknowledged what?'*

Carefully, I open my Sent Mail folder and find the email, correctly addressed to her chambers account. More games, no doubt. I close it again.

#

The queue for bag drop is mercifully short. On seeing me struggle to make the machine work, a member of the airline staff approaches and kindly helps me print my luggage tag. 'Might need to charge you extra for that one,' she says, looking at my neat little holdall.

'Not exactly huge, is it?'

'Well, you'll have plenty of spare kilos for souvenirs and stuff on your return.'

'Return?'

'Oh, emigrating, are we?'

'You tell me,' I oblige.

'Gate number 40,' she chuckles, and beckons the next person forward.

#

Three frisks, a shoe swab and full body scan later, I am allowed through to Departures. I down a free shot of Baileys, then make for the bar where I grab a seat by the Departures screen.

A young man approaches me with a tray of éclairs, packaged in smart little multi-coloured boxes on which are written, *'Eat the world a better place'*.

'Chockie for charity?' the man asks.

'Excuse me?'

'Half of every one sold goes to leukaemia research,' he says.

I frisk my pockets for loose change. 'How much are they?'

'Five pounds, sir.'

'What!'

Committed now, I find a fiver and hand it over.

'Think of it as more like two fifty,' the man says, without looking at me.

I pop it in my pocket, look for my flight number on the Departures screen, and see that we are boarding. Up and off I speed, past dithery couples, airport buggies, parents and errant children.

At the gate, one queue is considerably shorter than the other. I slip in as inconspicuously as I can.

'Speedy boarding?' asks a stout man at the desk.

'Alex Donovan,' I respond, holding out my hand.

He sighs. 'There's always one. Back of the queue please if you've not paid the extra.'

I look over my shoulder and see a large group of school children joining the main queue. 'I'll pay the extra,' I say authoritatively. 'And a seat with extra legroom if there are any?'

'I'm afraid we can't take money at the gate,' comes the response.

I think for a moment, then ask the man if he will consider payment in kind. He looks confused, then shocked, as I reach slowly into my inside pocket. But when I produce the éclair, his expression shifts to happy surprise.

'Yummy, yummy,' I whisper, and place it carefully on the counter, as if it were a fragile antique.

The man appears to vacillate. Then subtly, without looking down, rakes the bribe towards himself and scoops it under the table. 'Our secret,' he says, and disappears behind his computer a moment. 'Seats 18b and 18c are unreserved, but you'll have to nab them quick...'

\#

Queueing on the airstair to board the plane, I receive a WhatsApp. Amy? I feel my heart jump.

Nope, it's Danso.

'Al, you're never going believe this! That room? The Bolton room? It was her mother's, mate! She did it to wind me up and...well it fucking worked, didn't it!'

'Gotta be quick,' I text back, *'but that's hysterical! She sounds like a keeper, no?'*

'As in, one of the loves of my life?' he replies.

'I give up.'

'Lol. Hey, Al, another thing.'

'Quick.'

'I meant to tell you, the bloke we talked about, the violinist guy? Well, guess what? His surname's "Azam". It's him.'

'Crap...'

'No, it's OK. His barrister says it's a clear-cut case, "in the bag".'

'Well, he should know,' I respond. *'It is Fletcher, right?'*

'Yes!' comes the excited reply. *'Spoke to him after our music session. Seemed really sound.'*

'Great!' I reply, summoning all my enthusiasm. *'Glad he's being looked after. OK, gotta go. Hey, listen, gonna be off grid for a bit – catch up when I resurface.'*

#

As I board, I find myself wondering what kind of lawyer would pre-empt the outcome of a case to that extent, let alone relay his opinion so unequivocally to his client? What if they were to lose, for instance? The fallout would be terrible – to say nothing of the punishing guilt he would be left with. Then again, I reflect, this is Anton Fletcher KC…has the man ever even lost a case?

The plane is filling up fast and already the cabin is replete with the pitter patter of Spanish chatter. My bag safely stowed, I stretch out my pins in front of me as far as they will go and hit the call button. A familiar young steward appears.

'You look well, sir,' he says politely.

'Ah, hello again,' I reply. 'Yes, I suppose I am, thank you. How is yourself?'

'Oh, you know, up and down…'

I snort. 'Say, is there any chance of getting a…'

'Cuba libre?'

'Wow, you're good!'

'I know,' he says wistfully. 'I'm wasted up here.'

And so I intend to be.

37

Another drink in and somewhere over the west coast of France, I pull out the in-flight magazine. It contains many of the usual features: 'Wonderful Warsaw', 'Pisa Pizza?' and other, generic weekend away plugs. A feature on page 13 catches my eye, however. There, under a recruitment advert for the Home Office, is a 1,000-word leader piece on none other than Ms Khadija Osman. I rub my eyes in disbelief and retrain them on the page.

The opening reads a bit like the introduction to a legal argument, factual and contextualising.

'Exiled and educated in Kenya, Ms Osman graduated in Anthropology from Nairobi University and returned to her native Mogadishu in 2006, with hopes of, one day, standing for government. Lamentably, however, her return coincided with the rise of the Islamist youth militia, Al Shabaab. And when, in 2010, they murdered her family and wiped out her minority clan, she was forced to flee for her life.

'With the help of an agent, she sailed to Mombasa and travelled on to the UK by plane. Her asylum claim was refused and her initial appeal dismissed. Yet, her luck would change when her solicitors instructed a certain Anton Fletcher KC to prepare her onward appeal. Not only did he go on to win it for her, but it became the landmark case for other, vulnerable women in her situation to rely on.'

Yeah, all seven of them, I think, and instantly feel bad. Were it not for Fletcher, no doubt Ms Osman would not be alive today, let alone working for…what the fuck? I hit the call button and order another drink.

#

Refilled and ready, I return to the article. No, I haven't dreamt it. Khadija Osman, '…*a fluent English speaker, completed the law conversion course and was hired by the Home Office as an immigration officer to do "status determination" – in other words, to decide asylum claims.'*

'Well fuck me backwards,' I exclaim, a little loudly as it happens.

'Certainly not,' comes a posh, elderly voice from a row or two behind me.

Eagerly, I read on. The piece presents Ms Osman as a benign adjudicator and human rights defender, motivated by identifying and helping refugees as others helped her before. Wonderful stuff in principle. But as the article develops, she reveals her true colours and I recognise her as the very same, repressive Home Office inquisitor whom Amy and I complained about: Officer 31.

'*Naturally,*' she reports, '*I was obliged to refuse the odd, bogus case along the way.'* And the example she gives is of Kenyans claiming to be Somalis in order to obtain refugee status in the UK. '*It didn't take long to expose their ignorance of Somali traditions,'* she gloats. '*I even tricked one into speaking Swahili in his asylum interview. I'm afraid he got the wrong interviewer!'*

Hilarious fun, apparently, but for the possibility that some of those she dismissed were, like her, Somalis who had been exiled in neighbouring Kenya and spoke Swahili, but who were perhaps less familiar with Somali traditions. Even as regards those who *were* actually Kenyan, I simmer, the fact that they pretended to be Somali did not necessarily mean they were safe in Kenya. Perhaps they were fleeing post-election violence there, for instance? In my experience, buried under a false account, can often lie a true and more compelling one.

I take another gulp of rum. And I'll need it. '*In late 2017,'* the article concludes, *'Ms Osman was elevated to the role of senior fact finder for East Africa, under Country Policy and Information Team manager, Mr Jon Price.'*

'Shit the bed!' I blurt out.

'Won't do that either,' comes the voice from behind again.

I turn around and to my happy surprise see it is none other than the man I had met earlier on the Express. 'You!' I say enthusiastically.

'No,' he replies, pointing at a book he is reading.

'I'm sorry?'

'It's not me yet. We've still a good hour to go and I want to finish this chapter.'

#

The captain announces we have begun our descent into Jerez airport, and I feel a tap on my shoulder.

'We can talk now,' the old man says. 'What did you want to say to me?' He looks at the row of empty Bacardi miniatures on my table tray. 'You can still speak, can you?'

I affect an embarrassed look. 'There's more leg room in this row...'

The man groans, hauls himself up and hobbles over to join me. 'So, where were we?'

'You were about to reprimand me for my language,' I reply.

'Ah yes – and you might want to get a handle on this drinking habit of yours too, don't you think?'

I bite my lip and the man cocks his head to one side. 'Are you going to tell me what was so remarkable about that piece you were reading, then?'

'Oh, nothing much. It only revealed that the repressive immigration officer, Ms Osman, who dismissed my client's asylum claim a couple of years back, was herself a former refugee!'

He is unmoved. 'Ah, yes, the old drawbridge mentality – "I'm all right, Jack" et cetera – nothing surprising about that, is there?'

'No, not in of itself…' I reflect, 'but it's all so…connected? OK, the immigration officer's own asylum case was a high-profile one.'

'In what sense?'

'It carried a special status – they call it "country guidance". Basically, it became binding precedent for decision-makers to follow in all subsequent Somali asylum appeals. It was a big deal. And, here is the thing,' I whisper. 'The barrister who acted for Ms Osman at her appeal, Anton Fletcher KC, has a close friend at the Home Office, Jon Price, who Ms Osman now works directly under!'

'Sorry, and?'

'Well, doesn't that seem a bit of a coincidence?'

The man combs his long, white eyebrows with his stiff-looking, dappled index finger. 'Perhaps the KC introduced the other two, then? So what? Why the excitement?'

'Almost certainly he did,' I reply. 'They were opponents in the case!'

'Well, there you go then.'

'No, look, you need to understand something. Politically, claimant lawyers and Home Office lawyers are sworn enemies.'

'All right…'

'None of our lot would wish to help anyone to get work at the Home Office. That is, I seriously doubt it. It's like…it's like Yoda help-ing Luke to join the Dark Side: not gonna happen. Help her become a dismisser of asylum claims? No way!'

The man looks at me quizzically. 'Presumably, they grant a few too?'

'They do,' I concede. 'And, all right, I did also hear that Jon Price may be more sympathetic than some…'

'Well, that's your answer then.'

'Plus,' I think aloud, 'the word is they met at law school. It's possible they forged an inextricable bond there or something, I suppose? One that' – I gesture with my arms – '*transcends* their political differences.'

'I would imagine perfectly possible.'

'Still though, really? You help to get protection for a refugee, then help her refuse it to others? Doesn't make sense, does it?'

He looks me in the eye. 'Not if that were all the Home Office did, perhaps. But you accepted yourself that they grant protection too. Maybe, erm, the KC had hoped he might improve the institution, by diversifying its workforce?'

'With her?' I laugh. 'That woman is as crooked as they come!'

'Or became so, perhaps?'

Again, he has a point. What's my problem? Despite all I've learnt in recent weeks, I seem to want to paint them all as villains, as if I myself were somehow infallible. Even so, I can't help myself. The knowledge alone that the Home Office, that impenetrable cesspit of an institution, allowed a person suspended for bullying to climb to a position of such power sickens me to the core, and god only knows what other horrors they hide behind those concertina-covered yellow brick walls. I rip out the article, fold it up and stuff it in my wallet.

The captain's voice comes over the PA system. 'Cabin crew, ten minutes to landing,' and the steward returns.

'I'm going to have to ask you to return to your seat, please, sir.'

'Gladly,' he replies, and winks at me. 'Sensitive soul, aren't you? Cheer up, that's a good thing.'

#

The cabin crew open the door. Then follows the wave of warmth and the intense aroma of the surrounding pine forest, as I step out onto the airstair and into another world.

There are only ever one or two planes on the tarmac here but you can always guarantee a decent wait. Still, knocking around in Arrivals, listening to the local lingo, is a perfect way to acclimatise – and who would wish to deny our baggage handlers their cherished smoking breaks?

I first discovered this place while interrailing and haven't looked back. Friends would encourage me to consider alternative destinations – 'Hey, have you ever tried skiing?'; 'What's wrong with France?', et cetera – but why would I? Cádiz, this authentic, unfettered, warm, wondrous province on the southernmost tip of Europe, is more than a destination. It's where I go to catch my thoughts, a sanctuary in an olive grove bordered by the sea.

#

Once through passport control, I pick up my hire car – the naffest available, naturally – search for Radiolé and make for the Costa de La Luz.

On the open road, passing Conil, I find myself singing along to a ballad by la Nina Pastori and Miguel Poveda. The lyrics are on point: *'I no longer want to be the person I was yesterday; I no longer want to be with you; I want to fly'.* Or, almost. If I had only actually been with you, I might be able to fucking leave you, I despair, correcting my steering to avoid the central reservation.

Soon though, I am zipping through the golden hills, past La Zarzuela to the sea. On arrival in Zahara de los Atunes, I find a room for the night in Hotel Gran Sol, dump my bags, close the shutters and climb into bed. Tomorrow is another day, I remind myself. Besides, I'm in Zahara, and however challenging my situation, however uncertain, it is of course not a patch on what my old clients were forced to tolerate.

FACE

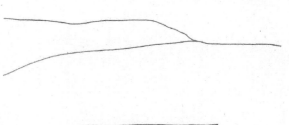

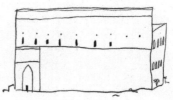

38

Two days left

Turns out there's nothing like accepting failure to secure a good night's sleep. It's past ten in the morning when Novak comes to wake me. Into my cell he bursts, brandishing two documents for me to sign. He speaks quickly, even for him, and with a fixed chinny grin. I sit up and pay attention.

'First things first. These docs are all provisional, OK? What does that mean? Means if you change your mind, we'll tear them up for you. Simple as that. You with me? Why do we get them signed now? Routine. Helps us to have everything in place should you decide to cooperate with your removal to Armenia.'

'Argentina,' I remind him. He knows, he tells me – he was pulling my leg. He hands me a standard document headed 'ETD', which I pretend to scrutinise.

'It's an application for an Emergency Travel Document,' explains the officer. 'Basically, it lets you back into Argentina without a passport. Ah, you need to sign this one too.'

He passes me another familiar document, this one waiving my right to appeal the decision to refuse my asylum claim.

'What is this?' I ask innocently.

'This one? Ah nothing important, really, let's see…' He snatches the document back and holds it at a distance from his eyes, squinting. 'Basically says you understand your asylum claim was refused.'

'Liar,' I mutter involuntarily.

'I'm sorry?'

'Like ah…to show that I know I lose my case?'

'Pretty much, yes,' he says.

I do not believe a word of it, of course. But new horizons beckon. I sign both documents.

'Right then, all done,' he announces breezily. 'Actually, there was something else I meant to tell you. What was it now…?'

He is a terrible actor; it is perfectly obvious he's milking the moment.

'Yes, here it is.' He pretends to read the papers in his hands. 'You're booked on a flight to Buenos Aires tomorrow, first thing. I'll see if I can get you a nice little seat by the window, shall I?'

'What?' I reply dutifully. 'I still have my…?'

'Appeal? Not anymore!' he gloats. '*Bon voyage, amigo.*'

'It's *buen viaje, imbécil.*'

'Whatever. All being well, you'll be back where you belong in a day or two, where you can chat Spanish to your heart's content.'

'All being well?'

'Yes. Sometimes people resist and we have to – how to put this? – get heavy with them…' He steps right up in my face, as it were (he reaches my sternum) and doubles down (up) on his threat. 'But I'm sure you wouldn't do anything like that, would you?'

I look at him pityingly.

'You know, for a moment there, I thought you were a nice guy.'

'Got what I wanted, didn't I?' he laughs. 'You didn't have to sign either form, thicko. Byee.'

Off he bounces.

'Wait!' I call after him.

'Be quick.'

'I'll tell De Rossi what you did.'

'Good luck with that.' He laughs and carries on his merry way.

#

Later that day, I see Priya in the corridor. I try to blank her but she grabs my arm and pulls me in towards her.

'I need to speak to you!' she whispers.

'Shouldn't you be with Ian, your lover boy?' I reply.

'I'm serious, Alex, it's urgent – come.'

#

On entering my room, I see the bottom bunk had been made up for the next poor soul.

'You moving in?' I ask.

'Listen,' she whispers. 'I'm told you signed the emergency travel document and waiver forms? Is that true?'

I nod.

She clutches her head with both hands. 'What the fuck? OK, don't you think this has gone far enough?'

'I thought we were only just starting?'

'Not now, moron!' She muffles her mouth with her hand, desperation in her eyes. 'I need to know if you're serious about going through with this?'

'Why do you ask?'

'Why do you think?'

'Honestly? I don't know,' I reply. 'If you're worried about me grassing you up, then don't be. I've got nothing to gain from it, and besides…'

'Go on.'

'I…'

'Yes?'

'I like you.'

For a nanosecond I think I can detect a hint of a smile, but am quickly disabused of any such notion:

'Yes, well, I am flattered, but you know perfectly well I am taken.'

I cough. 'That's one way of putting it.'

Priya slams her papers on the wall in frustration, dropping them all over the floor.

'Seriously, I don't have much time, OK?' she says, hastily gathering them up.

She slaps my hand away as I bend down to help her, and as she does so, I catch sight of a familiar name in the email address bar of one of the print-outs.

'Was that an email from Amir?' I ask.

She closes her document wallet again.

'No.'

'It was. I saw it.'

'So, what if it was?'

I look her in the eye, hoping to elicit an explanation.

'What did he tell you?' she asks nervously.

I put my hands in my pockets and rock back on my heels. 'Oh, stuff. He told me he had been in the UK a long time, that he was a whizz with a computer...'

'OK, you can't blame me for trying, can you?'

'Erm...?'

'I needed to know who you were.'

This throws me a little. I decide to wing it. 'And...did you like what you found?'

'Bah. He barely found anything on you, not even professional stuff. Seems you never even made it onto the firm's website, did you?'

My head sinks. 'No indeed. That spot's reserved for *solicitors*.'

Priya's turn to laugh. 'And there was I thinking we had a hotshot in our midst.'

'Drop it, will you?' I take a moment. 'Wow, I didn't think I could be made to feel much worse, but you are succeeding.'

'Oh, chin up, Alex. Seriously, though, I can't believe the sneaky git told you I was looking into you. After all I did for him.'

She rummages in her handbag, pulls out some gum and offers me one.

'Is that it, then?' I persist. 'Is that all he was able to tell you about me?'

'Pretty much, Alex. Oh, he also told me you had been single for two years and that you were the go-to brochure model for your university languages department...'

'Fucking hell, he's good!' I reply, laughing. 'The onion necklace and beret weren't my idea, OK? That it?'

'All right, no.' She is now whispering so quietly I can barely hear her. 'He also told me you asked him to hack Gian's computer.'

'Fuck, he told you!' My heart is racing. 'And? Anything?'

Slowly, she reaches out an arm and pinches my cheek. 'Come now, you didn't seriously think he would do it did you? The bloke has only just been granted status, you dingbat.'

'Fucking twat...!' I compose myself. 'Not you, him.' I'm struggling to stay calm. 'Amir was all I had...'

Out of the blue, I feel her hand on my back. 'It's been a long week, Alex,' she says. 'Are you sure I can't convince you to stay? Think about it. The sooner you confess to this prank, the sooner we can begin your mitigation. I can even put in a good word with De Rossi, if you like?'

It ought to be persuasive, all this: her soothing hand on my back; her soft, measured voice; those disarming, almond-shaped eyes. But the more she speaks, the more defiant I become. Seek clemency from De Rossi? That corrupt, three-piece egoist, who would help a puffed-up prat like Frank and shaft a gent like Tapa?

'I've nothing left here,' I say.

'Nothing?' she replies.

I pause. 'My work was my life.'

'And your family? Your friends?'

I stay firm. 'They'll wait for me. I'll drop them a line, let them know I'm OK.'

'I don't get it. What are you going to do when you get there? Assuming they even let you in?'

'Fucked if I know. But I'm doing it.'

'Why?'

Why? For a moment, everything seems to stop. This ludicrous situation I find myself in reminds me of a documentary I once saw about French high-wire artist Philippe Petit, and his perilous, unharnessed tightrope walk between the Twin Towers. On completing it, he is asked by a journalist that same, simple question: why? And for the first time, I feel, I understand his response. I quote him: 'There is no why'.

#

There is a loud knock on the door and Novak bursts in. Priya tucks her hair behind her ear and makes to leave.

'You OK, madam?' he asks.

'Perfectly,' she responds. 'Can we look into getting Mr Guerrero some new bed springs for the top bunk, please? Plainly they've seen better days.'

The little thug peeps under the bunk to inspect it. 'All looks OK to me, madam.'

'Are you questioning my judgement, Novak?'

'I can get 'em looked at for the next detainee, madam. This one's off tomorrow, see? Or he's meant to be. His flight friend's off sick and De Rossi's looking for a volunteer to escort him.'

'It's OK,' I interject. 'One night more will not harm me.'

'Well, that's mighty good of you, sire,' he replies, sarcastically. 'As I said to the lady there, just fixing up someone to hold your hand on the flight to Spain. Stop you misbehaving.'

'Spain?' I respond.

'Flights to Buenos Aires are staggered, mate. They go via Madrid.'

'Good,' I reply defiantly. 'I need a holiday.'

'Holiday? You've never travelled in the hold, have you?' He grins and opens the door for Priya.

'Goodbye Mr Guerrero,' she says, without looking at me. 'No doubt you'll think twice before making a bogus asylum claim again.'

'One is enough,' I reply, setting my eyes on her one last time.

#

With one evening left, I take a turn around the centre to say my goodbyes. Pausing by the 'viewing gallery' I feel a soft tap on my back.

I turn to face her but find De Rossi standing there instead.

'Beautiful, isn't it?'

'You come here to watch your deportations?' I ask.

He takes his hand away. 'I prefer to call them flights home at His Majesty's expense.'

'The homes we run from.'

He sneers. 'That's putting it a little high, don't you think? Last time I checked, you had made a false asylum claim and signed voluntary removal papers…'

'Are all the claims you receive false, then?'

'Don't be ridiculous. The genuine ones we grant. Oh, before I forget, I received a message for you from a certain Abayomrunkoje Adeola. I gather you overlapped before he was transferred? He wanted to apologise for his poor manners, and to give you this.' He passes me a piece of paper with a number on it. 'It's the fixed line for the common room at Grouper Hill, Manchester. Bear in mind they don't always answer the phone.'

'Manchester?'

'We transferred him there so he could be as close as possible to the hospital. Oh, didn't you know? Royal Infirmary is the country's first specialist sickle-cell unit.'

He pats my shoulder again. 'You've done the right thing, you know. And look on the bright side, you'll only have to wait ten years before you can re-enter the country and pull this shit all over again. Goodbye Guerrero.'

'*Adios, boludo.*'

De Rossi slinks off and I turn back towards the glass. A plane taxies in and out of view, leaving only darkness behind. I remember Abay the giant, his deep velvet voice, the stunt he pulled on me, the tacky green and white striped smartwatch he spoke into. *'Take it from me, you have contact with the authorities, you document it!'*

Sure Abay – I close my eyes – but who's ever going to listen?

39

Abayomrunkoje's Voice Files

Voice 001 – 15 July 11:43 – Battery Level IIIII

» Police picked me up last night – Immigration came – told them
about Boko Haram – my escape from the camp to my father's flat
and – gak – my throat got tight – there'll be time for this later
officer said – put me in a van and brought me to this place – Har-
rinwuth – or some shit

Voice 002 – 15 July 21:36

» Man interviewed me around 7 – short one – asked about school –
age I left – work – shit like that – told him I want to claim asylum
– seeing a lawyer tomorrow on the legal aid

Voice 003 – 16 July 05:15

» Officer came for me – little man – big attitude – you're coming
with me – the hell I am – tells me they're moving me to a better
cell – OK – now waiting outside office

Voice 004 – 16 July 05:32

» Seen second officer – bigger – pulling a brother along by his hair
– man shouting and cussing – clinging to officer's arm – let go I
told him – officer dropped him – get up monkey he shouted go
get your stuff – shot me a look – I'll see you later

Voice 005 – 16 July 08:29 – Battery Level IIII
» Big officer came back – snap – cuffed my hands tight – pair of them drove me to portacabin by runway – Domestic Transfers on door – taking me to different removal centre – more space they said – confirmed I can see lawyer there

Voice 006 – 16 July 09:45
» Getting rammed in here – people from all over talking different languages – officers wheeled in disabled woman – headscarf – large – 50s maybe – tipped her out and left her collapsed on floor – some of us helped her sit up – dress torn – crying

Voice 007 – 16 July 11:46
» Boarded small plane – letters LL on tailfin – no stewards – packed us in

Voice 008 – 16 July 12:01
» Squashed up can't breathe – knees touching my face – officers gassing with the pilot – ringing the bell and no one coming

Voice 009 – 16 July 12:07
» OK – moving off

Voice 010 – 16 July 12:11
» [Screams in background] Spray – coming from panels

40

One day left

My removal from the UK is conducted in the standard way. At 5am I am pulled from my bunk by a psychopath – in this case, Novak – held under a cold shower for 30 seconds and ordered to get dressed.

In place of breakfast, I am given a stale doughnut in a sealed packet with 'Best Before 1900' written on in permanent marker.

'Gotta love it,' I mutter.

'Eh?' Novak responds.

'I said I love your English humour,' I reply.

'Gimme that.' He grunts, holds the doughnut up some five inches from his eyes and chuckles before handing it back. 'Probably older than that.' He smirks and whips out some handcuffs.

'What are those for?' I ask, as he slaps them on me.

'Anyone on the Watch List gets the cuffs – standard.'

'The Watch List?'

'Anyone considered suicidal or disruptive. Last thing anyone wants 36,000 feet up is antics.' He snots into his left hand, shoves me forward with the other and chortles. 'Come on, we've got you a plane to catch!'

'You are my "flight friend"?' I ask.

'Don't be daft, I'm her security.'

\#

Outside, dawn is beginning to break. He pulls out his walkie-talkie. 'No sign of Transit, over.'

There is some crackling, then a lethargic voice responds, 'On their way – give it five, OK?'

10 minutes later, Novak lights up a cigarette. 'Don't tell the boss, yeah?' he laughs, and takes a long, contented drag.

Lights. A car appears in the distance. As it draws close and comes to a stop, I can barely believe my eyes.

'Fiat 500?'

'Discreet, nippy and cheap to run – De Rossi's brainchild – you can take the Italian out of Italy…'

'Wait…you want to get three of us in that thing?'

'Plus her,' he replies and points towards a taxi coming down the slip road in front of us. 'Bit cosy, but it's only a couple of minutes to the terminal building.'

Perhaps it is the lack of sleep but I had not realised quite how close the Removal Centre was to the airport. They literally built it slap bang on the end of the runway, probably to keep those they return in a maximum state of panic.

The taxi draws up, and out steps a familiar figure.

'Priya?'

'Ms Basu to you. Now, are we going to be cooperative today?' she asks.

Sensing an opportunity no doubt, Novak draws his baton, but she stops him in his tracks. 'Oh no, officer, I am sure that won't be necessary.' She turns to me. 'Will it?'

'I will be good boy, *señorita*,' I reply, earning myself a scowl.

The short transit to the terminal is as confusing as it is cramped. Halfway through, the chauffeur removes his flat cap, looks over his shoulder and reveals himself.

'Now I hope you're not getting too close to that lady next to you – she's mine,' he quips.

Priya responds before I can. 'Can we keep this professional please, bunny? The less interaction with the detainee the better, OK?'

Ian makes a pretend, wounded animal noise and she blows him a kiss. 'Bah,' he says. 'I doubt he understands much anyway, *verdad compadre?*'

'*Qué?*'

'See?'

All of this is proving a lot to take in for De Rossi's henchman, who is clearly not used to being kept in the dark. 'So, you guys are together?' he asks hesitantly.

'Priya and I met through your manager, Gian,' Ian announces proudly. 'I head up the transport and reception wing of the OTT.'

'Oh, I'm sorry. It's a pleasure to finally meet you. Mr Large, right?'

'Yes...'

'Novak,' he says proudly, sticking his hand through the gap between the front seats.

Ian ignores it. 'As you can see,' he says, 'I'm switching it up for the next few days, so the little lady and I can spend some quality time together. And I for one cannot bloody wait.'

They smile at each other and she strokes his hair.

'How is the money?' I chip in, unable to help myself.

'Excuse me?'

'*El dinero.* It pays well, what you do?'

'I'm sorry. I'm not sure that's any of your business, Mr...'

'Guerrero,' Priya clarifies.

'Ah yes, Guerrero,' he repeats, his tone becoming calmer again. 'What is it about Hispanic names beginning with "Gue"? I always want to pronounce them "Gwe".'

Unamused, I return him a half-smile and look out the window. We are arriving.

41

Voice 011 – 17 July 02:31

» [Laboured breathing] Woken up in old fortress or something –
freezing – no roof – no GPS – bodies lying next to me on the sand
– some moving – place smells rancid like rotting meat

Voice 012 – 17 July 03:29

» Found disabled lady – Mouna – retired doctor from Sudan – everyone awake bar one – no pulse

» Place size of football pitch – four walls – old stone – crumbles in
your hand like pound cake – gate – took dead man outside – people prayed – man I recognised came up – Joseph – Caribbean –
thanked me for stepping in that time

» Drugged for sure – benzo – benzodi – Mouna knows – huddling
together to keep warm – stomach empty – sunrise we go find food
and water

Voice 013 – 17 July 07:25

» Climbed the walls and felt to vomit – desert – far as you can see –
that's it – nothing else but someone's old white hat and tyre tracks
going west to the dunes

» Probably an old market people reckon – row of hooks along each
of the walls about a metre off the ground – women tying together

jackets jumpers and scarves – threading sides into north east corner to make shade

Voice 014 – 17 July 08:32

» Four of us heading out – Sofia coming west with me – Saudi – tried to stop her – looked at me hard – asked me how many Saudi women I know with an HGV licence – laughed – other pair will go east

Voice 015 – 17 July 09:36

» [Coughing] Mouth dry and sun hot already – Sofia removed headscarf and tore in two – using to shade sun from our heads and necks – found long grass with small white flowers and ate the seeds – halfway to big dunes

Voice 016 – 17 July 10:46

» Reached dunes – stopped to rest – Sofia praying – next we climb

Voice 017 – 17 July 11:24

» Hard climb – wind picking up – sand covering tracks

Voice 018 – 17 July 11:56

» [Interference] Striped animals in dip other side of peak – sand stinging our faces – maybe gazelles and something bright like water – rushed closer – froze – eleven hyenas I counted – all staring – pointed ears – stripes on cheeks – waited – one – two – then charged and watched them scatter

» Human body where the animals had been – mauled – bald head cracked in two jelly on sand – no face – arm skin dark dimpled like old bread fruit – backed away – scavengers came forward but stopped at corpse

» Wind too strong – heading back

42

We drive past a portacabin towards the runway side of the terminal building and look set to collide with it until Ian hits the brakes hard, releases, hits them again and draws us all to a standstill.

'I thought you were going to stack it then!' Novak says excitedly.

'Cadence braking, my friend. One of the first things you learn as a pilot.'

This is evidently the cue for Priya to fill us in. 'Ian flies,' she says, and I fight the urge to groan.

The chauffeur-cum-entrepreneur-cum-pilot now reaches into his jacket pocket, pulls out a little remote-control device and directs it at the wall, whereupon a tiny garage door opens. In we drive.

'We had this built for tricky removals,' Ian brags, staring at me. 'More discreet, should a detainee kick-off.'

'What do you do to them?' I probe, earning myself a thump from Novak.

'Oh, control yourself, will you?' Ian snaps. 'Or do you want to be a low-level lackey all your life?'

Again, Priya defuses the tension. 'Actually, erm, you can leave us from here on, Novak. Thank you for all your help, but we won't be needing you.'

He looks confused. 'I'm meant to be flying with you guys, right?'

'That's right, you were, but Ian is here now.'

Novak leans forward, cups a hand to her ear and whispers, 'Are you sure about this, madam? What if the spic, you know…?'

She shakes off his hand. 'I am a hundred percent sure. I know this one – wouldn't hurt a fly, seriously. Besides, Ian's a black belt, aren't you darling?' She pinches his dimples and feeds him a stuffed bagel.

'Licence to kill,' he confirms, brie dripping from his bottom lip.

'But De Rossi said…' protests Novak.

'De Rossi said what? That you were doing the removal? Well, you were. And now you're not.' Priya pauses. 'It's not that hard to understand, is it?'

'No. But…'

'I'm officially giving you the day off, OK? Now scarper before I change my mind.'

Slowly, the man grabs his travel bag from the footwell, opens the door and bids us a safe trip.

Ian seems equally bemused, however. 'Puh-ri-ya,' he says emphatically. 'Are you *sure* you're allowed to do…'

'Oh, I see. So a woman can't call the shots round here, is that it?'

He seems a little startled, but she feeds him more bagel, pats his tummy and urges him to live a little. 'We've got lots of catching up to do – and I mean lots…' she says, breaking into a whisper. 'Can't you see? I don't want anyone getting in the way, OK?'

She squeezes his knee, and he makes a sort of squeaky noise.

#

There is no check-in, no bag check and no passport control. We simply walk up some noisy metal stairs, through a little door and into a mini, makeshift departure lounge with nothing but a few tired bench chairs and a solitary vending machine.

Priya and Ian embrace and take a seat. I, still cuffed, go to join them.

'Could you, err, you know – give us some space? Sit over there somewhere?'

'Ehem,' I cough. 'You are meant to be looking after me, no?'

'Watching over you, you mean? Yes,' Priya replies. 'Looking after you? Ahm, no, I'm afraid not.'

Ian laughs.

'When all's said and done, they're all the fucking same,' he says. 'So…what's the word?'

'Entitled?' she replies.

'I can have a coffee?' I try to interrupt.

'And illiterate,' he adds.

'Ahh, come now, Mr Grumpy. It's not his first language.'

On saying this, she flings her arms around his neck, looks directly at me and raises a finger to her lips to make a 'shh' sign.

#

After twenty minutes or so, Priya receives radio confirmation that the air crew are ready for us. We grab our things and stand up to go.

'Wait for me,' I quip, eliciting a flicker of a smile from Ian.

'He's quite an amusing little fucker, isn't he?' whispers Ian. 'Shame he's a pathological liar.'

'You know him?' replies Priya.

'I took the liberty of reading his file. Gian gave me access. Never heard such a load of bullshit in my life!'

Priya cocks her head, straightens it again and leads us out through the commercial gate, which is now closed to the public.

The plane is a little over half full. Instead of sitting together in a row as arranged, they invite me to sit on my own a couple of rows in front. I oblige on the condition that Priya removes my handcuffs. Done. The pilot reads out the usual spiel. As expected, we shall be transiting in Spain where we shall change planes and pick up some additional passengers before flying on, direct to Buenos Aires. There will be a drinks service throughout the flight and in the transit lounge.

I shut my eyes and listen to Ian and Priya bickering for a bit. 'Bunny, where's your ring? What do you mean it's in the hold? What if they lost your luggage? No, the insurers wouldn't touch it, which is why you should keep it on your blessed finger!'

Bored, I find the little button and recline my seat. A hostess passes and tells me to put it upright, do my belt up and fold away the tray table in front of me. I smile nicely and ask for a drink.

'At least wait until we are in the air, perhaps?'

#

When the seatbelt sign eventually goes off, I press the bell for attention. After a short delay, a dapper young man appears, pulls down my tray table and on it carefully places a little paper mat, a plastic glass and a miniature bottle of Spanish brandy.

I half sit up and look round.

'No,' the steward whispers, placing a hand on my shoulder. 'The lady said expressly not to thank her.'

Slowly, I slump back into my seat.

43

Voice 019 – 18 July 16:24 – Battery Level III

» Mad storm – walls of sand – scrambled up small dune scarves over faces – huddled – ground shifting – slipping – climbing back up

» Waited till winds eased – reached camp at dusk – sand high against the walls – collapsed and woke this morning – Mouna pouring water on my lips

» Good news – rescuers here – six men in blue gowns and turbans – Mouna says Sahrawis – came in dump truck with water – bread – vegetables – blankets and small gazebo shade – tomorrow they evacuate sick and elderly – then the rest of us

Voice 020 – 18 July 17:11

» People crying – other pair not back – Joseph led search party this morning – failed

Voice 021 – 19 July 09:28

» Rescuers now taking first wave – Mouna chose to stay

Voice 022 – 19 July – 10:02

» First wave gone – big relief – three diabetics – man with heart problem et cetera – last on was an old Ghanaian lady – Cindy – retied yellow and green headdress sat down and blew us kiss

» Mouna said she stayed for Sofia – one of the rescuers giving her eyes – fat one she said

Voice 023 – 20 July 10:48

» Sahrawis still not returned

» From wall can see smoke trail rising up behind the dunes – provisions limited – rescuers not back in three days we head out towards the source

Voice 024 – 22 July 10:01

» Rough 48 hours mood here dropping fast – fighting over rations – shade – who sleeps where – madness – children here – hungry – breaks your heart – tomorrow we go

Voice 025 – 23 July 10.01 – Battery Level II

» [Whispering] Went out at first light – took Sofia – got to foot of dunes and Sahrawis' truck came – picked us up – fat one driving – other men in trailer with food crates a long wooden box and a big brown sack – Sofia asked a bearded man about the smoke – said he had not seen it

» Got to camp and driver opened tailgate – climbing down I stopped dead – a ripped piece of cloth poking out from under the sack – yellow and green – Cindy's headdress

44

Barajas airport, Madrid. I step out of the cabin doors and am enveloped in the warm embrace of Castilian summer.

'That is more like it!' I enthuse to my minders, forgetting for a second that I am not on holiday. It is then I realise they have forgotten to put my cuffs back on.

I see a sudden flash of light and when my focus returns, there's a man on the tarmac below pointing a long-lens camera at me. I look behind to see Priya and Ian have also clocked him.

'Get used to it, *señores*,' I tell them. 'I am big noise in this country!' Neither react; both remain staring at the man.

This time there are no special doors, no secret stairs. We follow the flock into the main building and wait in the queue for passport control where Priya pushes past us, fishes around in her bag and pulls out a large, plastic document wallet.

'They do know there's a change in personnel, right?' asks Ian.

Priya nods and hands him one of the documents. As she does so, I can just make out the heading: 'Emergency Travel Document'.

'What the fuck?' Ian whispers to her, clearly agitated.

'Oh, relax, will you? You must know, we do this all the time.'

'Do we?' he replies, incredulous.

'Makes things smoother.' Priya turns away from him to face the front of the queue.

Ian grabs her by the back of the neck and puts his mouth to her ear. 'What does? *Juan Carlos Grande*?' he reads out. 'Who the fuck is this?'

I try not to laugh. 'Someone with an unfortunate name,' I reply. 'Maybe don't abbreviate it…'

For a split second I think I see Priya smirk too but, if she did, when she turns to address Ian, it is gone. 'Having got you along last minute, I couldn't change yours and the officer's details in time for the removal.'

He raises his eyes to the ceiling.

'Forgive me, bunny,' she continues, 'this seemed the most expedient way to get us through immigration with zero fuss.'

'By pretending I'm being removed to Argentina too?' he whispers angrily, sweat appearing on his brow.

'No,' she says. 'The document states you are an Argentinian citizen whose passport was lost and is voluntarily returning home.'

'I barely speak Spanish!'

As she pleads with him to keep his voice down, I notice a team of armed officers looking over in our direction. Meanwhile, the queue in front of us has already halved and the Spanish immigration desk is fast approaching.

Ian is in such a flap now he can barely hold the document still enough to read it. He stares at his feet then looks her directly in the eye. For at least two seconds, she stares back with equal intensity.

'This is how it's going to work,' she says calmly. 'I'll go through first with Guerrero. You give us some space. Then you go through.'

'But…'

She holds her finger to his lips. 'Just show the pre-cleared document to the officers and meet us in the transit lounge. Got it?'

Ian glances around, looking for a way out. But with the queue now down to three people, he's left no choice but to comply.

'OK,' he says, wiping the perspiration from his head. I watch him drop back a few places in the queue, then try to scramble forward again, but a chubby-looking man in spectacles and a Ralph Lauren polo shirt sticks his arm out to stop him coming forward.

'Wait!' he mouths to Priya.

'Well, that was easy,' she says, drawing breath and looking around. 'Now to get us out of here.'

'What did you say?'

Priya squeezes past an elderly couple, dragging me behind her. We board a moving walkway and follow signs to the transit lounge. On the way, she briefs me. 'When we get there, I want you to ask them the quickest route to the train station, OK?'

I feel a smile forming on my face. 'Whatever you say, boss.'

'God knows what shit Ian will be chatting back there.' She pauses a moment and stares up at a large TV screen showing 24-hour news. 'Ahh…' she says coolly. 'It's out.'

I follow her gaze and see live footage of someone who looks very like Ian being escorted by Spanish police. I do a double take. 'What did that document you handed him say exactly?' I ask.

'Oh, nothing much. I copied it from one of your fellow detainee's files and subbed in a different name.'

'Yes, I heard the name.' I laugh, boarding the mini travellator. "Juan Carlos" – "Juanca" for short – "Juanca Grande" – "Big wanker", right? Nice touch!'

'*Gracias*,' she replies, eyelashes fluttering.

We dismount and run back a few paces to the television.

'Quick, translate for me!' she shrieks.

'Shit!' I yell. 'This is…unbelievable!' I turn to her: 'You…!'

'Translate it!'

'OK, OK!'

45

Voice 026 – 23 July – 14:07

» [Whispering] OK that long box – rifles – fat man sent women and children to west wall and told them to take off clothes – inspected them and wrote numbers on their backs with marker pen – said tomorrow you start new journey – Sofia translated

» Woman next to bearded man went for his rifle – turned barrel on her – two shots to the chest – dragged her body out and slung it in truck

» Came back with sack and took out handcuffs – came straight for me – struck me across jaw and cuffed my arm to wall hook – locked Joseph to next hook along – then the rest – every last one of us sat on his ass – shackled to wall

Voice 027 – 23 July 15:57

» Not chaining women and children – good – but the fear on their faces I can't look – tomorrow they'll be gone – and next it will be us

» [Faint cracking sound] Wait [Same sound] When I cup hands and lean away hard

Voice 028 – 23 July 15:58

» [Whispers] Hook giving

46

Above a sub-heading reading, *'Breaking: document dump reveals slave trade alive and well in North Africa'*, a sombre looking reporter describes intelligence showing how asylum seekers are being unlawfully removed from the UK and disposed of at a trafficking site in Western Sahara.

'The leak, made just six hours ago to Canal News 24, reveals what would appear to be the auctioning of asylum seekers of different nationalities to traders, primarily, it seems, from Eastern Europe, Russia and the Middle East. The documents also reveal strong evidence of forced disappearances and a large scale project to dispose of remains.'

The report pans in on a satellite image of what appears to be a makeshift bonfire site in the middle of the desert. I take a step back and steady myself against a pillar.

'I knew something was off,' I gasp. 'But...what the actual fuck?'

'I could scarcely believe it myself,' Priya tells me. 'Didn't want to believe it...'

'Why didn't you tell me?' I ask.

'When Amir cracked the...'

'He did it! I knew he would.'

'Yep, when he cracked the code, I was desperate to tell you. But you know De Rossi. He sees things others don't. He'd have smelt a rat. I had to maintain the illusion I knew nothing.'

'Hold on!' I stick my arm out to silence her as Ian's picture flashes up on the screen again.

'Dr Ian Large of Large Logistics Ltd,' the bulletin continues, *'has been*

named as the chief coordinator of operations between the UK and those man-
ning the trading site, referred to in the leaked papers simply as "The Market".
We understand his arrest was authorised a short while ago, and that he was
intercepted by police in Barajas Airport, Madrid, attempting to transit to
Buenos Aires under a false identity. We are informed that in a coordinated
move, the manager of a British immigration detention facility near Stansted,
Herringsworth Immigration Removal Centre, has also been arrested and taken
into custody. Stay tuned – more to follow.'

I can barely believe what I am seeing.

She takes my hand. 'Come, our train awaits.'

'Where to now?'

'You'll see.'

47

Voice 029 – 23 July 17:07

» [Whispering] Joseph wants in

Voice 030 – 23 July 21:07

» They let Sofia bring us water – got to me – coughed – pulled hook out few inches for her to see – whispered be ready

Voice 031 – 23 July 21:15

» Announcement just now – women and children to sleep by gate on west wall – men to ask permission to go to toilet – guard to accompany us – OK

Voice 032 – 23 July 22:02

» Fat one by gate with the women – bearded one guarding us – other four laying down in middle by water supply – two-on/four-off looks like – OK

Voice 033 – 23 July 22:32

» Got it

48

The AVE train is every bit as smart as I remember. Priya finds our seats, and I help squash her clumpy wheelie bag onto the overhead shelf.

'The joys of travelling light…'

'Hey, that's not fair,' she replies. 'If a lady can't have a summer wardrobe in Cádiz…'

'Wait, what…? You're really taking me to Cádiz?'

'No, you're taking me. I want to see what all the fuss is about.'

It's a lot to take in and my first instinct is to seek out the buffet car. Minutes later, I return with two half bottles of Cava.

'Seriously? No champagne?' Eyes crinkling, she stretches and holds out her hand. I take it and shiver with excitement. 'Right,' she says, 'two and a half hours before we reach Seville. I'll fill you in on what the fuck just happened if you tell me more about the Costa de la Luz. Oh, and don't worry about money. I pawned my engagement ring – we're flush.'

#

It takes her all the way to Cordoba to explain everything, and I am still struggling to process it.

'You don't need to make that face,' she teases.

'I'll try to summarise, and you tell me if I'm right, OK? You believed me.'

'Yep. Ultimately, I think I always believed you, yes.'

'But you played me?'

'I had no proof. And De Rossi was on to you. I needed to throw him off the scent.'

'And what better way than to expedite my Refusal and volunteer to remove me?'

'Exactly.'

'But, how did you know I'd sign my removal papers?'

She laughs and pours out the drink. 'Because you're a self-sabotaging madman, riddled with self-doubt, you have no ties to speak of and you are obsessed with the Latin world. Or are you going to tell me otherwise?'

Laughter.

'Ian was easy to dupe,' she continues. 'I was his weak spot. He believed we were eloping to Buenos Aires for a dirty weekend.'

'And he didn't ask any questions?'

'He was excited to be led for once. I packed a skimpy cocktail dress and told him to pack his Tango shoes…'

'Ouch…'

'I even bought us two nights in the Hotel Madero as I knew he'd check my accounts. It's OK, they're refundable.' She glances at her phone. 'It's going berserk,' she says, scanning down an article on the BBC website. 'Holy fuck! Look at this…'

She shows me the headline: *'Home Office in Modern Slavery Murder Scandal'*.

'It's all here,' she confirms, scrolling down faster than I can read. 'Take it. Read it. Then join me in the buffet car.'

I hesitate a moment, then dive in. The piece describes how De Rossi has engineered and presided over a classified Home Office pilot scheme, referred to as 'NUU Beginnings.' The so-called 'NUUs' are essentially the group I identified: asylum seekers who are non-white, unrepresented and either unskilled or unwell.

Before considering asylum claims, the leaked guidance reveals, specifically trained caseworkers were to assess whether the individual applicants met the 'NUU' criteria. Those who did would then be taken out of the asylum system and passed directly to the OTT for 'onward transfer'.

Conversely, if an applicant was white and/or represented and/or skilled and healthy, the asylum claim would be processed and determined in the usual way.

More than familiar with the dark sense of humour employed by the Home Office, I google the acronym. '*Nuu,*' reads the online entry in the Urban Dictionary '*is the British way of saying no in a rather cute way*'. Yet the worst is still to come.

The second half of the exposé makes reference to another piece of leaked guidance innocuously entitled '*Summer Camp*', which contains details of what befell the NUUs once they were handed over to the OTT. Though the picture is still emerging, it makes for extremely distressing reading.

In a nutshell, the so-called NUUs were not only deprived of an asylum claim but transferred to an off-grid black site in North Africa, thought to be in Western Sahara. There, the article alleges, they were paraded in front of traffickers, who proceeded to bid for those they considered of any worth to them.

'And the others?' I mutter to myself. The rest of them, it says, are officially still unaccounted for, but rescue services are combing the desert in and around an improvised bus stop a couple of hours outside the City of Semara, where an undisclosed number of fresh corpses have been discovered by a shepherd…

I put Priya's phone down and simply sit there inert, paralysed and nauseous, while related stories of fearful relatives of missing migrants break around me. Some minutes later, I feel her delicate hand on my shoulder. Slowly, gently, she pulls me to her chest.

'Do we have any news on Abayomrunkoje?' I ask eventually.

'Not yet, as far as I know,' she replies tenderly, 'but they are doing all they can, OK?'

'They?'

'MI6. They have agreed to share information they find on any of those transferred to my secure email address.'

'Seriously? They agreed to that?'

'I made the leak conditional on it,' she says.

'Amazing.'

'They mentioned something else too,' she says gently. 'The foreign office has agreed to repatriate Tapa's body to his next of kin in Chechnya.'

'Poor Tapa. That is the least we could do.'

'Quite. Here, give me that,' she says eventually, reaching for her phone. 'You need to drink that, and I need to contact Amir.'

49

Joseph's Voice Files

Voice 034 – 23 July 22:45

» [Whispering] Testing testing – we good

Voice 035 – 24 July 06:20

» [Background voices and crying, Joseph whispering] We freakin' did it – all the children and least half the women – big man gonna pay for this – if he not dead already – atmosphere super tense – guards flippin' out – Abay out cold – women out there digging graves for them two he kill

» I can't lie – had no idea what the man was up to – first he shuffles close – hands me his watch and explains me how to record – next he says real stern – document everything you can – and Joseph – tell them that I tried – and that's it – we just wait

» Four in the morning I feel sand in my face – Abay – on his instruc-tions I raise my hand – guard comes over and takes me outside – I drop my drawers – and I'm squatting by the wall when I see him leap out of the darkness – like a panther – and throttle the fella with the handcuff chain – must have made noise – movement by the door – seconds later big guard comes out – sees me then look at the body on the ground – I throw him a face like I am straining real hard – and before the man can twig – chain round his neck – I telling you – my boy is quick – two down

» I grab the first dead guard's gun – you fired one of these before he whispers – uh uh – he reaches down into second guard's pocket – pulls out some keys – children first he says real focused – we sneak back in and start waking them – quiet as we can – get as many of them onto the truck as will fit – more and more – until big man signals to Sofia and she climbs into the cab – he turns to me – you value your life you go sit back down – I creep back in – and I've just clamped the cuff back around my wrist when the engine starts

» Other four guards wake up grab their rifles and rush out – but they are late to the party – you can hear a scuffle and next thing they are marching Panther back in – halfway into the yard – he drops to his knees – then – crack – they strike his head hard with the rifle butt – tall man topples over like a tower – and they turn their anger on the women

» Mouna the doctor's name was – she took a bullet for the others

Voice 036 – 24 July 06:24
» I hear something – guards stressing – vehicles?

50

When I look out of the window again, the flatlands of Castille have been replaced by olive groves, rows of citruses and cypress trees.

'Is that the lot?' I hear her say. 'Great. And my official resignation letter? OK, yes please. Send it.'

I look at her quizzically and she pulls the phone from her ear and passes it to me.

'Amir. He wants to speak to you.'

'Hi mate,' he greets me. 'Turns out you may have been onto something after all.'

'You think?' I reply. 'Where are you?'

'They're putting me up in a safehouse until these gits are accounted for. Looks like they've pretty much got 'em all though. At least this side of the pond.'

'De Rossi?'

'Detained. As is Novak. And Carole.'

'Carole was in on it?'

'Nah mate. They found a bag of 70 ready-rolled spliffs on her when they searched her clinic!' he laughs. 'She handed them out like paracetamol, mate – trust me!'

'Always the last to know, me,' I reply. 'Amir, listen. Thank you so, so much for doing all this.'

'Ahh, shut up. All in a day's work for me. Besides, I couldn't stand the twat. And to think what he did to our poor brothers and sisters…'

Priya shoots me a glance as if to say hurry up.

'Totally. It's horrific, isn't it? Look, I've gotta run, OK? Just quickly though – I need to know – did you use the click incentive?'

'The Trojan Anti-Dandruff lotion bait? 'Course, I did! Fucker swallowed it hook, line and sinker.'

Laughter.

'Take good care, Amir. This lot are nasty.'

'Don't I know it. I will, mate. And, er, Alex?'

'Yes?

'You did good, son.'

I hesitate. 'I think you mean well?'

'Just take the fucking compliment, smartarse.'

#

'*Otra, por favor.*'

'*Cava? Vale, en seguida – y para la mujer?*'

'She'll have the same.' I wink at her. '*Qué sean dos.*'

Ever reliable, the booze is doing its thing. I sigh, drop my shoulders and look admiringly at my travelling companion.

'Your resignation letter – what does it say?'

'Here, read it for yourself,' Priya replies, passing me her phone which is open on her Facebook profile page. 'It's more of an announcement really.'

Taken in by my boss, my partner and my own naïvety, I awoke to find myself at the heart of a vile, unprecedented and inhuman abuse. Tipped off by an anonymous source, I obtained incontrovertible evidence of our systemic detention and disposal of large numbers of asylum seekers, all of whom possessed a common characteristic: their perceived worthlessness.

*The perpetrators are named directly in the evidence and include senior civil servants, businessmen and the Home Secretary herself, as well as a handful of dignitaries from Greece, Hungary and other European states. More names are still emerging. For anyone keen to know more, all the relevant leaked documents are available here [download]. For security reasons, I shall be keeping a low profile for now. Thanks.'

When I look up again, Priya has been replaced by a woman with a short bob, large pink sunglasses and loose-fitting 70s clothes. Or so I think. When I stand up to go and find my companion, the lady grabs my arm.

'Not so fast,' she says in a faux-Australian accent.

'Priya?' I laugh. 'What's with the attire?'

'When in Cádiz…'

'It's not carnival season, you know?'

'Hey, take that back!'

'Hang on.' Something's troubling me. 'The investigation? Shouldn't we…'

'I've disclosed everything I have, including my computer, my old sim and every piece of correspondence between me and those pricks. I've no more to give them.'

'They'll want to speak to me, presumably?'

'Inevitably. But the evidence speaks for itself. What can you usefully add that they don't already know?'

I think for a moment, then shrug my shoulders.

'Exactly,' she continues. 'So' – she strokes my thigh – 'what say you to showing me some of these places you talk so lovingly about?'

'Honestly?'

'Yes.'

'Nothing I'd rather do.'

'Good.' She puts a hand in her bag and pulls out an Australian slouch hat, a razor and foam, and two ID badges. 'Cheers, Shane,' she says, holding up her glass.

Bewildered but game, I raise mine too. 'Yes, cheers…erm…?'

She flashes one of the badges at me.

'Sheila!' I exclaim. 'Inspired!'

'We can blame Amir for these,' she replies. 'Oh, I'd grab a shave, if I were you.'

'This is only a few days' growth!'

'No…your head,' she replies, passing me the other ID. The photo is of a bald man.

'Whaaa?'

'OK, I'll break it down for you. The more different we look, the more time we buy. The more time we buy, the more of Cádiz I get to see. The more of Cádiz I get to see, the more I get to know you, and…' she winks.

'And…?'

'And I cannot bear your ridiculous two-tone mohican a day longer!'

I make for the improvised changing rooms.

#

'It's not *that* knobbly,' she lies, rubbing the back of my head, before walking round to my side of the table, sitting down next to me and resting her head on my shoulder. 'Now, if you'll forgive me, I've been up 24 hours and…'

#

While she sleeps, I read more about the skullduggery the journos have uncovered. Already, the interest seems to have shifted towards which of the multiple felons was the prime mover, responsible for masterminding the abuse. On that, of course, the jury is out.

Stories are also emerging about how De Rossi and Large met – the Young Conservatives club, would you believe it? – along with your token, barely relevant testimonials from shocked neighbours; universal condemnation from lawyers, journalists, and politicians at both ends of the spectrum, as well as celebrities, commentators and oblivious Home Office employees, horrified by what their colleagues have done. The response is heartening, if scarcely surprising. Indeed, on any view, what these men and their underlings have achieved is utterly indefensible. It is hard to imagine they will be able to wriggle out of this one. On a much happier note, a connected piece reports on a group of women and children reaching safety in the city of Semara, having succeeded in fleeing their captors.

The train begins to slow. Priya opens her eyes, throws me a startled look and checks the time on her phone. 'Quick, grab your stuff. We're here.'

51

Voice 037 – 24 July 06:42 – Battery Level I

» [Women's voices screaming] Holy Christ! – Arabs and Europeans
  – armed to the teeth and real hacked off – guards rushed over to
  greet them – big argument – shouting – then – clack clack clack
  clack – all four of them – dead

» Now fighting over the women – not good

Voice 038 – 24 July 07:21

» [Sound of rotor blades] Fuck is that sound...? [Gunfire] Jesus!

Transcription by Amir Tech Solutions Ltd

52

We alight at Santa Justa, Seville, and set off in search of a coffee and our connecting train to Cádiz.

With ten minutes to spare before boarding, we pop outside for some fresh air… And pop straight back in again.

'Bloody hell, it must be 40 degrees in the bloody shade!' Priya bursts out, pulling up a chair on the terrace of a large, noisy café.

'And not a cloud in the sky,' I reply, joining her. 'Relax, it'll be a good five to ten degrees cooler in Cádiz.'

'Not ideal for baldies all this sun.' She winks.

I point to my head. 'This is my fault, is it? You didn't think to pack some factor 50 when you compiled this genius plan?'

'Sorry…we'll sort you out in Cádiz.'

'Oh, will we?'

'Depends how you play your cards, I guess…'

A waiter appears and Priya makes a series of bizarre hand gestures. 'Ehhhh…'

I rock back on my chair and enjoy the spectacle.

'*Dos caffé por favor,*' she says eventually, 'with milk.'

'OK, two cafés weeth meelk,' he repeats.

'*Sí, sí,*' she confirms enthusiastically, turning to me for recognition.

'*Brava!*' I clap, losing myself a moment in her electric gaze…surreal to imagine that just a few hours ago, this quite sublimely lovely person was removing me to Argentina…

\#

When we've finished our coffees the waiter returns. More comic gestures.

'*La cuenta*,' I translate.

'*La cuenta*?' the waiter asks, his voice doubling in volume.

'*Sí, por favor*,' I reply instantly, damned if I am going to be mistaken for a regular, monolingual Brit, '*que nos vamos ya, sabe*?'

The waiter comes back with the bill and she taps her card on the reader.

'*Gracias*,' she says with a smile.

'*Las que tu tienes, mi alma*,' he replies, and she nods politely.

'What did he just say to me?' she asks me under her breath.

'Literally, "the grace that you have, my soul",' I confirm.

She blushes and I raise my eyes to the vast, steel support arches overhead.

'What?' she says. 'Well, he was rather dishy…'

'Women,' I mutter back, as we make for the train.

'Men,' she retorts and climbs into the carriage.

Once we are both aboard, she curls up next to me and, together, we drift into a delicious sleep.

#

I awake to find Priya tugging on my arm.

'Look!' she says excitedly, shoving her phone in my face.

I sit up and read the title aloud: '*Freed captives describe their ordeal*'.

'The photograph,' she asks. 'Is that him?'

I maximise the screen to get a closer look. It shows a gathering of reporters, local police and dozens of others. And there, towering over them all, unmistakable, in an undersized shock blanket, a bandage around his head, is Abay.

'It couldn't be anyone else.' I am going to burst with happiness. 'Thank god!'

'We have our key witness,' she says coolly, grabbing her phone back and moving off down the carriage. 'I'll let the you-know-who know – if they don't know already.'

'Priya?' I call after her.

'Yes,' she replies, returning to me.

'Do you think…' I hesitate, deep in thought. 'Do you think this could have a wider effect?'

She cocks her head to one side. 'Wider than breaking up a state-sanctioned trafficking ring?' she replies.

'I mean, could it make us care more? About the people we reject?'

'Unlikely.' She sighs. 'Then again, I did reject you…'

I fan my face with my hand.

'Now, will you let me make this call before we lose track of our key witness?'

#

A second strong coffee in Cádiz bus station and we are soon on our way again, rolling through parched hills to the coastal town of Barbate, home to the best tuna in Spain and enough marijuana to keep the entire province ablaze.

From there, we hitch a ride east and watch in awe as the Phoenician village of Zahara de Los Atunes rises up between the mountain and the sea, shimmering white like a burning magnesium sun. And there on the right, lining the entire route, is la Playa de la Virgen del Carmen, wild, golden, unchanged.

'Who are you texting?' she asks.

'My brother from another mother,' I say. 'Give me a moment, and I'll introduce you.'

We are dropped outside a little shop called 'Colors' opposite the medieval walls of Palacio de la Jadraza. The shopkeeper, an unmistakable bronzed lady in her early 40s with sea bleached golden hair, piercings and a vest that reads '*Cádizfornia*', runs out to greet me.

'Oysters, Alejandro! Baldy *mío*! So good to see you!' she yells. 'And who is this *preciocidad?* This…this Moorish beauty on your arm, eh?'

'Priya, Sur Ali; Sur Ali, Priya!' I reply.

'He calls me that because I am from the south – 'sur' – I am Alicia.'

'It's lovely to meet you.' Priya beams, one hand shielding her eyes from the sun.

'*El gusto es mío,*' she replies. 'How you say it?'

'The pleasure is mine,' I reply. '*Cerveza?*'

'*Sí, claro.* My brother, Javi, is in El Castillete ordering some drinks and tapas. I come in a minute, *vale?*'

#

'Here you are, *chiquillo,*' Javi says, after a bite to eat, passing me a small set of keys. 'This one's the boot and this one's *la moto.*'

Priya takes a step back.

'Don't be nervous,' I reassure her. 'No one's abducting you – ha, if anyone's been abducted here, it's me, right?'

'Shall I book a hotel or something?' she asks.

'A little presumptuous, perhaps?'

'I didn't mean it like…'

'All right, all right,' I level with her. 'We have a choice: stay in a regular hotel, *hostal* or something, or…stay in the hotel of a thousand stars.'

'You mean…?' she points at the beach.

'Yep,' I say, smiling back. "There's a gentle *Levante* tonight. Alicia will lend us a throw or two and we can chuck our stuff in Javi's boot.'

'I knew you were up to something,' Priya says, sidling up to me and kissing me on the neck. 'I'll take option two.'

I try to wrap my arm round her and she pushes me back. 'Wait, what was the other key for again?'

'That's for your chastity belt,' I reply, the *Cruzcampo* already taking effect.

'I lending you my little Vespa,' Javi explains. 'Is nothing special – only a 125 – but this is all you need around here, neither of you is very fatty nor nothing.'

'I'll take that as a compliment,' she replies.

'I'll get this.' I throw a hand in the air. 'Rocío, *la cuenta, por favor*!'

'You know everyone round here,' Priya comments.

'That's what happens when you can't keep away, I guess. Come, I've got things to show you.'

#

Off we scoot, inland past the little village of La Zarzuela, onto the main road south and off up a glorified dirt track into the mountains. Once at the ridge, we pause to watch a committee of griffon vultures circling above a herd of retinto cattle, then begin our descent to the sea. Moments later we can see the wide, curving sands of Bolonia, its shallow, turquoise waters, enormous sand dunes and umbrella pine forest.

'What's that?' she shouts in my ear. 'Across the water? Is it what I think it is?'

I come off the throttle, cut the engine and let the moped roll the last part.

'Tangier!' I reply.

'My god, it's beautiful!'

'Come, there's more to see.'

We park up and dismount, then I take her hand and lead her past the ancient Roman settlement of Baelo Claudia to the sea. With barely a soul around and the dusk setting in, I take off my clothes and hand them to her.

'What are you like?' she shrieks with laughter.

'Here,' I say. 'Can you put these with yours?'

'With mine?'

I stare at her imploringly.

'Ah, what the heck! I hate you, Donovan!'

Moments later we are immersed in bracing, Atlantic waters.

'It's fucking free-zing!' she yells, swimming over to me, throwing her arms around my neck and pressing her salty lips to mine.

'You're telling me,' I stammer back, unable to stop kissing her. She takes an arm away and drops it under the water.

'Doesn't seem to have affected you though, does it?' she asks, tilting her head to one side.

I pick her up and she wraps her legs around me. 'This is...you are...'

'Shhh,' she says, placing her finger on my mouth as the water laps against our naked bodies.

The sun slowly disappears behind the dunes and the moon casts a silvery path across the sea to Africa.

FIND

53

Hotel Gran Sol, Zahara de los Atunes

I climb out of bed and open the shutters to reveal, in all its glory, la Playa de la Virgen del Carmen, *wild, golden, unchanged.* In the absence of other plans, this will be my home for a few days.

I begin unpacking my bags and folding away my clothes with the calm deliberation of a well-heeled holidaymaker embarking on his long summer vacation. Plainly, I have lost the plot. It's a month since the GP signed me off and today would be my first day back, yet here I am, incognito in the south of Spain with limited savings and a future about as certain as a two-week weather forecast. And the strangest part? It feels OK. Better than OK.

I blame my novella, the detention story. It began as a sort of indignant legal thriller, inspired by Amy's talk at the Human Rights Lawyers Awards – the ill-treatment of refugees was a metaphor for our neglect of unprofitable migrants. Quickly, though, I started to experience a creative freedom that I barely remembered existed; the writing allowed me to take my real life and to turn it into a fantasy, to explore the love that had eluded me and to interrogate the arbitrary legal landscape that I blame for my disaffection – along with my idealism, of course, my prejudice, my irreverence, my woeful admin skills and my lack of self-awareness…

The writing also forced me to examine why I love this place so much, what it gives me that I don't ordinarily have. Conclusion: it is the glimpses of peace it provides, of calm and safety, of beauty and hope, of humour and wonder and light. I would say it was my sanctuary, but it is more nuanced than that. It is, I now see, the warm and hospitable place I come to in *search* of sanctuary, to recover a fraction of the peace I lost that day, all those years ago, when, staring at the Rosetta Stone, I felt the shelter of my childhood belief begin to crumble around me.

With the last of my things put neatly away, I store my empty baggage in the wardrobe and walk into the shower with one last thought on my mind: what will tomorrow bring? Indeed, what writing the story did not teach me was where on earth we go from here. And at the risk of continuing to sound like the young romantic fool I have been all this time, maybe that is the point? There is this line from a poem by the Sevillian poet, Antonio Machado, that I cannot get out of my head: *Traveller, there is no road; you make your own path as you walk.* Could it be that the path to sanctuary lies in accepting that there is none?

#

By the time I have showered and dressed it is mid-morning so I make for la Calle Real, a narrow, cobbled little street and home to some of the best restaurant bars in Zahara.

On arrival, I hover outside el Zoko, a pop-up restaurant I discovered last time I was over. It was here, in fact, sitting at a table adapted from an old sherry barrel, that I met the woman I had that 'dalliance' with. She was the waitress and I remember it vividly. Despite my efforts to 'move on', this was the first time since meeting Amy that I had even looked at anyone else. And I am ashamed to say, that was only the start...

'*Qué desea usted?*' she had asked me, and I knew straightaway she wasn't Spanish.

'*Una cervecita, por favor.*'

'*Ya mismo.*' She turned to fetch my beer.

'*Bonarense?*' I guessed.

'Close. Uspallata,' she answered playing with her wavy, sun-bleached hair. I'd never heard of it. Soon, though, she was reminiscing fondly about her little village in the Andes between Mendoza and the border with Chile. 'I loved the riding, singing, shooting…it was all so free, so untamed! I guess you could say it suited my character, you know?'

I fanned my face with the menu. 'You never told me what brought you to Spain?'

'Guess,' she replied.

I studied her carefully.

'Hmm, let's see…your grandparents left Spain as refugees from the Spanish Civil War?'

She laughed.

'Am I warm?'

'Keep going.'

'When the law changed in the 2000s, you became entitled to Spanish citizenship. You thought: *¡che boludo!*, here I am, 18 years old, and I've never even learnt to dance flamenco…'

'Erm…' She giggled. 'No. I came here in 2004. I was 16, alone, no visa, no papers.'

'My god, that sounds tough.'

'It was at first. But then, in 2005…

'They granted the amnesty,' I interrupted excitedly.

'That's right…you know your stuff, *loco*,' she said, blinking. 'You are a lawyer?'

'Is it that obvious?' I replied. 'Tell me, do you miss Argentina?'

'Some things…'

'Your family, right?'

'No, they are here now.' She shot me an intense look. 'I miss my fresh *yerba mate!*'

'I can't help you with that,' I laughed. 'But what time do you finish?'

Later, I had asked her name.

'Guillermina,' she replied, pulling up a bar stool. 'My grandparents on my mother's side were Italian.'

'I bet you have some beautiful surname,' I flirted, 'like – I don't know – Firenze-di-Ferrero or something?'

'Yeah, something like that,' she said, moving closer to me. 'And your name?'

'Alex.'

'Alex,' she whispered back. 'Good choice, by the way. I love this spot.'

Behind us, a fellow in a top-hat and patchwork waistcoat soundchecked his microphone. 'Welcome to El Pez Limon,' he opened, then introduced the rest of the band who rose from their seats, one by one, and joined him on the stage.

'Wow,' I commented as a waiter approached to take our order. 'You used to have to queue for a drink here. What are you having, *guapa*?'

'You, *bonito*,' she said, dimples appearing at the corners of her mouth, 'and a *ron-cola*.'

There was a sudden hush and the frontman stared at the floor for a few seconds, before slowly raising his head. '*En los olivaritos, niña, te espero*,' he began, '*con un jarro de vino y un pan casero*,' whereupon the unmistakable sound of flamenco guitar broke out and coursed through the audience, mellifluous and mesmeric like the cool mountain waters of the Acequia Real, flowing through the Alhambra palace.

The drinks arrived. We ordered more. Soon, fast-paced *bulerías* slowed to intimate *soleás* and lyrics of young love morphed into beautiful lost laments.

'You know, the acoustics are better out there by the water,' she said, holding out her hand.

#

The sand beneath my back was still warm from the fallen sun.

'No, like this,' she whispered, pulling me up onto my knees.

'I...'

'Shh, no one can see us.'

As I moved up to her, she threw her head back and fixed her eyes on mine.

'Do it,' she whispered.

Soon, remote sounds of revelry were fusing with cries of ecstasy. I looked up at the black sparkle sky, closed my eyes and felt myself falling backwards.

#

I awoke with a mouthful of sand and a fly buzzing round my ear. The only trace of the night before was the beach, blushing pink with the new dawn. I did actually see her again just before I left and I would have approached her, only she was hand in hand with some meathead fellow in a muscle vest – the bloke I described as her husband in my story.

After careful reflection, I give el Zoko a wide berth and ten minutes later, on the sandy approach to *chiringuito* La Luna, whom should I spot behind the bar but dear old Hans. Takes me a moment to recognise him, mind, the peroxide mohican he had last time I was over having grown out into a sort of two-tone shagpile carpet.

'*Qué pasa, inglesito?*' he greets me and ridiculous as it sounds, I have to remind myself that he did not, in fact, sell me a false passport.

#

I spend what remains of the morning ferrying between the *chiringuito* and the water, and I find I am able to think less about Amy. I have even made peace, I think, with her pretending not to have received my email. After all, it is not every day that someone essentially writes a story in your honour, let alone such a cryptic and elaborate one. Unable to reciprocate my feelings, no doubt, she was probably embarrassed on my behalf and/or afraid of hurting me. In other words, same old same old.

It does also cross my mind that Amy could have been telling the truth, that she genuinely has not read my manuscript. However, the days of second guessing are over: either Amy's heart belongs to another, or she genuinely loves me but lacks the courage to do anything about it. Either way, it is time to let it go. For if writing the story has taught me anything about love, it is the value I place on conviction. All that time pursuing Amy, I reflect, when the woman I was really after was but a fictional version of her, a braver, more romantic woman: Priya. Hindsight can be as cruel as it can be liberating.

#

I go for lunch with some old friends in El Castillete in la Calle Jara. Halfway through a plate of *chocos fritos*, I make the mistake of checking my phone. The top message is from Toby. *'Hey chap, where the hell are you? Made contact with your Congolese guy's new solicitors in Glasgow – turns out he requested the transfer himself – said he had wanted a change of scenery!'* Could not make it up.

Also there, buried amongst a string of concerned emails from work, is a further message from Amy. *'Alex, are you OK? People keep asking where you are. Listen, can we talk, please? Jon and Anton found some last minute deal on a sailing holiday in Spain, so I'm free for the rest of the week. Xx'*

'Que te folle un pez,' I say aloud, turning my phone off and addressing my friends. 'You know, I think that could be one of my favourite Spanish expressions?'

'I'd keep that thing off if I were you,' one of them advises. And so I do.

The rest of the afternoon is a carbon copy of the morning, only now without my pesky phone: dips, chats, *cañas de cerveza*, tapas, dips, smokes, *siestacitas*, dips, *cañas*, *pipas*, and so on. It feels almost meditative. At one stage, I borrow a pen and some serviettes from Hans and have a stab at summarising my detention story in the pithiest form I can muster, to put my finger on what it's really about.

Turns out it's far from easy. Is it about my character overcoming his self-doubt to expose the abuse and find love, for instance? Or is it more about the insight he gets from Priya into his own prejudices and limitations? Or is the main point perhaps the deeper one, that appalling abuses will continue to occur for as long as we prioritise profit over humanity?

When I get nowhere with this, I begin to wonder whether the story is, in fact, about all of the above, and if so, whether there is any one theme that unites them. And when this enquiry also hits a brick wall and I'm back to wondering what the point of any of it was, just like that it hits me that the answer is in the question. Most fundamentally, my story is about Alex's naïve quest for certainty, and his deeply held fear that without it, somehow his life will be meaningless.

I fold up the serviette and put it in my pocket. Then I stretch out my legs in front of me and relish the moment. All that angst – two thirds of my life spent searching for the other, missing third, when the only place it existed was in the past. Uncertainty was never the problem. It was my fear of embracing it.

#

When the sun disappears behind the waves, I pick up my sunburnt body and retire to the hotel for an early night. A glance at the BBC website reveals some wild story about a purported government plan to outsource refugee status determination to Africa – they'd never be so brazen, surely, but it makes me do a double take. Other than that, it's just the usual stuff – weather, football and who's wearing what at what event (yawn).

I shut my eyes and let the sound of the sea lull me to sleep. Only once do I wish she were lying next to me...

54

I spend the next morning mooching around in the narrow back streets of the village, poking my head in and out of artisanal shops, cafés and kiosks, and greeting the odd friendly face along the way. It is thirsty work and as midday approaches, the sun is beginning to bite. I hang a right down Calle Extremaduros and towards that beautiful spot I once told Amy about.

#

Restaurante El Refugio. Unauthorised absence well underway. Weather: warm, breezy, sublime. I choose a table and order a cold beer.

The fig tree is coming into bloom again and the white, low-lying wall separating the patio from the beach has had a lick of paint. Other than that, little has changed. I shut my eyes and listen to the sounds of the new day: waves breaking on the wide, golden beach, soft indistinct chatter and the faint put-put of an engine. Bliss.

Thoughts of Amy come and go. Musing again over our recent exchanges, I remember her relaying some trouble she was having with her emails and it begins to seem more plausible that she did not read my novella I sent her. Instinctively, I reach for my phone, only to discover that I have left it in the hotel. Saved by my own chaos, I reflect, and have a sip of my drink.

The engine sound stops and some movement on the near horizon catches my eye. I watch with interest as a couple of figures, silhouetted against the sky, haul their sailing dinghy ashore and make their way up the beach towards the restaurant.

As they draw closer, the taller of the two walks straight up to the perimeter wall, removes his sunglasses and says in a smooth, recognisable voice:

'*Buenos dias, señor Donovano.*'

'Anton? Jon?' I shuffle back on my seat.

'What? Don't tell us you weren't expecting us?'

'Nice tan by the way,' mocks Jon, pointing at my face. 'Big fan of the lobster look.'

Struggling to assimilate their presence, I watch the men walk round to the makeshift entrance, point me out to the waiters, then saunter over to join me.

'Now, I hope we are not intruding?'

'Not at all,' I reply. 'You can drop the act. What is this?'

Fletcher ignores my question, leans forward and rests his hands on the table in front of him. 'Permit me to save you some time. It will be best if you cooperate with us.'

Bemused, I say nothing.

'I should remind you,' he continues, pulling up a chair, 'I have 25 years' witness handling experience.'

'Sorry, I don't follow.'

'I mean I have a rather acute radar for when someone is trying to deceive me.'

A waiter appears and leaves again.

'Respectfully, what are you talking about?'

Fletcher nods to Jon, prompting him to reach into his bag and pull out a thin, lever-arch file. Opening it in front of me, he affects a little cough. And there, on the first page, I can see a print-out of my email to Amy, subject: *'For your eyes only'*.

'What?' I gasp.

Jon turns the page and there at the top, sure enough, I see the words *Stansted Airport, Immigration Control. Spanish holiday over.*

'My story?'

'That's right,' Jon says in a baby voice. 'Your story.'

'I don't get it. How did…' I interrupt myself. 'I told Amy not to share it with anyone.'

The men glance at each other.

'All right guys, what is this? And what are you doing with my book?'

Jon leans in towards me. 'Keep your voice down, prat.'

'Get out of my face!'

He withdraws and the waiter reappears.

'*Ehm, ya puedo tomar nota?*'

'He's asking to…'

'Take our order,' Fletcher interrupts.

'Don't tell me you speak Spanish too?'

'*Un poquito.* Look, it's not exactly the hardest language to learn, is it?'

Before I can retaliate, he is off again.

'Now, I am a little peckish. What do you tend to prefer, young man? *La carne o el pescado*? Or both, perhaps?'

Fletcher winks at me then turns to Jon. 'Local slang, my friend. It means "What's your sexual orientation?"'

Jon sniggers, while I stare at him pityingly.

'Seriously, what would you recommend, Alex?'

I sit forward on my chair. 'I'd recommend the What, followed by The Fuck Are You Doing Here?'

Unflinching, Fletcher continues perusing the menu. 'Now, now – no need for that. I'll explain everything. Just as soon as I've tried these homemade *croquetas*. I think I'll have a glass of something too. *¡Oiga, camarero!*'

#

The *croquetas* look delicious as ever. Nonetheless I decline them.

SANCTUARY

'A little early for our Spanish friend, I'd expect,' quips Fletcher, before wiping his mouth and getting down to business. 'Your story,' he begins. 'With whom have you shared it?'

'With Amy,' I respond, my eyes dipping towards the floor. 'I asked her to keep it to herself.'

'Does it matter?'

'Erm, yes it does actually,' I reply.

'Why?'

I pause. 'Now, let me see. It's unedited, I'm yet to completely decide on a title for it...and...'

'Yes?'

'I trusted her not to.' I am struggling to understand why on earth she would forward it to them. Are they all laughing at me? 'Why did she send it to you?'

Fletcher puts his hands in his pockets and rocks back on his chair.

'Search me, sunshine. Shouldn't she have?'

'Not if I asked her to keep it to herself!'

He picks up his wine and swishes it around in his glass. 'I quite understand. To be clear, though, Amy, Jon and I are the only privileged three to have had sight of your *magnum opus*, correct?'

'Easy on the sarcasm, all right? As far as I'm aware you're the only three so far. Who knows who else she's bloody told!'

'So far...?'

'Yes, well, irrespective of what you think of it, I plan to get it published.'

'Reeeeally,' Fletcher chortles, a hint of a quiver detectable in his voice.

'When I'm happy with it, yes,' I reply as resolutely as I can.

'And who is the lucky publisher, might I ask?'

I look down then back up at my interrogator. 'I haven't approached any yet.'

'Ah,' Fletcher replies, glancing at Jon. 'Well, early days. A tip though: if you must write about yourself, at least give your protagonist a different name?'

'Drop the first-person thing too, if I were you,' Jon piles in, 'unless you actually want it to sound like a witness statement?'

I put both hands on the table in front of me and take a deep breath. 'Are you two going to tell me why the fuck you're here?'

'Simmer down, tiger,' drawls Jon. 'There's no need for that.'

'Then. Tell. Me.'

'We came to find you,' he answers.

'Yes, that much I gathered!'

'Come, come, Alex, what did you expect? Disappearing unannounced? Telling no one of your whereabouts? People have been worried sick about you.'

'I've been away barely three days!'

'It's my fault,' Fletcher declares. 'When I read the book, it occurred to me you might be here in Zahara. And I felt it only responsible to check.'

I scratch my head in disbelief. 'Oh, come off it! You're a busy man. You could have told someone else to look for me here. I don't know, the police, anyone…'

'A certain junior colleague of mine, perhaps?'

Jon flinches and I gather my strength. 'Well, now you mention it, yes,' I reply, and take a gulp of beer.

Jon gestures to speak but Fletcher holds out an arm to stop him. 'Is that what this is all about, old fellow?' he asks me.

I spit out my *Cruzcampo*. 'You tell me, o great one.'

'All right, I shall,' he says, glancing out towards the horizon. 'You wrote the book to capture Amy's attention, didn't you? You wanted to show her what you were capable of.'

I look at Jon, who is wiping his nose on the back of his arm.

'Maybe…not exactly.'

'And also, perhaps, what she was capable of,' he emphasises. 'Like Priya, she too could be with a gutsy, perceptive man, if only she could find the courage of her convictions and ditch Jon?'

'I have never asked her to ditch Jon,' I reply, indignant.

'Never directly…'

I stare Fletcher in the eye while he patiently prepares to deliver his next question. Love or loathe him, he is good at this.

'And when she didn't read it,' he continues, 'you tried a different technique, didn't you?'

'Excuse me?'

'You disappeared.'

'Scarcely, I…'

'You left London?'

'OK…'

'Your colleagues?'

'Well, I…'

'You didn't tell them where you were going, did you? That's right, isn't it?'

Silence. As ever, it is difficult to dispute Mr Brain-on-a-stick's analysis. But there is something odd in what he just said.

'Wait a moment. How do you know she didn't read it?'

'I'm sorry?'

'You heard me. I said, how do you know she didn't read it?'

The waiter returns and Fletcher places a 50 Euro note carefully on his little silver tray, half smiling as if to say, 'There. Now, off you trot.'

'That, Alex, is a good question,' he replies a few moments later, 'and I'm afraid the answer is a little sensitive. Too sensitive for here, in fact. Shall we?'

The men stand up.

'Wait! She's OK, right?' I ask, grabbing Fletcher's arm, earning myself a glare from Jon.

'Yes. Why wouldn't she be?' he replies. 'Do you sail?'

I don't respond.

'Well?'

'Yes.'

'Good. Come, I'll explain everything.'

FIND

I stand up. What can be so sensitive he can't whisper it – in English – in El Refugio?

285

55

The dinghy appears relatively new. A simple, open hull four-seater about the size of a small fishing boat, it is equipped with smart, beige sails and an outboard motor. In the open hull a hip flask and a couple of life jackets rest on a tatty holdall, from which some spare rope is poking out.

'Right, next stop Bolonia beach!' Jon announces. 'Give us a hand pushing off, would you, chaps?'

On gripping the stern, I notice two large kettle bells stowed under the front deck. Who anchors a dinghy?

'What are they for?' I wheeze.

'Anchor, mate,' Jon replies. 'Bit makeshift, but does the job.'

I look at the two men, then back at the kettle bells, and feel my chest tightening. I step back from the boat in horror, my eyes now fixed on Fletcher who produces another unconvincing smile, somewhere between a grin and a grimace. Jon begins to move towards me, but a piercing cry rings out, startling us all.

Shielding my eyes from the sun, I can just make out the outline of a woman running towards us across the stirring sands, her arms flailing like the wings of a pigeon in a gust.

As she draws closer, I begin to recognise her.

'Amy?'

I turn to the other two, who look equally stunned. Her cries are now discernible. 'Stop! Stop! Don't get in!'

'Well, well,' Anton remarks, while Jon clasps his hands behind his head and turns to face the sea.

She makes directly for me, flings her arms around me, then squares up to the others. All of this appears to amuse Fletcher.

'Now, now, Amy, there's no need for histrionics,' he chortles.

'Fuck you, Anton.'

Silence.

'Ah, I take it you've read our friend's great literary work?'

'Yes,' she replies, turning and looking me in the eye. 'Yes, I have. And…'

'It's wonderful, isn't it?' Fletcher interrupts, stepping up and putting an arm around me like a proud father. As he speaks to me, his eyes remain trained on Amy, as if he were telegraphing something to her. 'It's hard to believe that – as you explained just now, Alex – to date, we are the *only* people to have had sight of this original and imaginative work. I feel truly privileged.' He turns to face me. 'I hope you've backed it up, by the way?'

'What do you mean?'

'You must save it securely if you haven't already. It would be a terrible shame if you were to lose even a word before it's published.'

'Published?' I respond. 'Moments ago, you scoffed at the thought…'

'Nonsense. I think it's a marvellous idea. Not an easy thing, of course, but I can think of a couple of literary friends who I am quite sure would give you an honest view. I'll send it to them for you if you like? I take it you saved it somewhere?' he asks again.

'Why does it matter? You've already got it…' I shoot an angry glance at Amy who tries to speak but is interrupted a second time.

'Wait please, Amy, dear,' comes Fletcher again. 'Alex, I must explain something. Amy and I share our emails, for work reasons.'

'Do we?' she says.

'Amy, please!' he says firmly, holding up his hand to her. 'We have invited young Alex for a sail. Like him, no doubt you are wanting some explanations. And we shall give them to you, shan't we Jon?'

'You deleted his email to me, you…'

'Of course, we shall,' Jon confirms, shutting off her allegation and turning to face us. 'I think we owe you *both* an explanation.'

He walks around the bow and offers his hand to Amy. She refuses to take it.

'Don't you think it's a bit late for that?' she asks, her voice quivering. 'You two are out of control.'

'What?' they respond in unison.

'How long?'

'How long what, darling?' Jon replies.

'Don't lie to me! How long have you been profiting from our refugee system? Well? That's why you're here, isn't it?'

'Amy, what are you…'

'You read Alex's book and believed you had been rumbled.'

There's a pause.

'What on earth are you on about, Ames?' Jon asks – though it might as well have been me, such is my own confusion.

What follows is as astonishing as it is surreal. Amy declares that the villains in my book, De Rossi and Ian, were even more unnervingly like Fletcher and Jon than I had imagined them to be, and she accuses them of conspiring to select refugees according to their profitability.

On hearing this, Fletcher seems as flabbergasted as I am and insists there must have been a 'woeful misunderstanding'. Yet his denial only seems to strengthen her conviction.

'I'll give you woeful,' Amy begins. 'Woeful is closing the door to Somalis fleeing militias because they lack the education, skills or health to be deemed *valuable* to us!'

'What in god's name are you saying, Amy?' Fletcher snaps back. 'I have fought for and won refugee status for multiple Somalis, and you know it!'

She steps up to him. 'Multiples you could count on one hand.'

'Amy, honestly, I…'

'Khadija Osman's case!' she shouts, now shaking.

'Yes, what about it?'

'How many asylum seekers did the guidance you secured in that case actually assist? Well? Five, ten people? 50 max?' she asks, prodding at him at each interval.

'50 lives, Amy. 50 people who would otherwise have been seriously harmed or killed.'

'Certainly, that is the line you fed us!'

'What the dickens are you talking about? Good grief, girl, you've read the Osman Decision yourself. You know perfectly well what it says.'

'Yes.' She is undeterred. 'And tell me how many thousands of would-be refugees the guidance excluded?'

'Excuse me?'

'How many Somali asylum claims were actually *weakened* by the tribunal's guidance in that Decision?'

He produces a hearty laugh. 'This is nonsense on stilts!'

'You and Proudfoot knew what you were doing. You worked out the narrowest possible class of refugee to protect and played down the plight of the rest.'

'Oh bollocks.'

'Is it? How many young women in Somalia – or anywhere – could ever be said to be '*without any support whatsoever*'?

Silence.

'You set the bar impossibly high for 99.9% of applicants, didn't you?'

'We did nothing of the sort.'

'And with great effect,' she persists. 'Before your wonderful case, the Home Office weren't removing anyone at all to Somalia, were they? And with good reason. It was a bloody war zone!'

'A lot has changed since then, Amy dear.'

'Don't patronise me, you fuck!'

I can barely believe what I am hearing. It appears that Jon and Fletcher manipulated the country evidence on Somalia to produce a false picture of the situation on the ground, thus ensuring that far fewer asylum seekers were granted protection than were eligible for it.

'Oh come on, Amy,' Fletcher interjects again. 'You know perfectly well we serve the evidence that best suits our clients' interests, in accordance with the Code of Conduct.'

She laughs. 'Tell me – where in the Bar Standards Board's Code of Conduct does it says it's OK to make up evidence and mislead the court?'

For a moment – for the first time in his life? – Fletcher seems genuinely lost for words. And Amy is unremitting. Fixing her stare away from him, she dishes out consecutive allegations in close succession, a savage advocacy technique she once told me about known as the 'bounce'.

'You have wilfully neglected a great many of those most in need.'

'Oh, rot!'

'Thereby condemning them to misery, torture, death even.'

'Stop this!'

'You are in effect, the pair of you…murderers!'

'About Khadija Osman…' I chip in. 'Turns out she went on to become that notorious asylum interviewer. You know, Officer 31?'

Her jaw drops. 'What?'

'Not only that, she now works for your man, there,' I add. I open my wallet and produce for her the crumpled rags-to-riches story from the in-flight magazine.

There is a stunned silence. She looks at Jon who merely shrugs, and now Fletcher steps back into the breach.

'All right, all right, this has gone quite far enough.'

'You don't say?' She reloads and fires again. 'Tell me, who in god's name would contrive to exclude evidence of widespread violence in Afghanistan?'

'Oh, for heaven's sake, what now?'

'It's what you've done, isn't it? In your Afghan violinist case.'

'Zalmai Azam,' I confirm.

'Amy dear, as you well know, I am not at liberty to discuss

confidential…'

'He's the Afghan equivalent of Khadija Osman, isn't he?' she interrupts.

'No, he is not.'

'A decoy. A vehicle for excluding unwanted refugees in the name of reaching out to them! That is what you two do, isn't it?'

'I'll say it again, Amy. As you well know, the Decision in that case is yet to be handed down. Who knows what the tribunal will find?'

She shakes her head. 'You do.' Her tone softens. 'I am ashamed of myself.'

'What for? For winning challenging, high-profile cases with me?' he mocks, but no amount of gaslighting can stop her now.

'Can't believe I didn't see all this sooner. And, to think I helped you. *'High net worth professionals between the ages of 20 and 45'*. It makes me sick.'

Silence.

'You made protection contingent on desirability.'

'Enough!'

'And you used me.'

'I did nothing of the sort!'

'To keep your reputation clean, massage your ridiculous ego and of course, to line your silken pocket.'

'All right, calm down,' Jon interrupts. 'We get the message.'

'And as for you…' She turns to him.

A stout little seagull flies by, barely clearing his head.

'As for you,' she begins again, 'you told me you loved me…said you wanted us to start a family together. To think that I could be so naïve. There never was any "us", was there? Just "you". You…' She gathers her breath. 'You made me complicit in something so unthink-able, I couldn't even see it.'

There is a pause and she looks over at me.

'Thankfully, though, someone did.'

Did I? I wonder, struggling to keep up. It must show on my face.

'Oh, you pathetic half-wit,' Jon sneers. 'Look, we wanted to do this the more civilised way. You know, praise your efforts, persuade you that publishing the book would adversely affect your career, result in legal action against you, et cetera – Christ! – we were even prepared to offer you a job! But my darling clever clogs here has joined up the dots... My god!' he starts laughing. 'Even now, despite everything you just said, he still doesn't have a clue what we're talking about!'

'I have some idea, Jon,' I say. More laughter. 'I know that by writing the pair of you into an environment befitting of your arrogant, egomaniac selves, your story revealed itself. How about that? *I* might not have imagined you were capable of conspiring to shaft refugees,' I add, 'but my protagonist did.'

Jon affects a slow clap. 'Your pathetic, punky alter ego?'

'Well, not alone he didn't. Without that woman there,' I continue, pointing at Amy, 'without her wit and her determination, I would never have known the full extent of just how shitty you are.' This is starting to feel good...

'I said enough! It is all too easy to criticise,' Fletcher interrupts. 'But know this and know it well: our actions have not only saved the lives of many refugees...'

'The ones you wanted,' Amy reiterates.

'...but have served to *preserve* the Refugee Convention,' he continues.

'He's right, you fools,' Jon chips in.

'You are deluded,' she says, aghast. 'What good is a refugee convention when it is used to exclude refugees? It is exclusive enough already, without your help!' Amy takes a moment, then turns to Jon with a look of utter contempt. 'Well, we now know where all that money came from, don't we? All those fact-finding forays...tell me, how many governments have you bribed? And how many kickbacks have you received?'

'I told you.'

'Bullshit!'

Fletcher, who has been propping himself up on the side of the boat, stands up to his full height, clasps his hands together, then reaches into the hull and pulls out the holdall. Slowly and deliberately, he unzips it to reveal two smaller bags. He picks one of them up and lobs it at my feet.

'Go on. Open it.'

I dig my hand in and pull out a tightly bound wad of £50 notes.

'You have got to be joking…' I respond.

'Alex. Wait.'

'Eh?'

'Listen to her, chump,' Jon interjects. 'Go on, Amy.'

'OK. Is…this what I think it is?'

Fletcher's turn again. 'You may not agree with our approach,' he begins. Amy scoffs and he resets. 'We did what we thought was right. For our country. For the fragile heirloom that is the Convention. And, yes, to the extent that we were remunerated, for ourselves.'

I am now beyond bewildered. 'Are we really expected to swallow this?'

'I'd be grateful if you'd let me finish, Alexander.'

'Don't "Alexander" me.'

'Let him finish!' exclaim Jon and Amy in unison.

'Thank you. In fairness to Alex here, everything has a value, and everything has a price. What I was trying to say, if you would only let me, is that value takes multiple forms, correct? And, whatever we do professionally, then, we work for value. The price we are paid is only a part of it – a small part, in my case, I assure you.'

'Come off it, Anton,' Amy retorts. 'Everyone in chambers knows your receipts are through the roof.'

'When you don't like something,' he carries on, 'the price needs to be high to compensate for the relative lack of value. Why do you suppose all those corporate lawyers get paid so much? I'll tell you. Because no one wants to do such work, to be at the constant beck and call of demanding clients in different time zones, to go days on end without seeing their children or their loved ones.'

To my irritation, I catch myself nodding along.

'What is your point, Anton?'

'Everyone has a price, Amy. Alex. Everyone has a price for doing something they don't want to. And what is more, I have calculated yours.'

Amy balks. 'Are you trying to buy our silence?'

'Two million, two hundred and twenty thousand, four hundred and forty-seven pounds thirty-three pence is your price,' he says proudly. 'Count it if you like – it's all there. Oh, and that's for both of you by the way. I worked it out on the inevitable assumption that you will get together.'

Amy and I look at each other, speechless, while Fletcher turns to Jon.

'Sorry, old boy, but no use fighting the tide and all that.'

'Who else?' Amy asks.

'I beg your pardon?'

'Before we consider your offer, we need to know who else we're being asked to cover for.'

'Consider your offer?' I repeat.

She takes my hand. 'Yes,' she says, squeezing it to the point I think it might break.

Fletcher bows his head for a moment, apparently consumed in thought. Then, 'No, I think not. You know quite enough already.'

'Proudfoot?'

Silence.

'Look,' Amy continues. 'If we're to protect you effectively, we at least need to know how high up this goes.'

Jon approaches Fletcher and they confer for a moment. 'Very well,' he says. 'Proudfoot is, let us say, wilfully unaware of what goes on.'

'Explain.'

'He puts himself forward to sit on certain, high impact cases.'

'The ones you are listed to appear in? Yes, I saw that. I've also seen how he adopts any Draft Directions you ask him to make without so much as blinking.' She composes herself. 'What is in it for Proudfoot? Besides kickbacks, I mean?'

'Kickbacks?' Fletcher laughs, and disabuses her of the notion. 'Have you been listening to anything I've been saying? Value, Amy. Not only is Henry Proudfoot fiendishly bright but, like me, he is a Convention man. He lives and breathes refugee law – reads everything, knows everything.'

'And?'

'Again, like me, Proudfoot is keenly aware of the central role Britain has had in shaping and preserving the international refugee legal framework.'

'As are we,' she says, jollying him along.

'OK, the point is a simple one: to protect some, you must neglect others, which is better than protecting no one. Full stop.'

'So, he knowingly sits as a judge in cases where evidence has been skewed?'

'I prefer the term "shaped".'

Hand on her mouth, Amy takes a moment.

'And you, Jon?' she presses. 'You don't contrive and collate the evidence on your own, I take it?'

'Drop the act, Amy,' he snarls. 'I can explain my actions too if you'll let me.'

'The kickbacks?'

'Like my learned friend here, I have no regrets about any of this – zero.'

'Go on,' Amy beckons.

'Many – most – of my fact-finding missions were straight-up, uneventful information gathering exercises. I swear. But what you have to understand, see, is that everything – everything – requires a trade-off of some type or other.'

'How much did they pay you, Jon?' she asks coldly.

'My salary.'

'Stop! Stop lying to me, Jon.'

He sighs. 'Look, I can't remember the exact figure. Not much, all things considered. Besides, I barely touched the stats in that Country Report.'

'You massaged them to within an inch of their life, Jon. They were completely at odds with the stats in the experts' report we commissioned and that you, Anton, managed to discredit – and to think those experts risked their lives to gather that evidence!'

'And you don't think I risked my life?'

'Oh, do fuck off, Jon.'

He steps towards her aggressively, and I stand in his path.

'Let's get something straight,' he says, eyeballing us intermittently like an axe-murderer choosing who to chop up first. 'Brave folk like us don't risk our necks protecting the national interest for comfortable, lefty, activist lawyer snowflakes like you to lecture us. It makes me sick!'

'Us?' Amy asks.

'What about us?'

'No, not "us". You said "brave folk like us". There are more of you dodgy "fact-finders" out there, are there?'

'Oh, come on! Wakey, wakey, counsel, of course there are. Khadija Osman, for one!'

'And?' she replies, quick on her feet. 'Who else?'

But Jon's expression shifts from frustration to suspicion. He bolts over to the hull, fiddles around a bit, then pulls out a small handgun. Fletcher moves to disarm him, but he bats him off.

'Look at her shirt, Anton!' he yells, shaking. 'The lapel – she's wearing a lav.'

'A what?'

'A lavalier. A mic. Frisk her!'

But before he can, Amy has already disentangled the microphone which I can see is plugged into her phone. Calmly, she puts it on speaker mode, raises it to her mouth and asks:

'Got it?'

'Yep, it's a wrap,' replies a warm, familiar voice. 'All live streamed as requested, my dear, with a neat little button link to your statement.'

I reach for the phone.

'Danso...?'

56

The mainsail flaps slack against the mast and little waves gather expectantly around the hull.

The wind is picking up.

'It seems you have a choice, gentlemen,' Amy says coldly. 'Turn yourselves in, or fuck off in your little boat.'

Shoulders slumped, fringe lifting in the gusts, Fletcher turns to his accomplice for instructions.

'We'll take our chances,' Jon says, and he kneels to pick up the money, only to find Amy's foot.

'Uh-uh. That stays here, tosspot.'

'As does the gun,' I tell him, holding out my hand.

A small crowd of concerned onlookers begins to gather a little way up the beach from us. Jon hesitates a moment, then slings the revolver into the sea. 'Come on, let's go.'

'Where to?' Fletcher asks.

'I don't know, away from here.'

'But…'

'Just shut up and get in, will you? If our chat's just been uploaded, the Guardia Civil, Interpol and fuck knows who else will be on us in no time. Anton, the outboard.'

'No,' he replies. 'With this wind, we're better off using the sails.' He unravels the gib sheet, snatches the halyard and turns to face Amy. 'A question,' he says. 'Why the head start?'

'Simple,' she replies. 'If you can't imagine what it's like to be desperate and fleeing for your life, then you had better experience it.'

'Amy.'

'No time, Anton!' Jon yells.

'Know this,' he continues. 'We never meant any harm to come to anyone.'

'And nor do I. Good luck, gentlemen. And good riddance.'

As Jon pushes them off, Amy turns on her heel, looks down at the sand and clasps her hands together in a gesture of prayer. Five seconds later, she lifts her head up and looks me in the eye.

'Are you OK?' she asks.

'Am *I* OK?'

#

As we stand there, Amy reveals to me the extent of the operation. When none of my colleagues knew where I was, she contacted Danso. 'By the way, he's seeing Claire,' she adds nonchalantly, and I did not see that coming. Danso was worried too. So, when she forwarded him my confusing text and told him about the email problems she was having, he went round to look at her computer, and recovered the email and attached story. As she read it, she tells me, she could not believe how blind she had been.

'*You* were blind?' I reply. 'I wrote the bloody thing and still didn't see it!'

I explain how the crazy idea for my story came to me the last time I was over. Hans had been bragging about his black-market contacts and I asked him if he would be able to get me a false Spanish passport. I was taking the piss of course but when he took me seriously, I began to wonder what might happen if someone like me did actually return to England on a false passport and claim asylum…

'I found that I couldn't stop thinking about it,' I explain, 'but the bit I was stuck on was imagining a crime so heinous and flagrant the Home Office hadn't already committed it. When I hit on the crime, the story virtually wrote itself.'

Amy frowns. 'I don't get it. Clearly, you based the villains on Anton and Jon. You must have known something was up.'

'I knew I didn't like them…'

'That's it? No,' she insists. 'Your story fits too neatly with what Anton and Jon were doing in real life. You *must* have known.'

'God, I don't know – subliminally, perhaps? I do remember feeling that the refugee groups Anton's cases protected were a little niche, considering all the praise he got.'

'So I recall.' She drops her head.

'Then, there was the Peru evidence…'

'Yes, of course.'

'Anyone who read that report of Jon's would assume Peru to be the safest country on earth!'

'Yes. Yes, so you did know?' she asks me again.

'Did know what? That the Home Office often try to play down the risk of sending back vulnerable asylum seekers? Yes, of course. But for the life of me, I never imagined they would actually conspire – with opposing counsel – to choose the asylum seekers they wanted, and reject the rest out of hand. I mean, Jesus…'

'It does beggar belief…' She looks pensive for a moment. 'Then again, I suppose, in one sense, it's not a million miles away from what we do…?'

'Go on?'

'I mean, into battle we go each day on our white chargers, fighting to protect refugees and those acutely vulnerable enough to meet the stratospheric threshold for human rights protection – but what about the ones we effectively ignore?'

'Those irregular migrants, you mean, "who risk their lives just to get vital medical treatment, or clean water, or enough food to feed their families"?'

The traces of a smile appear on her face. 'I see *someone* was listening to me that day…'

The penny is beginning to drop.

'As I said at the time, Amy, it was a great speech. Short. But mighty powerful. "We cannot continue to pick and choose the people we admit, without proper regard for what befalls those we discard."'

A sudden intake of breath. 'Hang on...'

You have to admire her. She has cracked it already: her speech at the Awards night was the true inspiration for my plot.

'Wait! My god...! Your story was an allegory of our neglect of irregular migrants.'

'That was the idea.' I blush. 'Shameful as it is, though, I am not sure even our neglect compares with what Fletcher and crew have done...'

She scoffs. 'You mean skewing the evidence, manipulating – breaking – the law and then pretending to be heroic protectors of the vulnerable?' Her expression changes to one of disgust. 'You know, I think I'm most angry with Anton. There he was, the self-professed guardian of the Convention, subverting it before our very eyes. The sheer audacity of the man!'

I take stock a moment, then ask her what it was that made her twig.

She confirms that it was essentially all the weirdness: Jon asking for my number; the cryptic message I sent her, followed by my disappearance; the sudden announcement that Jon and Anton were going abroad... It all started to ring alarm bells, 'And there was the sailing, of course. Sure, Fletcher was keen. But Jon? He literally gets seasick in the bath...'

I glance at the boat, which is making erratic progress against the incoming tide and receiving a righteous buffeting from the waves, then I pick up the bag of money, turn away and together we begin walking slowly back along the beach towards the village.

#

It is lunchtime and the nosy little crowd has now dispersed. When

Danso recovered my email, Amy explains, something clicked in her mind. She recalled having told Fletcher about those emails she had received showing as 'read' before she had read them, and how casual his response was. Uncharacteristically so, 'I started to feel sick and began to wonder whether it was he, Fletcher, who had accessed my account, he who had deleted my email.'

The next question was why? All Amy could safely assume was that my story contained something he did not want her to see. And, scanning through the pages, she suddenly found herself barely able to breathe. 'I rushed back to chambers and looked up all similar cases Anton had been involved in since Khadija Osman's case. I found seven. And, guess what? Just as I feared, not one resulted in protection being given to anyone unskilled or unwell. The only winners I could see were the kind of asylum seekers who would have qualified under our immigration laws anyway – essentially, well off professionals and skilled workers.'

'The people our government actively recruits.'

'Exactly. And – surprise, surprise – a disproportionate number also happened to be white or light-skinned. Are you *sure* you didn't suss them out?'

'In my dreams…' I laugh. 'No, I was in full flow with my story. As I said, the idea was to use it to make your point about vulnerable migrants, you see?'

'Well, it worked! And you have exposed Fletcher and Jon, Proudfoot and Osman, and god knows how many others in the process.'

'Pure chance. I never stopped to imagine those bastards could actually be flouting the Refugee Convention in real life, right under our noses…' I pause. 'Thankfully though, someone did. Fuck, Amy – thank god for your wonderful brain!'

'Oh, bollocks,' she replies. 'If I were smarter, I would have seen all this sooner. You know, without your story, I might never have…'

She takes a deep breath.

'The play's the thing…' she begins.

'…wherein I'll catch the conscience of the king,' I conclude, still in shock.

'You rumbled them,' she says triumphantly.

'Unwittingly, perhaps.' But something is still plaguing me. 'How on earth did they know where to find me?' I ask.

'They may have tracked your phone, I guess…or just found you the same way I did.'

'Home Office contacts, or something?'

'Scarcely. No, this place is all you ever talk about,' she says with a chuckle. 'And you go on about it in your novella, don't you?'

Before I can get too offended, however, she puts it right. 'Of course, I can see exactly why you would…'

'Oh, you can?' I reply, my smile returning.

'It's beautiful, Alex, simply beautiful.'

#

'He's back,' she says, nudging me. The chubby little seagull has followed us down the beach.

'Our very own, feathered bodyguard.' I drop the bag and ask to borrow her phone, then text Jedrek to ask him to reopen Gema's asylum file, closed on the basis of Jon's bogus report on Peru.

'Wow, always thinking of others, you.' She beams.

'Oh, rubbish. Anyway, like you don't?'

I hand the phone back.

'Speaking of which,' I continue. 'What do you suppose will happen to Azam? I mean, I am assuming his appeal will have to be reheard?'

'Yes, in all likelihood. The Home Office may wish to exercise their discretion in his favour, given all that's happened – you know, to try to make the story go away.'

'Good luck to them with that…'

She smiles. 'On the facts I saw, Azam has more than a fighting chance of winning regardless.' She pauses. 'The issue will be what guidance a newly-assembled panel will give, and how it will affect others like him whose cases aren't as strong…'

'Like Nasir…'

'Precisely. His case will largely depend on the level of violence in Kabul at the time the Country Guidance appeal is reheard – whenever that may be.'

I nod. Then she fixes me with those eyes. 'Alex, you know I…I never meant to…'

'It's OK,' I reply softly, putting an arm around her.

'No. It's not OK. I hated hurting you – I just felt so helpless. God, and then that night we nearly kissed…'

'Before I slipped and broke my leg in two?'

'I felt so guilty…'

'You didn't put the stupid saucer there. And you came with me in the ambulance.'

'No, I mean about Jon. Deep down, I knew something didn't feel right. I even tried to break up with him. But he wouldn't accept it. He kept calling, texting, telling me I was his world. He adored me. Or so I thought…'

Her lip begins to quiver. She tells me how attentive, committed and reassuring the man was, at a time in her life when so little else seemed certain. She is now fighting off the tears. 'Most of all,' she persists, 'I felt I had committed to him. Our lives had become so intertwined. When you appeared, it was like a dream and a nightmare, all at the same time…'

'Cheers, I think…'

She pretends not to laugh. 'Here I am pouring my heart out, and all you can do is…'

'I missed you so much, Amy,' I cut in.

'I know,' she whispers softly back.

'I couldn't…it just didn't feel right to try to prise you away from him, like a, like a…'

'Go on,' she implores.

'Limpet?'

'Right...'

'So, I did my best to block you out, to forget you. But, then...'

'Yes?' she asks.

'...I couldn't stop wondering what might have been.'

I take her hand in mine and confirm that the book was always written with her in mind, that I wanted to show her how much she meant to me, and what we could be together.

'So, you wrote it about a fancy Bengali/Italian immigration officer?' she replies, discretely wiping a tear from her eye.

'I wrote it about a blisteringly smart, kind-to-a-fault, non-conformist beauty, whose name happens to mean...'

'Beloved,' she interrupts. 'As does mine.'

More tears.

'Priya was always you, Amy. My only question was whether you were her. And it seems you have answered it.'

'I...you...' she is struggling for words. But I'm not stopping now, not this time.

'I guess, what I am trying to say is' – a gust of *Levante* blows her into my arms – 'I adore you, Amy.'

#

Peering over her shoulder, I think I can just make out the last of the dinghy, disappearing into the Rif mountains beyond. Tenderly, she tilts my head back towards her own. In the white light of the afternoon, her eyes are viridescent and serene, like the waters of an enchanted grotto. 'Now,' she whispers, moving her lips closer to mine, 'remind me how your story ended...'

I close my eyes, and can hear the distant sound of harp music, rising and falling with the tide.

#

The melody grows louder, closer. I open my eyes again to find Amy, phone in hand, staring at me apologetically.

'Actually, Alex, do you mind if I take this?'

57

Turns out the call is for me.

'Alex? Alex Donovan?' The voice on the other end sounds breathless, almost. 'My name's Andrea Sorton-Mayner, I'm an editor at Minerva Press. Can you talk?'

Is this real? I stare at Amy, who's shaking her head as if to say, 'Who is it?'

'How did you get this number?' I ask in disbelief.

'Mr Gayle gave it to me.' Danso. 'I've just seen the Statement.'

'Statement?'

Amy smiles up at me.

'We would like to acquire the detention fantasy.'

'What?' It's a lot, all this.

'And the true story around it, of course. I'm thinking we might even elide the two somehow, make them into one narrative? Sort of, autofiction meets true crime, if that makes sense?'

Yes – I find myself nodding – each can inform the other...

'Wait,' I say. 'You can't have even read it...'

'Don't need to.' She laughs in that fast-twitch way brainy people do. 'Think about it. We could even end it right here – with this scene, I mean!'

I don't hear the rest. Eyes shut, warm sun on my face, I picture my old desk in the open-plan at Hatton Taylor. On it there sits a single engraved hole punch, but the initials aren't mine.

List of Spanish terms and other references

Chiquillo (p 8): Literally, little boy; colloquially, friend.

Picha (p 8): Used a lot in Cádiz – literally, penis; colloquially, friend.

Tío (p 9): Literally, uncle; colloquially, pal.

Qué cojones haces? (p 66): Essentially, 'What the fuck are you doing?'

Chiringuito (p 122): Pop-up restaurant on the beach.

Boludo (p 229): Argentinian slang for jerk (vulgar) – can also mean friend (colloquial).

Levante (p 266): Warm east wind.

Traveller, there is no road; you make your own path as you walk (*Caminante, no hay camino, se hace camino al andar*) (p 272): *Caminante no hay camino*, by Antonio Machado.

Bonarense (p 273): A person from Buenos Aires.

¡Che boludo! (p 273): A popular Argentinian interjection, expressing amazement.

En los olivaritos, niña, te espero, con un jarro de vino y un pan casero (p 274): In the olive groves, girl, I wait for you, with a jug of wine and some homemade bread (opening lyrics from '*Homenaje a Federico*', by Camarón de la Isla).

Que te folle un pez (p 276): That you are fucked by a fish.

Endnote (warning: contains spoilers)

Thank you for reading my novel. While it is loosely set in the immigration world I know, all its characters and the events that Alex narrates are imaginary.

The same goes for Herringsworth. I have visited several immigration removal centres through my work as a lawyer,[1] but I have never explored the inner sanctum of any. Alex wouldn't have done so either, and my portrayal of life inside one is imperfect by design.

Even so, I was able to draw on my experience of representing detained clients and on reports, cases and other documents available in the public domain.[2] And occasionally I did so directly. Novak's words, *'You fucking piece of shit...I'm going to put you to fucking sleep'*, for instance, are those spoken by a detention custody officer to a detainee in the 2017 BBC Panorama exposé on Brook House[3] (and quoted in the Brook House Inquiry Report six years later[4]).

As such, there were always likely to be some similarities between Herringsworth and its non-fictional counterparts. But I had

---

[1] For legal visits to clients, detention advice surgeries, on-site bail hearings and asylum appeals, and so on.

[2] Indeed, just as Alex would have been able to.

[3] 'Undercover: Britain's Immigration Secrets' first aired on 4 September 2017.

[4] 'One of the most shocking incidents I considered, which was central to the Panorama programme, was the moment Detention Custody Officer (DCO) Ioannis (Yan) Paschali placed his hands firmly around the neck of one detained person (referred to by the Inquiry as D1527), leaned forward over him and said in a quiet voice: "You fucking piece of shit, because I'm going to put you to fucking sleep".' (The Brook House Inquiry Report: A public inquiry into the mistreatment of individuals detained at Brook House immigration removal centre, p. 3, paragraph 14: https://assets.publishing.service.gov.uk/media/650964844cd3c3000d68c-c65/11199-HHG-BHI-Vol_I_Brook_House_Inquiry_Vol_I_ACCESSIBLE__1_.pdf).

not anticipated quite how closely much of the conduct that Alex describes in the detention story would reflect real, current examples of mistreatment.

Staying with Brook House, on 18 November 2024 HM Chief Inspector of Prisons published a report of his unannounced inspection of the facility.[5] Troublingly, he found that it was less safe than it had been two years earlier; more to the point, of the thirteen key concerns he raised, most, if not all, appear to mirror practices depicted in the novel (for ease of reference, the list is appended to this note).

Lest readers be misled, Brook House is by no means the only immigration removal centre in which mistreatment of detainees is reported to have occurred.[6] Nor, it would seem, do the similarities between Alex's story and real-life abuses end there. It may surprise some readers that a close parallel appears to exist between the most savage – and, this writer believed, far-fetched – part of the detention story plot, and real-life abuses recently alleged to be taking place in North Africa.

Arguably, there were already loose parallels between Alex's removal plot and the United Kingdom's (abandoned) Rwanda policy. But on 21 May 2024, when *Sanctuary* was on submission to publishers, I read a story reported by James Crisp in The Telegraph that made me

---

[5] https://hmiprisons.justiceinspectorates.gov.uk/hmipris_reports/brook-house-immigration-removal-centre-2/

[6] See, for instance: https://www.independent.co.uk/news/uk/home-news/yarls-wood-detention-centre-home-office-b2422992.html; https://www.independent.co.uk/news/uk/home-news/immigration-detention-torture-migrants-prison-handcuffed-b2492004.html; https://www.theguardian.com/uk-news/2018/oct/11/life-in-a-uk-immigration-removal-centre-worse-than-prison-as-criminal-sentence; https://www.freedomfromtorture.org/real-voices/one-womans-account-of-life-at-yarlswood-detention-centre

do a double take, then feel physically sick.[7] The title read as follows:

'EU accused of funding units that dump migrants in North African desert. Black refugees in Morocco, Mauritania and Tunisia are 'driven to the middle of nowhere' where they face torture and death, says report.'

The article went on to cite a report by Lighthouse Reports, which alleged that refugees and migrants in Morocco, Mauritania and Tunisia were being *'apprehended based on the colour of their skin, loaded onto buses and driven to the middle of nowhere, often arid desert areas'* without water or food, while others were being taken to border areas where they were allegedly *'sold by the authorities to human traffickers and gangs who torture them for ransom'*.

You couldn't make it up (even if you thought you had). At the time of writing, the report is still available to read online.[8]

A word or two more before I end:

The Human Rights Lawyers Awards are fictional, though the points Amy makes in her speech about the limited scope of the Refugee Convention and the high threshold a migrant would need to reach in order to secure protection under human rights law are well-founded.[9]

The descriptions of London in the novel are faithful to reality, but neither Hatton Taylor Solicitors nor Ascham Chambers exist outside it.

As for the characters' respective speech patterns, these are only as plausible as Alex might have made them – in the time available to

---

[7] https://www.telegraph.co.uk/world-news/2024/05/21/
eu-funds-units-that-dump-migrants-in-north-african-desert/

[8] https://www.lighthousereports.com/investigation/desert-dumps/

[9] Consider, for instance, the law in respect of medical cases – a straightforward introduction to which can be found here: https://righttoremain.org.uk/human-rights-cases-based-on-medical-grounds/. Another invaluable resource worth consulting in this and other regards is the Free Movement blog – https://freemovement.org.uk – which offers regular updates, commentary, training and advice to all those affected by immigration control: migrants themselves, their families, their lawyers and their judges.

him, and with the benefit of such cultural exposure as he would have had courtesy of his job, his outlook, living in a metropolis, and so on.

The portrayal of the immigration judge is something of a caricature, built in part on an unsubstantiated rumour I once heard about a judge who did not know how to allow an appeal on account of never having done so. At the other end of the spectrum, I should stress, there are many compassionate, professional and fair immigration judges sitting in our immigration tribunals, as there are barristers and Home Office presenting officers who appear before them.

As to the novel's central plot, I am aware of no circumstances in which lawyers acting for the Home Office have conspired with opposing counsel to play down the risk of harm asylum seekers face on return to their countries of origin. This is something I have simply dreamt up.

Or at least, so I believe.

Tom Gaisford
24 November 2024

List of 13 concerns identified by HM Chief Inspector of Prisons in his Report on an unannounced inspection of Brook House Immigration Removal Centre, 5–22 August 2024 (published 18 November 2024), pp. 5-6

Priority concerns

1) The number of recorded fights, assaults on staff and uses of force had risen substantially since the previous inspection, and leaders had not made sufficient use of data to understand why this was the case.

2) Policies and procedures to minimise the length of detention and protect the most vulnerable were not effective enough. The centre was unaware of 31 detainees assessed at the higher levels of the adults at risk policy, and Rule 35 reports (see Glossary) were not always submitted when necessary. The length of detention had increased and case progression was often slow.

3) Over half of operational staff had less than two years' experience, there were pockets of immature and unprofessional behaviour. Some officers continued to congregate in offices instead of pro actively managing the wings.

4) The centre continued to look and feel like a prison, and not enough had been done to improve the environment.

5) There were serious problems affecting the staffing, culture and morale of the health services team, which was not delivering a good enough service to detainees. Partnership working to help resolve these issues was poor.

Key concerns

6) Not enough care was given to detainees on arrival and during their early days in detention. The reception area was chaotic, and induction was not carried out consistently.

7) Some security measures were disproportionate. In particular, the centre was now routinely handcuffing detainees on external escorts.

8) There was increasing availability of illicit drugs in the centre, but planning and resources to tackle the problem were inadequate.

9) Leaders had limited awareness of diverse needs in the centre as protected characteristic information about detainees was not systematically captured on their arrival.

10) The education provision had been poorly attended for a long time, but little had been done to review the curriculum to make it more appealing to detainees.

11) The library was poor and little used. The room was no longer suitable for library activities, and most of the book stock had been removed, with the remaining collection held in cupboards.

12) The welfare service was under-resourced and staff lacked space to see detainees privately.

13) In the previous year, at least 20 detainees had been released homeless, including people assessed as vulnerable.

Acknowledgments

Enormous thanks to all who read my novel during its various stages of development, and to the brave people who inspired it, clients and colleagues alike.

My first reader was my dearly cherished mother, the journalist Sue Gaisford, who delivered her verdict one midsummer's afternoon in her garden. 'Better than I dared hope,' she said, whereupon my legs gave way and the smelling salts were fetched.

In the weeks and months that followed, a peal of incredibly kind siblings and friends chimed in with their own thoughts and encouragement. And when London's most charming literary agent, Tom Cull, agreed to represent me, I began to believe it might really happen.

Sanctuary is not a conventional novel. We needed a bold, enterprising publisher prepared to take a risk on it, and in Cinto Press we found one. I shall be forever grateful to David, Helen and Hannah for taking it on, for their expertise, of course, and for being such fun to work with. They also had the vision to instruct Katie, Claire and Olivia, the brilliant team at Read Maxwell Communications, and to commission Mark Ecob to do the cover design and Magdalen Hashimi to do the illustrations. To each and every one of you, my heartfelt thanks.

Did I mention my supremely wonderful wife? Thank you, dearest Sarra, for supporting me unconditionally in this mad endeavour – yes, and thank you too, Minnie and Lulu – at last Daddy's finished his boring book!

The last toast is to my magnificent late father, Rob Gaisford, to whom I owe the novel's title, and so very much more.

For discussion

1) Alex's judgement and stability are questioned early on in the novel. While reading it, how much did you feel able to trust him as a narrator?

2) Later, as Alex muses about penning a memoir of the mess he is in, he reflects, 'And, yes, my imagination is running away with me. But what's a man to do in a lock-up but explore his thoughts?' How might this be read as a summary of the novel's wider story?

3) How does *Sanctuary* differ from other novels you might have read which concern the plight of asylum seekers?

4) The great Erma Bombeck wrote, 'There is a thin line that separates laughter and pain, comedy and tragedy, humour and hurt.' How closely does the author tread this line in *Sanctuary*, and to what effect?

5) '…if somebody dies, disappears, or has something stolen, and somebody else investigates, it counts (as a crime novel). Build that foundation and you can pile as many other genres on top as you'd like' (Stuart Turton). How does *Sanctuary* meet his definition, and what other genres does it cross into?

6) While reading, how similar or different did Priya and Amy appear, and did you relate to one more than to the other?

7) In what ways do the events of the novel alter Alex's vocation and perspective?

8) 'Is there anything people won't do for money?' Alex asks at the opening of Act II; 'Everyone has a price for doing something they don't want to,' Fletcher answers in Act IV. Is he right?

9) To what extent do you agree with Alex's conclusion that 'appalling abuses will continue to occur for as long as we prioritise profit over humanity'?

10) In Act IV Alex quotes from a poem by Antonio Machado, 'Traveller, there is no road; you make your own path as you walk'. How closely does this resemble the process of creative writing?

11) How might the plot of this novel be read as a vindication of fiction itself?

12) The plot lines are tied up and the story is resolved – but what, do you suppose, will the characters do next…?

BETWEEN THE LIES

The debut novel from award-winning journalist and broadcaster, Louise Tickle.

When it comes to families, is anyone a reliable witness?
Cherry Magraw can never forget the date her mother and brother were killed – the night of her ninth birthday. When her father was jailed for their murders, she lost everyone she loved.

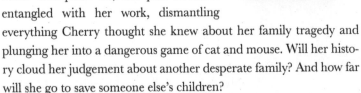

Twenty years later, Cherry is a freelance journalist investigating domestic abuse and the secret world of the family courts, when she gets a letter from her father – still in prison for the killings – which contains a startling request.

From that point on, her past becomes entangled with her work, dismantling everything Cherry thought she knew about her family tragedy and plunging her into a dangerous game of cat and mouse. Will her history cloud her judgement about another desperate family? And how far will she go to save someone else's children?

About the author
Louise Tickle is an award-winning journalist and broadcaster who specialises in reporting on domestic abuse, family courts and child protection. *Between the Lies* is her first novel.

> "This book is brilliant: gripping, powerful and one of the best thrillers I've ever read – I could not put it down."
> *Victoria Derbyshire*

COMING SOON FROM CINTO PRESS

TAINTED LOVE

A policeman's wife dies in an unexplained fall from her flat. As journalist Cherry Magraw digs deeper, whistleblowing, corruption and her own past are exposed in this gripping crime thriller.

The second Cherry Magraw novel picks up the story from her near death clifftop chase in *Between The Lies*. Recurring themes of deceit and domestic abuse remain at the heart of Cherry's fearless reporting, this time leading her into the centre of the very organisation that should be policing the crime.

Publication due September 2025.

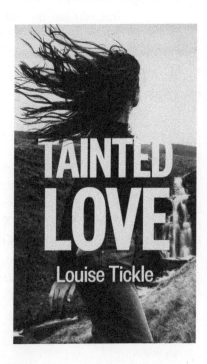

THE GREAT POST OFFICE COVER-UP

The Great Post Office Cover-Up reveals for the first time the full story behind the largest miscarriage of justice the nation has ever seen. Building on *The Great Post Office Scandal*, freelance journalist and broadcaster, Nick Wallis, uses the fresh evidence uncovered by the statutory inquiry and Nick's own journalism to chronicle the legal obstruction and embedded cultural attitudes that led one of the nation's most respected institutions to become a byword for corporate callousness and incompetence. Along the way, he recounts hitherto untold stories of the human cost of their actions.

The scandal sparked national outrage in January 2024 when the ITV drama, *Mr Bates vs The Post Office* was broadcast, but we now know

that was not the full story. With the statutory inquiry over, *The Great Post Office Cover-Up* stands as the definitive account of one of the darkest episodes of modern British history.

About the Author

Nick Wallis is an award-winning freelance journalist and broadcaster. He has worked with the BBC, Private Eye and ITN. His Radio 4 series on the Post Office scandal has been nominated for national awards. He also acted as series consultant for the ITV drama, *Mr Bates vs The Post Office*.

Publication due Autumn 2025.